Dear Reader,

Thank you so much for reading *A Perfect Amish Romance*! This series, which combines my love for libraries and the Amish, has been a dream of mine for quite some time, and I'm so grateful it has finally become a reality.

Do you remember your first visit to the library? My first library was made up of two double-wide trailers in the suburbs of Houston. It was a temporary building while a brand-new library was being built, and I thought it was the most magical place in the world. I especially loved how "my section" was in the second trailer, and my mom would let me stay there looking at books while she went to the adults' section. It was cramped and hot (Houston in the summer, y'all!), and there were tons of picture books on shelves and in stacks on top of tables. It really was my favorite place in the world—especially after I found *The Little Match Girl,* the first book I found and checked out by myself.

Years later, I remember checking out stacks of Victoria Holt and Barbara Cartland romances and Agatha Christie mysteries in junior high and high school. I was the girl who had to count how many books I was holding so I wouldn't exceed the checkout limit.

I guess you never know how something will make an impression on you. That first library inspired a love of reading that has never waned. Consequently, that love of reading encouraged me to write my first "Chapter 1" during a lunch break back when I was teaching elementary school. That moment led me down a whole new career path.

I hope you enjoy *A Perfect Amish Romance* as well as the rest of the books in the Berlin Bookmobile series. If you have time, write and tell me who inspired your love of books. I'd love to hear all about your story . . . after all, I think we might have a lot in common.

With blessings and my continued thanks,
Shelley Shepard Gray

"Gray tells a beautiful story of friendship, love, and truth born out of pain and grief. This story reminds us to hold those we love close."

—Rachel Hauck, *New York Times* bestselling author
of *The Wedding Dress*

"Gray has created an endearing cast of characters . . . that both delights and surprises—and kept me thinking about the story long after I turned the last page. Bravo!"

—Leslie Gould, #1 bestselling and
Christy Award–winning author

"Like sunshine breaking through clouds . . . readers who love Amish stories and/or Christian fiction are sure to take pleasure in following the saga of this wonderful group of friends [who] learn to support each other and follow their hearts as they attempt to discern God's will in their lives."

—*Fresh Fiction*

THE PROTECTIVE ONE

"A slow-burning, enjoyable romance . . . Embedded in this quaint story is a poignant message about the importance of community, compassion, and doing what's right rather than what's easy."

—*Publishers Weekly*

"Gray deftly weaves the threads of abuse, friendship, love, and faith into a thought-provoking, emotional story."

—Patricia Davids, *USA Today* bestselling author
of *The Wish*

"Filled with heartbreaking and uplifting moments, this love story stars Elizabeth Anne, or 'E.A.,' as she reevaluates her life . . . Now, E.A. must go on a heart-opening journey that may lead her to everything she's been searching for."

—*Woman's World*

THE TRUSTWORTHY ONE

"Gray's biblical themes are nuanced and well integrated into the narrative."

—*Publishers Weekly*

"Hope is found in unexpected places as this sweet Amish love story unfolds."

—*Woman's World*

Also available from
Shelley Shepard Gray and Gallery Books

THE WALNUT CREEK SERIES

*Friends to the End**
The Patient One
The Loyal One
*A Precious Gift**
The Protective One
The Trustworthy One
*Promises of Tomorrow**

*ebook only

A PERFECT AMISH ROMANCE

Shelley Shepard Gray

GALLERY BOOKS

New York   London   Toronto   Sydney   New Delhi

Gallery Books
An Imprint of Simon & Schuster, Inc.
1230 Avenue of the Americas
New York, NY 10020

First Gallery Books hardcover edition January 2021

GALLERY BOOKS and colophon are registered trademarks of Simon & Schuster, Inc.

For information about special discounts for bulk purchases, please contact Simon & Schuster Special Sales at 1-866-506-1949 or business@simonandschuster.com.

The Simon & Schuster Speakers Bureau can bring authors to your live event. For more information or to book an event, contact the Simon & Schuster Speakers Bureau at 1-866-248-3049 or visit our website at www.simonspeakers.com.

Interior design by Erika R. Genova

Manufactured in the United States of America

10   9   8   7   6   5   4   3   2   1

The Library of Congress has cataloged the trade paperback edition as follows:

Names: Gray, Shelley Shepard, author.
Title: A perfect Amish romance / Shelley Shepard Gray.
Description: First Gallery Books trade paperback edition. | New York : Gallery
    Books, 2021. | Series: The Berlin bookmobile series
Identifiers: LCCN 2020027763 (print) | LCCN 2020027764 (ebook) |
    ISBN 9781982148393 (paperback) | ISBN 9781982165161 (library binding) |
    ISBN 9781982148416 (ebook)
Subjects: GSAFD: Love stories.
Classification: LCC PS3607.R3966 P47 2021 (print) | LCC PS3607.R3966
    (ebook) | DDC 813/.6—dc23
LC record available at https://lccn.loc.gov/2020027763
LC ebook record available at https://lccn.loc.gov/2020027764

ISBN 978-1-9821-6516-1
ISBN 978-1-9821-4841-6 (ebook)

For my mother, Barbara, and my daughter, Lesley.
I've been blessed to share my love of books—
and bookstores—with them.

Now Faith is confidence in what we hope for and assurance about what we do not see.

—Hebrews 11:1

The trouble with reaching a crossroads in life is the lack of signposts.

—Amish proverb

prologue

"Well now, that's it," Ron Holiday said as he led the way out of the bookmobile. "Good luck to you. I'm sure you'll do just fine."

Sarah Anne Miller froze in the doorway. "Wait. That's it?"

He scratched his head. "Don't think there's anything more to say, Sarah Anne. You've got all the route information and times. What else would you need to know?"

"A lot more. A whole lot more." This part-time job she'd signed up for on a lark was beginning to feel real. Really real and more than a bit foreboding.

Now that she was about to head out and service the literary needs of the whole community, she was starting to combat a whole army of worries and doubts. "Ron, I have no idea what to say to these people."

"What do you mean, what to say? You give them the books they've requested and take their orders. You'll help them get on the Internet, talk about books, maybe even let them look around for a spell." He paused. "Smile. Chat. Some of our patrons are lonely, *jah?*"

Ron had grown up Amish. Now, even though he was *Englisch* enough to be wearing a pair of white leather tennis shoes, jeans, and a sweatshirt emblazoned with *See Rock City* across the front, he was as folksy as Mr. Rogers in his neighborhood. Sarah Anne had always found him to be mildly irritating, and right now she felt like he was being especially vague and unhelpful.

"Jah," she echoed in a dry tone.

If Ron caught her sarcasm, he was polished enough not to let on. "There you go. That's what you do."

But it wasn't that easy. People would no doubt have questions for her. Expectations. "Although I took a couple of online classes, you know I'm not actually a librarian, right?"

He stuffed his hands into his pockets. "To be sure, I haven't forgotten that. But it seems to me that you don't remember you've worked in a library before."

"I volunteered." She cleared her throat. "I volunteered in a brick-and-mortar building, Ron. There was a whole staff there to assist people. I was just there for support. There's a difference between that and . . . this." She gestured to the bookmobile.

"You volunteered a lot, though. A whole lot. Plus, you've received some very impressive recommendations. You'll do fine."

Even though he held out the key, Sarah Anne made no move to take it. "What if I miss someone? Or if can't find some of my customers?" She lowered her voice as she at last voiced her greatest fear. "Ron, what if I let some of our customers down?"

He laughed. "You're delivering books, not blood. You're going to be just fine." He jangled the key in front of him and motioned for her to lock the door. "Come on now. It must be thirty degrees out here, and the wind's picking up." He sniffed at the air. "I think we're in for a bit of snow."

She looked up at the sky but couldn't see anything but a few fluffy clouds. How Ron was interpreting that as an approaching storm, she didn't know. However, it was more than obvious that she'd just about used up the last of her new boss's patience. Taking the key from him, she locked the door and turned back to Ron, but he was walking fast, as if the sidewalk was made of hot coals. She rushed to catch up with him.

She was almost out of breath by the time they entered the administration building for the whole library system. The sudden warmth against her skin felt almost uncomfortable. She pressed a hand on the wall to steady herself. It was time to get in better shape, that was a fact.

"I'll check in with you in a week or so, Sarah Anne. Good luck tomorrow. I wish you God's blessings, too."

"Thank you, Ron." As irritating as he was, she knew he was also sincere, so she softened her voice and added, "I am grateful for your belief in me."

He waved her off. "No need for that. Now, don't forget to have fun, Sarah Anne. There's no reason to fret, I can promise you that. Just go out there and get to know our patrons. Remember, you're providing them a valuable service. They'll be pleased to see you. I'm sure of it. And when they're pleased to see ya, they'll forgive most anything."

But Sarah Anne wasn't used to getting things wrong. She'd demanded perfection from herself, and everyone else did, too. She'd just retired from her position as an accountant after putting in almost twenty-eight years on the eighth floor of a big firm. In that capacity, anything less than perfect wasn't even an option.

"I know I'll make mistakes." And yes, she sounded frightened.

"No one expects perfection, Sarah Anne. Not even our Lord. Ain't so?"

She nodded, though she was still worried. Even though the Lord might not expect perfection, she did.

After taking a deep breath, she smiled weakly. "I hope I'll have a good report for you."

"I'm sure you will." Then, to her surprise, Ron chuckled softly. "After all, what could go wrong?" He strode down the gray-carpeted hallway before she had a chance to reply.

But perhaps that was a good thing. Driving a bookmobile along country roads by herself? Receiving orders, picking up books, taking care of all of the paperwork? She had a feeling it wasn't going to be a matter of what could go wrong . . . but rather what in the world was going to go right?

one

SARAH ANNE MILLER'S
BEST BOOKMOBILING RULES

(I've started this log in order to allow myself to see my
professional growth and learn from my mistakes.)

• RULE #1 •

Make sure there's enough gas in your bookmobile's gas tank.

ONE YEAR LATER

It was the second Friday of the month, Aaron Coblentz's favorite day. On this day, the bookmobile would park down in the empty lot near Zeiset's Furniture Store for three hours. The librarian, a very friendly *Englischer* named Sarah Anne Miller, would greet everyone with a bright smile. Then, she'd lean up against her small circulation desk and trade gossip from around the county and ask everyone how their families and pets were. She was, more or less, their link to the outside world.

Most importantly, though, she'd check out the books everyone discovered and deliver any books that had been previously ordered. And she did it all in the most pleasing way.

Aaron was slightly amazed that Sarah Anne had such a knack for understanding what everyone needed from her. With some folks, she hardly talked at all. With others, she was a regular chatterbox. And with old Mr. Sol? Well, she practically yelled, since he was nearly deaf but vain about not wanting to wear a hearing aid.

Aaron figured all of those things were good qualities to have as a librarian. However, what he cared most about was that she never, ever commented on what people chose to read. He liked that Sarah Anne Miller could keep a secret.

In the year since she'd started coming around to his part of Holmes County, Aaron had never once heard Sarah Anne judge anyone for what they asked her to bring them—not even the English lady who always requested a stack of romances, each with a half-naked man on the cover.

Aaron didn't care about any of that, though. As far as he was concerned, sixty-something-year-old Sarah Anne was an answer to his prayers. If she hadn't brought the bookmobile out to his neck of the woods, he might never have the chance to do what he wanted.

And he wanted his GED.

It was taking some time, but if all went well, he would finish his coursework by June, right around his twenty-second birthday. All he had to do was keep his secret a little longer. Then he could put this quest behind him and finally get up the nerve to ask Mr. Dwight Zeiset, his boss at the furniture store, to give him a promotion.

Zeiset's was the largest furniture store in town. Aaron delivered furniture and moved it all around in the warehouse, helped customers, entered information in Mr. Zeiset's ledgers, and arranged stock a pleasing way. Mr. Zeiset said he was indispensable, and Aaron intended to stay that way.

Mr. Zeiset really valued education, and Aaron feared that if he didn't have a GED, he was going to be overlooked. And he didn't want that. After all, he had big goals. He hoped that one day, if he did a real good job, Mr. Zeiset, who was getting on in years, would ask him to be the manager of the whole store. That was a possibility, Aaron was sure of it.

Feeling pleased with himself, and almost optimistic about his future, Aaron gathered his notes, pencils, and the library books that were scattered all over his room and stuffed them into his army-green backpack.

"Aaron, how soon are you going?" his younger brother, Jack, called out from down the hall. As usual, he was in a dither.

Aaron looked at his pocket watch. "I don't know. Ten minutes?"

"Can you make it fifteen? I can't find one of my books."

"*Jah*, sure. Fifteen minutes is fine." Though, it would be a true miracle if Jack found what he was looking for by then.

Aaron peeked into Jack's room, only to see his brother's backside sticking out from under the bed. "Where's Tiny?"

"Not here, though I'm starting to think she's the only thing that's not lurking under this bed."

Aaron felt like cringing. Ever since their mother had stopped cleaning under Jack's bed, the mess had gotten much, much worse. Now, Aaron reckoned, there were any number of crawling creatures living down there. "Any idea where she might be?"

"*Jah*, helping Mamm in the kitchen with Rebecca."

"Okay, I'll go see if she's ready." After throwing his backpack over his shoulders, Aaron headed down the old wooden stairs of their farmhouse, taking special care to avoid steps number three and six. Neither was in good shape. Their father always said he was going to fix them, but so far—like many things in the house—the repair had never happened. Aaron had an idea that his *dawdi* had often told his grandmother the same thing a time or two.

The noise coming from the kitchen grew louder with each step. Not only was the singing a surprise, but the voices were rather difficult on his eardrums, too. His mother couldn't carry a tune if it was stuffed in her purse.

All three quieted when he entered.

"Hiya. Uh, what were you singing?"

"Mamm and me are teaching Rebecca her ABCs," Tiny said.

So far, he hadn't heard a recognizable letter spout out of his baby sister's mouth. "Sorry, but I don't reckon it's going too well."

"It ain't. But it could be going worse," Tiny murmured. "I could be trying to get Mamm to sing in tune."

"I heard that," Mamm said from her perch in front of Rebecca's booster chair. Glancing at Aaron, she straightened. "Well, my stars! You already have on your backpack." She glanced at the beautiful cuckoo clock that her parents had given her and Daed on their wedding day. "Are you heading to the bookmobile already?"

"*Jah.* Hopefully, I'll be on my way in fifteen minutes or so. Jack is searching for one of his books."

Tiny smirked. "You might as well sit down and have a cup of *kaffi.* That could take all day."

"It better not." He only had ninety more minutes until Sarah Anne left the parking lot.

"Tiny isn't wrong," Mamm said. "Jack couldn't find his head if it wasn't attached so good. He's going to be a while."

"I don't have time for that. Miss Miller is only going to be there for three hours today and she's already been there half the time."

"You need to calm down, *bruder.*" Tiny pointed to her neat stack of books. "I have Becca's books in my tote bag. We'll wait a bit, and if Jack doesn't come down soon, we'll go without him. And *jah*, before you ask. I'm ready. I've been ready."

"That makes two of us, then." After tossing his backpack on the floor, he flopped into the chair next to Rebecca. When the three-year-old grinned at him, he smiled back. "You're getting smart today, Becca."

"*Jah!*" She smiled.

Their mother wiped her hands on the apron she'd tied around the front of her dress. "She's getting smarter, but she's also making a real mess of me. I don't know how this little thing always manages to get so much peanut butter off her graham crackers and onto her clothes. I don't recall any of you being such messy eaters."

"I'm sure we were. Anyway, she's only three, aren't you, Becca?" Tiny cooed.

Becca smiled and held up three fingers.

"Perhaps, though I don't recall." Their *mamm* picked up a

dishrag. "Are you going to be checking out another one of your history books, Aaron?"

"Maybe. I don't know."

"I've never known a boy so interested in history and geography. I'm proud of you."

"*Danke*, Mamm." He felt vaguely guilty, since his parents had no idea he was studying for the high school equivalency test, but not guilty enough to spill his secret. There was no way they could find out, either. They were too afraid about anything that might pull him away from them, too afraid of anything that would take him down Timothy's path of being permanently shunned from both their community and their conversation.

Just as he looked at the kitchen clock yet again, Jack came running down the stairs.

"Aaron, I found it!"

"Don't yell, Jack!" Mamm called out.

"Sorry." He held up his stack. "See?"

"I see." Aaron opened up his backpack and stuffed them inside. "Am I supposed to pick any up?"

"Yep. Sarah Anne has two mysteries for me. Can't recall the titles offhand, but they're filled with murder and mayhem." He grinned. "I'm sure of it."

"I'll get them for you. Bye now."

"Hold on, Aaron. Are you working today?" Mamm called out.

"*Jah*. I'll be at Zeiset's until dark."

She frowned. "He runs you ragged, he does. Remind him that you are needed here at home, too. With your family."

That's what she always said. It was another veiled reference to Tim, and how he'd gone out into the *Englisch* world in spite of their parents' best efforts. "I'm fine, *Mudder*."

"See you later," Jack called out as he poured a large mug of hot coffee. "I'd best get back out to the barn."

Aaron knew that Jack had already been in the barn since five that morning. For all his disorganized mess, Jack was a hard worker. He helped their father farm their land in the spring, summer, and fall, and did woodworking in the barn in the winter.

"Ready, Aaron?" Tiny asked. "As you can see, I have on my boots and cloak."

He stuffed his feet into his heavy winter boots. "I am. Bye, everyone."

Five minutes later, he and Tiny were on their way to the bookmobile. Tiny's real name was Elizabeth, but Aaron couldn't recall anyone ever calling her that. Their father started calling her "Tiny" soon after she was born, since she'd been born early and was so much smaller than he, Tim, and Jack had been. Though she was normal size, now, the name had stuck.

She was seventeen to Jack's eighteen and his twenty-one. At one time, they'd all walked to school together, but now that they were older, their days were as different as the three of them were.

Tiny was the most dependable. She flitted around, helping them all with one thing or another. Lately, she spent much of her time helping their mother can and sell their jams and jellies.

Tim had been handsome and loud. He'd also always questioned everything: their parents' rules, their church district's customs, the adherence to tradition. For a time it had seemed that he'd settled down. He'd gotten baptized and was even courting Suzanne down the street. But then they'd broken up, and he'd declared he wanted to leave everything they were behind. Their parents had threated to shun him. It had all happened so quickly, and he was lost to them forever.

Jack was the most easygoing and helped their father around the farm. He'd also been the best student, much to Aaron's dismay when they were younger. Jack had taken his good grades for granted, never thinking too much about school; he'd always preferred to be outside by their father's side.

Aaron, though he was now the oldest, was in many ways the odd duck. He'd been a dreamer, always thinking about his studies late into the night. He'd been the one making up stories he would have loved to one day publish and the one with all the questions about history. He hadn't just wanted to know about Lewis and Clark and their journey out west; he had wanted to know what everyone was wearing, what they ate, how they prepared for such an adventure, and even how they made their maps. Now, though? Well, now his dreams were of the more concrete nature. He wanted to be smart enough to manage Zeiset's.

Rounding out their family was little Rebecca, his parents' surprise babe. It had taken them all off guard when their parents had announced that their mother was with child. But little Rebecca had been a blessing. He had no idea what her gifts were going to be, though perhaps it was her sunny disposition. Becca had brought all of them so much joy.

Tiny was perhaps the closest to Aaron. In a lot of ways, they were like two peas in a pod. Well, that's what their mother always said.

"Do you ever wonder how the five of us ever got into this family?" he mused, voicing his thoughts out loud. "We're quite the varied lot."

Tiny nodded. "It has crossed my mind a time or two. But I'm glad we're different. I like our differences. I kind of like that our *haus* isn't like everyone else's."

Aaron knew what she meant. Their family was anything but a stereotypical Amish household. They were loud, disorganized, and rather messy. Their mother took the mess in stride and never thought to complain about her inability to keep a clean house, often thanking the Lord instead for giving her a pair of good eyes and a love of reading, cooking, and sewing.

A few minutes later, they reached the crest of the hill, and Aaron could see the bookmobile parked in the empty lot, just like always. He breathed a sigh of relief. They were going to make it there on time after all.

"Are you ever going to tell me what is really going on with you?" Tiny blurted.

He was not, but he played dumb. "I don't know what you're talking about."

"Sure you do. Sarah Anne practically sneaks the books you order to you under a shelf. It's obvious you're studying something you don't want the rest of us to know about."

"It is private, but it's nothing bad."

"I didn't think it would be." She gave him a curious look. "Aaron, if you ever want to talk about it, I can keep a secret, you know."

"I know."

"But?"

He smiled. "But I'm afraid I don't want to share right now."

She groaned. "Fine. But you're going to have to tell us all what you're really up to sooner or later."

"I understand." He just hoped it would be far later than sooner. "Just give me time, okay?"

"*Jah*. Sure." She smiled at him before waving to her friend Virginia.

Aaron breathed a sigh of relief. Virginia would distract Tiny from thinking about him for a while. Which was perfect because Sarah Anne said she was going to have some news for him today.

He just hoped it was the news he'd been praying for.

two

• RULE #2 •

*Be friendly and helpful. Also, never offer an opinion
if you can help it. Take it from me, lots of advice
eventually comes back to haunt you.*

Sarah Anne had known it was going to be a good day the moment she spied the likable Coblentz kids through the window. "Aaron and Tiny! It's good to see you," she said as she walked to the door to meet them. "I was beginning to worry that you wouldn't be in today."

While Tiny laughed and went to join her friend near the stack of new releases, the handsome, quiet boy nodded. "I was a little worried myself. At first, my brother couldn't find his books for you." He handed over two popular mysteries.

She took them with a grin. She'd come to appreciate all

the members of the Coblentz household, and indeed they were a varied lot. Aaron's brother particularly amused her, often reminding her of a human pinball, constantly zipping from one activity to another. "At least Jack found them. That's something."

He smiled back. *"Jah."* After looking out the open doorway, he lowered his voice. "Did you have any luck finding me some help?"

After making sure no one was around, she replied, "I did. I found you a tutor."

He couldn't believe she'd found him one so fast. "Really? When can I meet him?"

"First of all, *she* is a woman, and I took the liberty of setting something up for you tomorrow at four in the afternoon. If memory serves, that's when you get off work, yes?"

"Yes." He nodded, but he didn't look nearly as excited as she'd hoped. "Sarah Anne, I appreciate your help, but I don't know how I'm going to be able to meet this woman right after work. The furniture store is downtown, you know."

"I know. But guess what? Kayla just happens to work at the little sewing shop across the street from Zeiset's. You won't have to worry about not getting along with her, either. She confided in me that she almost left the faith, and while she was making her decision, she took the GED."

"Really?" He'd honestly thought he was the only Amish person around who wanted to take the notoriously difficult test.

"That's what she told me." Sarah Anne shrugged. "You'll have to ask her more about that, if you're curious."

"How old is Kayla?"

"Hmm. Twenty-five or twenty-six, perhaps?"

So she was a little older. "What's her last name?"

"Kauffman. Kayla Kauffman. That has a nice ring to it, don't you think?"

"I suppose."

"Well? What do you say?"

He was desperate, and though he was a little uneasy to share his secret with a woman close to his age, he knew he was being silly. "I guess we could meet to see how it goes."

"I think you could, indeed, Aaron. I think it was meant to be. I feel like the Lord has helped us set everything in the right direction. You need the help, and she needs the extra money. And her aunt is willing to let her tutor you in the back room of her shop."

"There?"

"Her aunt runs the place and has a real good work area in the back. You two will be able to work in relative privacy." Feeling awfully good about her efforts, Sarah Anne patted him on the shoulder. "That's why I've been so excited to see you today, Aaron. If you didn't show up, I was going to have to tell Kayla that the job wasn't going to happen after all."

"Thank you for helping me."

"I'm happy to help you." Deciding to comment on the worry lines she noticed, Sarah Anne added, "Aaron, sorry, but you don't seem very pleased."

"I guess I just realized that this is really going to happen. If my parents find out, I don't know what I'm going to tell them. They're going to be mighty upset with me."

Sarah Anne had met his parents, and they'd seemed nice enough. Rather easygoing, too. But perhaps they weren't always that way, or maybe not that way when it came to their oldest son. She'd certainly met more than a few people who had expectations for their children that caused nothing but pain and eventually failure for all of them.

"It's up to you, but I've always been fond of the truth myself."

"I reckon you're right, but this time I know what the truth will get me."

He still looked like he was about to meet the guillotine, but since more people had just walked inside, Sarah Anne decided to give Aaron some space.

"When you're ready to leave, I have the book you ordered and all of Kayla's information paper clipped to the inside of the front cover."

"Sounds *gut*. I am going to look around a bit."

"I'm glad." She pointed to a display of books just to the right of them. "Go check out the newest arrivals. There's a couple of good ones there."

"I will, *danke*."

"Of course, Aaron. That's why I'm here."

He smiled and, watching him turn away, Sarah Anne made a mental note to pray extra hard for him that afternoon. She'd begun to pray for eight or ten of her customers every day that she worked. She'd soon realized it was impossible to remain detached from the patrons she served. Almost immediately, she'd begun to notice all sorts of little things about them. They were slowly becoming her extended family.

Not a bad thing at all, especially considering that she'd been worried about taking the job in the first place. Besides, it was always easier to focus on all of them instead of her own troubles and worries.

The fact was, she was lonely. She was glad she'd accepted the early retirement her boss had offered at her accounting job, but when she'd left, she had also left behind a big network of friends and acquaintances there. Throughout the day, she'd have any number of conversations, even if just around the coffeepot in the morning or the watercooler in the afternoon.

Now, when she wasn't out in the community, much of her work was done alone.

When she got home, it was worse. Her three-bedroom, two-story house was too big for one person, especially one person with memories of a husband who'd loved her dearly and had always looked out for her. Now, there were so many special items that evoked memories from vacations or holidays that they felt like traps at times.

But what else could she do? She was sixty-one. She wasn't supposed to need excitement anymore. But it was hard to tell that to her heart.

"I think we're ready, Miss Miller," Tiny said, interrupting her thoughts. "Can we check out our books now?"

"Hmm? Oh. But of course." Smiling at Tiny and Virginia, she held out her hands for the books. "Let's get you checked out so you two can be on your way."

"*Danke,*" Virginia said. "Tiny and me are going to stop by *mei haus* before we begin our chores for the day."

"That sounds like an excellent plan. There's nothing like a good visit with a good friend, is there?"

When the girls just giggled, Sarah Anne grinned. Yes, she just needed to concentrate on the good things in her life. Good things like books and Aaron needing her help and the sweet teenage girls who giggled.

Those were all good things. Very good indeed.

three

"I know you're a grown woman, but I'm going to stick around during your lesson, Kayla," Aunt Pat announced. "Something doesn't feel quite right about this student of yours. All this secrecy never did anyone much good."

Kayla smiled fondly at her aunt. Even though her aunt was as worldly and English as she could be, they'd always been thick as thieves. Kayla's mother used to say that she was the daughter her sister had never been blessed to have. All Kayla knew was that ever since her life had fallen apart three years ago, she would have been lost without Pat. Her aunt had bent over backward to help her time and again—especially after her mother died and her father had ceased to care about much beyond his overwhelming grief.

"Thanks, Pat. I'll feel better knowing you are around." Kayla didn't feel good about this secret meeting, either. Even though she knew Aaron Coblentz was Amish, she didn't know him personally since she was New Order and he was Old Order. And though it was doubtful that he was going to be anything but polite, she also knew that some people did bad things. This man could be a secret ax murderer or something.

Immediately embarrassed that she was jumping to such conclusions, Kayla amended her fears.

Or, maybe not something as awful as that. There was a good chance he could just be plain odd. She did have experience with that.

Even though Sarah Anne had said Aaron was really nice and not at all weird, she was holding her judgment. She'd never heard of anyone wanting a secret tutor, and Levi, her former suitor, had made sure she'd never trust easily ever again.

Her aunt's reassuring smile faltered. "Uh-oh. Now I'm really getting worried. Usually you tell me to stop fussing when I spout my opinions."

Though she was pretty sure Aunt Pat was seeing right through her, Kayla lifted her chin. "I have a feeling that we're both letting our imaginations get the best of us. Hopefully I'll be able to tell you not to fuss at five o'clock."

"Fingers crossed." She held up two bejeweled fingers, crossed for emphasis.

Kayla was just about to tease Pat about her bright purple nails when the door to the shop opened and a serious-looking

Amish man entered. She straightened. "Hello. May I help you find anything?"

After a second's pause, he nodded. "I hope so. Are you Kayla?"

This was her student.

Oh my. He had a deep voice, a mop of dark blond hair, and hazel eyes. He was lanky but had wide shoulders and impressive muscles showing through the thin cotton of his gray shirt. He looked strong enough to lift the heaviest boxes that came in off the UPS truck on Monday mornings. In short, he was strikingly handsome, and she hated that she even noticed.

"Kay!" Aunt Pat whispered. "Say something."

Looking back at the man, she spit out a reply. "Sorry. *Jah.* That's me."

"You're Kayla? Kayla Kauffman?"

"I am. And I'm guessing you're Aaron Coblentz."

"*Jah.* I came here to be tutored," he explained. As if he still wasn't sure her mind was clicking along correctly, he said, "I assume that is still all right with you?"

"It is. I haven't forgotten."

Still staring at her intently, he nodded before glancing at her aunt. "I hope I'm not too late? It took me a little longer than I imagined to get off work."

It was only five minutes past the hour. "You're not late at all. We were just standing around talking. This is my aunt, Pat Rivers."

"Hello," he said before meeting her gaze again.

Pat smiled. "I'm pleased to meet you, Aaron."

He nodded, then turned to face Kayla again.

That was her signal to get started, she supposed. After giving Aunt Pat a look that said a silent "wish me luck," she walked toward the door of Pat's office. "We're going to meet in here. It will give us more privacy."

"All right."

Once they were alone in the room, Kayla started to feel even more awkward. This guy wasn't like anything she'd imagined, which made her kind of embarrassed. She'd taken a lot of guesses and questions and spun them up in her mind to make him into someone really strange.

She knew better than to let her imagination run rampant, too. Mamm always said it was better to give people the benefit of the doubt. She should have remembered that.

"Have a seat," she said, then took her aunt's wheelie chair. "So, you intend to take the GED?"

"I do."

"I heard you want to work on math?"

"*Jah.* And vocabulary. When I skimmed through a study guide at the library, I realized that there are a lot of English words I've never even heard of."

"I felt the same way." She wrote that down. "Back when I was preparing for the test, I made up a schedule. We might want to do the same thing. When is your test?"

"I'm not sure."

That drew her up short. "No?"

"I'm not in a real big hurry to learn everything. I thought we'd take it one step at a time."

"Are you sure you want to prepare that way? You might pay for lessons you don't need otherwise."

"I'm not worried about that."

"Really?" She was shocked. *Does he really have unlimited funds?*

He frowned. "I don't see how my financial situation matters to you."

"It doesn't. I was just surprised, that's all." Hoping to ease the tension that was brewing between them, she joked, "I forget that everyone isn't on a tight budget like I am. My mother used to say I never met a penny on the ground that I didn't pick up."

He didn't smile at her comment. If anything, he looked even more uncomfortable.

Starting to worry that they were never going to find a connection, she said, "Before we get started, maybe we could talk for a few minutes?"

He made a show of checking the time, which was a bit irritating since he had arrived five minutes late.

"*Jah*. We can talk. Um, what would you like to talk about?"

"You. Me."

His hazel eyes flared. "You want to discuss *us*?"

"*Jah*. I mean, *nee*. *Nee*, I do not." She felt her cheeks heat. "I mean, I have some questions."

"All right. Sure. What do you want to know?" He looked even more uneasy.

What is his deal? "Okay. I'm going to start with the most obvious. Did you read my fees? Are they all right with you?" Though he wasn't very forthcoming, there was something about him that she wanted to know more about. She found herself on pins and needles while she waited for his answer.

He patted a pocket. "*Jah*. I have your twenty dollars ready. Do you want it first? Is that how you like to handle your classes?"

"No. I just wanted to make sure you understood my fees."

"I understood them fine. Anything else?"

She wanted to ask why he was being so distant and prickly. After all, she was only trying to do him a favor. But because that seemed kind of harsh, she murmured the first other thing that came to her head. "Do you intend to stay Amish?"

His whole body stiffened. "I do."

For some reason, she'd offended him, but she wasn't sure why. Was asking such a thing really that intrusive, given the circumstances? She felt her cheeks heat. "I guess what I'm getting at is: Why are you studying for the GED on the sly? Aren't you done with school?"

"Is it any of your business?"

He could try the patience of a saint. "Uh, yeah," she blurted, giving his rudeness right back to him. "I might be getting paid for this, but I still need to help you. I can't help you study if I don't know what you're studying for."

He stared at her a long second. "Fine. I'm going to take the GED for a specific reason."

"Which is?" she asked before she could take it back.

"Beg pardon, but—"

"Sorry, but if we're going to be spending so much time together, I really do think knowing the reason will help me help you. So, are you going to try to go to college?" He was already stretching things by educating himself on his own, but to enter a college? Well, she seriously doubted there was a group of elders in any church district around here that would allow him to keep his faith and attend college.

"*Nee.*"

For a second, it had looked like he was going to add something, but he didn't. That pause felt like he was keeping something important from her, as if he were speaking in riddles.

She found it annoying. Though a bunch of questions were running through her head, she tamped them down.

If she pried into his life much more, she could be accused of acting exactly like he was—rude and intrusive. "Okay, I'll get some GED study guides from the library and help you with the math and vocabulary they suggest."

"What about today?"

"Let's work on vocabulary words." She had been going to work on math with him, but she wasn't sure what he knew. And he was so prickly that she didn't want to risk offending him even more by asking. However, she had stuck a list of SAT words in her tote bag that morning, a list from back when she'd been studying so hard. She'd had big plans then, plans to score so highly on the GED that she might even get a scholarship to college.

Of course, that was before she'd realized she had to make different plans.

Pulling out the list, she asked, "Did you bring a notebook?"

"*Nee.*"

"You're going to need one soon," she said as she flipped through her own and tore out a sheet. "But we can start on this." She slid the paper and a pen toward him. "Okay, here's the first word. *Frugal.*"

He picked up the pen but didn't do anything. "What do you want me to do?"

"Write it down. Do you want me to spell it?"

She could practically see the muscles in his cheek work as he debated answering. Finally, he nodded. "*Frugal. F-R-U-G-A-L.*"

He wrote down the letters in perfectly neat print. "Okay?"

"What do you think it means?"

"Not spending a lot?"

"Yep. Avoiding waste. Write either of those definitions down."

It took him a minute, but he wrote down the definition she'd given him. "Now what?" he asked.

She paused. Up until now, all of her tutoring experience had been helping kids with their homework assignments. She had no experience making up study guides. But she knew how she studied. "Use it in a sentence."

"Like how?"

"Like you were talking to me or one of your friends. Go."

"I'm not going to use that word in a sentence to a friend." He looked at her like she had two heads.

"How about a brother or sister?" What did it even matter? Why was he making it so hard? When he looked like he was about to argue again, she said, "Stop fighting me, Aaron. Believe it or not, I'm trying to help you. Now, please pretend!"

"Fine." He took a moment, then said, "We act real frugal when we butcher chickens. We use every part, even the feet, in the stew."

She felt like she was about to throw up, but just as she was about to grimace, she saw a look of amusement in Aaron's eyes. "That's good. Here's the next word: *ostentatious*. I'll spell it: *O-S-T-E-N-T-A-T-I-O-U-S*."

After he wrote it down, she said, "It means 'intended to attract notice or impress others.'" She felt a bit of satisfaction watching him write down the definition without her prompting.

Then he looked up. "Like one might wear ostentatious clothes to impress friends."

She noticed he was giving her a funny look. "What?"

"What do you mean?"

"You're looking at me like I'm ostentatious."

"You're the one wearing that necklace."

She pressed her palm to her chest before even thinking about it. Years ago she'd seriously contemplated leaving the faith. She'd had a rocky *rumspringa* and had spent a lot of her days among the English.

One of the jobs she'd taken had been at a big super center, and when she quit, the lady who'd been her confidant and mentor had given her the gold charm with the scrollwork that now bit into her skin. She noticed Aaron was staring at her chest and immediately dropped her hand.

This time he looked away with a faint blush to his cheeks. "Next?"

"Next? Oh." She scanned the page. "Um, *tenacious.*"

"I can't even begin to spell that."

"I never can spell it by myself, either." After spelling it out loud, she said, "It means 'to be stubbornly unyielding.'"

He narrowed his eyes. "I still don't get it."

"You know, like never giving up. Ah, like . . ." She thought fast. "That athlete is really tenacious. He keeps competing even though he's bruised and sore."

"I like that one," he said.

She smiled at him. "Me, too."

Something shifted between them, and before she knew it, her aunt Pat poked her head in.

"Sorry, you two, but your time is up."

Aaron started. "That went by fast."

"I thought so, too." Kayla closed her notebook and stuffed it in her backpack. "Do you want to meet again next week?"

"Yeah." He pulled out a twenty-dollar bill and handed it to her. "I'm sorry it took me a minute to get started."

"You mean that you were rude?"

He rolled his eyes. "Uh-huh."

"It's no big deal." Well, not anymore. Somehow she'd started appreciating his prickliness. "I just needed to know how to help you."

"The truth is that my family doesn't know about this."

"Why not? Would they get mad at you?"

"They just wouldn't understand."

"Because you want to go to college?"

"I wasn't lying. I don't. I have no plans to leave my faith or go to college. I . . . I just want to do something hard, you know? I want to challenge myself to do something I didn't think I could."

"*Jah.* I get that." Unfortunately, she really got that.

"Truly? Well, *gut.*" He stepped back. Now that their session was over, he looked a little more lost. "Well . . . thanks. I better go, and I guess you should, too."

"See you next week, Aaron." Just as he turned away, she remembered they didn't have a way to communicate with each other. "Hey, wait a sec."

"What?"

She ripped off a corner of one of her papers and scribbled down her name and two phone numbers. "The first one is my phone number here. The second is the phone in my kitchen."

"Are you New Order?"

"I am. Do you have access to a phone?"

"We have a shanty down the road. I work at the furniture store, too."

"Okay, we have a plan, then. We can call each other if one of us can't make it or something."

He looked at her writing and smiled. "You might be real smart, but you've got crappy handwriting."

She was so shocked that he had said "crappy" that she started laughing. "I know."

He grinned at her before walking out the door.

She stayed where she was, beaming at the empty doorway. She had to be at least four years older than him. She knew for a fact that she'd done a lot more than he ever had in his sheltered life. But he'd done something no one had been able to do for her in years. He'd made her feel like a girl again.

"Kayla?" Aunt Pat called out. "Do you want a ride, honey?"

"No. Thanks, Pat." When she met her at the door, Kayla noticed she already had her keys and purse out. "Thanks for waiting."

"No problem. But next week you can lock up."

"Yes, ma'am."

As they started walking to Pat's car, she looked at Kayla worriedly. "Are you sure you don't want a ride home? I could run you by a fast-food place."

Pat knew things were pretty sparse at home.

"*Nee*. I have my bike. Plus, *mei daed* said he was going to the store."

"Oh. Well, that's good."

She sounded skeptical. Honestly, Kayla was skeptical, too. Her father had a difficult time these days doing some of the easiest tasks.

There was a good chance he hadn't gone, but she was too old to tell on her dad. Or to try to make him change.

However, she'd learned to pick her battles. She already had a lot on her plate—her job at the sewing shop, her tutoring, and their constant financial worries. Then, there were her private sources of pain: she missed her mother, worried about her father, and regretted everything about Levi.

Jah, there was a lot about her life that she didn't want anyone else to know.

Aaron might be surprised to learn that she had just as many secrets as he did, and she was sincerely hoping he would never find out about them.

It was better if most people in her life never did.

four

• RULE #4 •

*Bring an extra set of clothes. I promise, one day you're going
to be glad you have them.*

If she hurried, Kayla could make it to the bookmobile near the
old Amish schoolhouse before it moved on to the next location.
After quickly saying goodbye to Aunt Pat, she slung her backpack
over her shoulders, hopped on her bike, and pedaled as fast as
she could down a back alleyway, across a vacant lot, and then
down an old county road that hardly anyone seemed to use since
the Troyers sold their land to a developer who was in no hurry to
do anything with it.

She knew it was silly to make such an effort to catch the
bookmobile instead of simply going to the library in town, but
Sarah Anne always knew what books she would like.

When she came to a stop sign, she barely stopped long enough to check how busy the intersection was before rushing through. She pedaled hard to reach the crest of the hill, and then she spied the bookmobile in the distance. Though she was too old for such things, she felt like pumping her fist in the air and giving a shout of thanks. She'd made it!

Sarah Anne grinned when Kayla pulled open the door and stepped inside. "Kayla! Now isn't this a nice surprise!" Taking in her pink cheeks, she added, "You look like the wind blew you in."

"I was afraid I was going to be too late." Seeing that it was almost half past six, she added, "I'm so glad we've had a spot of dry weather. If it had been snowing, I wouldn't have been able to ride my bike to work."

"I'm glad you made it here before I left, too."

"I promise I'll hurry."

"I don't need that promise. I can stay a few minutes later if need be."

"Are you sure?"

"Very sure. Now, try to relax, dear. After all, you're surrounded by friends."

By "friends" she meant the books. Perhaps it sounded a bit corny, but Kayla knew it was true. Books had saved her life a time or two. Well, at least, it felt that way. "I'd love to sit and visit, but I should probably leave as soon as I can. I'm sure *mei daed* is home by now."

"Of course, dear." Bending down, Sarah Anne pulled out a stack of four books and set them on the countertop. "I must have had a sixth sense about seeing you sometime soon because as soon as I saw these come in, I put them aside for you."

Kayla scanned the authors' names, the titles, and finally

the beautiful covers displaying handsome men and fresh-faced young women with white *kapps* on their heads. Everyone looked so very much in love. "Oh, *danke*! Thank you so much."

"It's not only my job, it's my pleasure, dear. Who else would I bring these Amish romances to if not my favorite Amish romance reader?"

She could feel her cheeks flush. Honestly, she was a little bit embarrassed by her love for the books. The moving stories, all filled with happily ever afters made her so happy. They were her secret addiction, her catnip, the way she was able to sleep at night. They were how she'd gotten through the last three years.

Before that?

Before that, she'd had hopes and dreams that one day she was going to have love and romance, too.

"May I have all four books? I promise I won't keep them long."

"Of course, dear. Hand me your library card, and I'll check them out so you can get on your way."

This was why she pedaled all over the county and had memorized Sarah Anne's schedule. She did things like this. *"Danke,"* she said again as she carefully placed the books in her backpack. "I'll see you soon."

"Be careful going home, dear. It's dark out, you know."

"I've got lots of reflectors on my bicycle, but I will. You be careful, too." After exchanging one more smile, Kayla hurried out to rush home, hoping her father had made it there all right, too.

She'd lied when she'd told Sarah Anne that she feared her father would worry where she was. Kayla was fairly certain that he wouldn't worry at all.

When she arrived home, she realized her guess had been right. Daed wasn't home. She bit back a sigh. This was why she always had a schedule and planned things out carefully. Her father was a good, but erratic, man.

Pushing her disappointment to one side—really, it did no good to start wishing he was different—she decided to do the dishes. As she'd expected, the sink was practically full.

But there was also a note that said he was going to go to the grocery store today. Knowing just how empty their refrigerator was, she gave thanks for that.

After making a cup of hot tea, she pulled out her books and decided to focus on them instead of stressing about her new student or her father's whereabouts. Yes, it was much better to think about getting swept away and falling in love instead of dwelling on things that couldn't be changed.

"Sorry I'm late, Kay," Kayla's father called out almost an hour later. "And even though I never made it to the grocery store, I did bring us home some dinner."

So, their cupboards were going to stay bare.

Getting off the couch, Kayla met her father in their small kitchen and shook her head when she saw the sack he was holding. "Taco Nacho again? Oh, Daed."

He almost looked embarrassed. "Sorry, but you know how *gut* these tacos are."

"I know they're good, but that doesn't mean it's okay to eat fast-food tacos all the time. Honestly, Daed. Sometimes I feel like I'm talking to a wall."

"Come now. I'm far more personable than any old wall."

"This is true." Knowing that it did no good to fuss at him, she dug into the distinctive red-and-green sack. "You got me a fajita bowl."

"I knew you'd be pleased."

"I am. *Danke.*"

He leaned down and pressed a kiss to her brow. "I may be a fast-food junkie, but I'm not completely oblivious."

"You're not oblivious about a lot of things."

His blue eyes softened, but he didn't say anything. Walking to the sink, he scrubbed his hands. Her father was working over at an RV factory in Millersburg. Every morning a driver hired by the company stopped at the end of their street, and her father ran out to meet the passenger van just like he was a boy trying to catch the bus. Every evening, it dropped him off, and he would slowly walk back to their place, unless he got off earlier and went to the store or Taco Nacho.

But there were also many days when he didn't feel up to working. On those days, he would use their kitchen phone and call in to work, making up a handful of excuses about why he wasn't able to go. On his worst days, he simply didn't get out of bed.

Mr. Edmonds, his boss, was a kind man. And a good one, too. So far he kept Kayla's dad on the payroll, which was a blessing. He never, however, gave her father a raise or a bonus and had said he wouldn't until Jay Kauffman went to work every day for six months.

Kayla didn't know if that would ever happen.

So, her father had a good enough job, and that was always good enough . . . if she didn't remember how he used to be before her mom died.

Their life had been so different before Mamm had gotten sick and Kayla had been burdened with her father's failings. That period of time had been so hard, but she'd had Levi to lean on and a future with him to look forward to. But then one day, just after the first anniversary of her mother's death, Levi broke things off with her, saying she simply wasn't worth the problems that she carried on her shoulders. His departure had changed her, too. Now Kayla just tried to get through each day and did her best to forget about the person she used to be three years ago.

That girl studied for the GED just because she'd known she was very smart. That girl had been giggling and fun and full of plans for her future with the cutest boy she knew.

But the Lord had other plans for her. For some reason, He'd decided that her mother needed to get a terrible, invasive cancer that took her life in five months. That her father would sink into a depression that he couldn't seem to pull out of. And that all her dreams would be smothered under too many responsibilities.

"How was your day?" he asked as he continued to scrub.

"It was *gut*."

"Anything new?"

"Jah." She paused, then decided to tell him about Aaron. "I got a new student to tutor today."

He turned off the faucet. "That's *gut* news. So, what's the story. Is it a boy or girl? Amish or English?"

"This time it's not a child. He's a grown man. And, he's Amish."

"Really? Who is it? Anyone I know?"

"Maybe. Maybe not. He's Old Order. I don't think I should tell you his name though."

He turned to look at her. "Why not?"

"He's trying to keep his lessons a secret. Since he's paying me, I think I should honor that wish."

"Why? How old is he?"

"Around my age. I'd say he was twenty or so."

"That old?" A line formed in between his brows. "Why is he wasting his time and money getting tutored? He should be working."

"He is."

"Then what does an Amish boy-almost-man need to be tutored in?"

"He's secretly studying for the GED."

A slow smile lit his face. "Secretly, huh? Well, I guess it's a good thing that you're his tutor, then. If anyone is good at secrets, it's you."

"I guess that's true."

He looked at her for a moment before pulling out two plates. "Grab your food, Kay. We might as well eat while it's hot."

She neatly placed her fajita bowl on her plate and then started fishing for salsa. "I don't know what to think of him, honestly," she said as they walked to the small, two-person table nestled in the corner of the kitchen. "He wasn't all that friendly."

"Not everyone is friendly, but that's okay, I reckon. Don't forget that you never know what someone else is going through."

This was a common reminder from him, but like always, she was grateful for it. His words were a small reminder of how far he had come since her mom had gotten sick, been hospitalized, and died, leaving him angry and short-tempered, with a broken heart, a motherless daughter, and more bills than he could afford to pay.

Everything had caught up to him about two months after Mom's funeral. He'd lost his job, yelled at everyone, and barely took care of her. But then things had gotten better.

Swallowing the lump that had suddenly formed in her throat, Kayla smiled at him. "You're right, Dad. That is something for me to remember."

"I've got some more good news for you. I got paid today." He smiled as he put a check and a stack of cash on the counter. "And, old Mr. Edmonds gave me a little something extra, since I've been putting in some overtime."

"Looks like we're going to be able to pay rent this month," she teased. He actually hadn't missed a payment in more than a year.

He pretended to look affronted. "It's better than that. I can pay rent and cable and give you a hundred bucks for groceries. You're going to be able to keep your money."

Her smile disappeared. They were in this together. "I'll still give you half."

"No need. Go to the movies or buy a dress or something." When she was about to argue again, he shook his head. "I'm okay, Kayla. Now you need to be okay, too. Life still goes on."

"Thanks, Daed."

He smiled at her before turning away, embarrassed.

After silently giving thanks for their food, they started eating. Kayla looked through a magazine Aunt Pat had given her that morning. It was an *Englischer* magazine, of course, chock full of beauty tips and fashion ideas. She read about designer purses and imagined using some of those beauty treatments that were supposed to make a woman look younger, thinner, and happier.

And, for a split second, she felt a little envious.

She looked up to find her father going through his cell phone, even though he wasn't supposed to have one. She wanted to ask what he was looking at so intently, but she didn't. Instead, she simply ate and remembered the two years during her *rumspringa* when she had carried a cell phone with her all the time.

It had been a most addicting contraption. She'd loved looking at people's posts and tweets and pictures. She'd loved pretending people who wanted to be her friends online actually were her friends in real life. Only when things had gotten so bad had she'd realized that none of those strangers meant anything to her . . . and that there was little shared online that was real.

Dad threw his trash away. "I'm off to the shower."

"All right. I'm going to sit here another minute."

He hesitated, then ran a hand over her hair before walking down the hall to his bedroom.

When she was alone again, she gazed at her father's abandoned cell phone. For a moment, she wished she had her old phone back and she could text Aaron. Though, what she'd say she had no idea, just something to continue their communication.

Pushing away that fanciful thought, Kayla wiped down the countertops and prepared the percolator for the morning's coffee. Then, with nothing left for her to do in the kitchen, she went to her own room and sat on the bed.

It was moments like this when she missed the way she used to be. Back when she was in school, she would trade notes with her girlfriends and read them all in her room at night. Sometimes, even Levi would write her something sweet and she'd sleep with his note under her pillow.

Then, too, there were the days when her mother was still

alive. Back when Kayla was a teenager, the three of them would sit in front of the fireplace on chilly evenings. Sometimes they'd talk. Sometimes they'd pull out flashlights and read whatever books they'd checked out from the library or play Scrabble. But most of the time, they simply sat together in the quiet. She'd loved that time, so loved her little family of three.

Now? Now, she was busy, busy, busy until she found the solace of her room. But hand in hand with that solace was the knowledge that she had little else, just her books and her dreams that she pushed aside over and over again.

Kayla set one of the romances she had checked out from Sarah Anne's bookmobile on her lap and tried to look forward to getting lost in the story. But all she seemed to want to do was think about the man she'd met today. The man with dark blond hair, a firm jaw, and enough magnetism to make her feel alive again years after she'd realized that feeling so much was only going to make her hurt inside. Nothing good lasted forever.

five

· RULE #5 ·

Pets should not be allowed in the bookmobile. Especially not
unaccompanied ones. Or puppies that are teething.

"It's Friday!" Tiny announced to her family when she entered the kitchen.

As usual, her proclamation didn't have much of an effect on the other members of her family. Aaron raised his eyebrows but only scooped up another bite of oatmeal. Rebecca smiled at her but seemed more intent on playing with her cereal.

Daed sipped his coffee. "*Gut meiyah, maydel. Danke* for the reminder about it being *Freidawk.*"

"No need to be sarcastic, Father."

He smiled and slathered some jam on his toast.

"Do you want oatmeal, Tiny?" Mamm asked.

"Sure." Feeling slightly deflated, she poured herself a glass of orange juice and a cup of coffee before joining her siblings and father at the large circular table that took up most of the kitchen.

Jack, being Jack, looked up at her and grinned. "Glad you're pleased to welcome the new day, Tiny. What's made you so pleased about it?" He waggled his eyebrows. "Do you have big plans for the day?"

"Not really." At least, not yet.

"Hmm," Mamm said as she placed a steaming bowl of oatmeal in front of Tiny.

Reaching for the fresh milk, Tiny poured a good amount on top of her oats, then added a generous helping of brown sugar and raisins. As usual, the simple breakfast was hot and filling. Usually she could think of nothing better, especially on such a snowy and cold morning, but now, oatmeal couldn't compare to the anxiousness she was feeling whenever she thought of Joel.

She couldn't imagine that anything in the world would. Whenever she thought of him, her palms got sweaty, and her heart felt like it was beating a little bit faster. Was it love? She wasn't sure about that, but she supposed it could be.

"Your food's getting cold," Jack said. "You'd best eat that oatmeal before it turns the consistency of glue."

Ugh. She hated when that happened. Hastily, she ate a large spoonful.

"*Jah*, you should eat up, daughter, as fast as you can," Mamm said. "We're going to be making some deliveries this afternoon just around the corner."

Joel's house! Tiny lifted another spoonful to her mouth.

Her father lifted his eyebrows as she took another bite. "I've rarely seen our Tiny eat so much so quickly." He looked across the kitchen at her mother. "Do you know something we don't know, Violet?"

"I might," Mamm said airily.

Tiny felt her stomach churn a bit. Their mother was a lot of things, but evasive wasn't one of them, which just proved that she knew something. Their mother could neither lie nor keep a secret.

Daed put down his spoon. "Well, don't keep us in suspense. What do you know that I don't?"

Her mother played coy. "Hmm. Well, I know that it isn't supposed to stop snowing until nightfall."

"That's it?" Jack asked.

Mamm looked back at her. "What do you think, Tiny?"

"I'm not sure to what you are referring."

"Well, now we know something is up," Aaron said. "Tiny always has something to say about everything."

"Don't be rude to your sister," Mamm murmured softly.

Feeling both of her brothers' gazes on her, Tiny ate her last bite and got to her feet. "I'll start on the dishes, Mamm."

Aaron grunted and scooted out of his chair. "*Danke* for breakfast, Mamm," he said politely, as he always did.

"Of course, dear Aaron," Mamm said with soft smile. "Don't forget your lunch, and please be careful in the weather."

"I will." He picked up the small cooler. "Bye all."

Just as Rebecca waved a hand, Aaron shot a look at Tiny. "Tell Joel hello for me. He's been around far too little of late."

"I—I . . ." Tiny stumbled over her words as Aaron shrugged on his coat and left the house.

Jack and her parents laughed as they put their bowls in the sink.

Perturbed, she turned on the faucet and pulled out the dish soap.

"You didn't really think you were going to get away with a secret like that, did you?" Jack whispered as he handed her his bowl.

"Maybe," she grumbled as she took it from him. She'd certainly hoped and prayed she could keep her new development with Joel a secret for at least a little while longer.

Jack laughed again before throwing on his thick coat and heading out to the barn. Her father followed soon after, leaving her with the dishes, Rebecca, and her mother's sparkling eyes.

Ugh. She loved her family, she truly did. But that didn't mean she didn't wish for a little bit of privacy from time to time.

Picking up the scrub brush, she started washing the bottom of the pot.

Her mother, her hands around a steaming cup of fresh coffee, leaned against the counter. "What is going on with you and Joel now, dear?"

Tiny ached to say nothing, to ignore her mother's question or announce that it wasn't her business, or even run up to her room so she could keep her news to herself for just a little while longer.

However, there was no point in doing that. Her mother would be mighty hurt, and she couldn't do that to her. They were too close for that. And besides, Joel was best friends with Aaron, which meant that her brother probably knew more about her relationship than she did.

"Joel mentioned that he would like to come calling one day soon, or that maybe I could even stop by to see him at the shop one day during his lunch hour."

"Oh my. That is news, isn't it?"

"I don't know . . . but I hope so." Which was a huge understatement. Joel had been her neighbor her whole life. Back when they were small, they'd all been thick as thieves. She'd practically been one of the boys, playing for hours with Aaron, Jack, and Joel. But then, right around the time she turned fourteen, Joel had begun to ignore her. She'd been crushed—until Aaron had told her he and Jack had told him to stop staring at their little sister. Even Tim, who always acted like his little sister was a baby, had gotten involved, pretty much threatening to beat up Joel if Joel even thought about flirting with her.

Tiny had been so embarrassed and mad. She'd gone to her parents and complained, but to her surprise, her parents had agreed that Tiny was too young to have a beau.

Joel had started avoiding her and even flirted with some of her friends at different gatherings they all attended. It had been so hard, especially since she soon couldn't seem to think about anyone else but him.

But then Tim left, their parents had basically shunned him, and Joel reached out to her. She'd clung to his friendship like a lifeline. Little by little, Aaron and Jack had stopped interfering, and her parents even started to sound as if they would allow him to come calling.

But Joel hadn't seemed to want to do anything but be her friend.

Until lately.

Her mother looked at her for a long moment. When she spoke again, her voice was tentative. Very un-Mamm-like. "Tiny, I know you and Joel have been kind of flirting with the idea of having a relationship for quite a long time. Do you really care for him more than Luke Yoder? Luke is such a fine young man."

"We don't need to talk about this, Mamm."

"I don't mean to embarrass you, but I do want to point out that just because you two have known each other for a long time and Joel is best friends with Aaron . . . that doesn't mean you shouldn't allow Luke to come calling, too."

Tiny felt like she needed to grab hold of the sink for stability, she was so surprised. "Multiple men?"

Mamm picked up the rag she'd just dampened and began to gently rub Rebecca's face with it. "You're a lovely and talented young woman, dear. If you wanted to maybe think about other boys courting you, that wouldn't be a bad thing."

"Mamm, I'm not interested in Luke. I mean, not that much . . ."

"I like Joel very much, Tiny, but, ah, he isn't exactly much of a suitor, is he?"

"I think he's ready now." She'd been waiting for years for Joel to finally make his move and declare he was ready to court her in earnest. With some dismay, she realized she needed to come to terms with the fact that his waiting could no longer have anything to do with Tim's threats, her age, or even Jack and Aaron's friendship. But as doubts began to form in her mind, she wondered if she'd gotten that all wrong. Maybe while she'd been waiting, Joel had been focused on someone else.

"Oh." Her mother smiled, a broad smile. "Of course. Sometimes I forget how young you both are."

"We aren't young. I'm seventeen."

"Seventeen isn't old, dear."

"I'm old enough to know my mind."

Just as her mother seemed ready to argue that fact, Rebecca fussed, saving the day.

Her mother frowned. "Goodness, Becca. You are a mess. Yet again." Hoisting Tiny's little sister up to her hip, her mother started for the stairs. "I guess I'm going to have to give her a quick bath. Somehow she managed to get oatmeal in her hair."

"I'll finish the dishes and pull out the jelly jars," Tiny offered. Anything to have a little bit of peace and quiet.

"*Danke*, daughter. Yes, you do that. But do a little bit of thinking while you're at it, okay?"

"All right, Mamm."

As she watched her mother head upstairs, she thought about Joel, with his wholesome good looks and sweet, if somewhat inattentive, manner. She'd been so excited to go visit him at work. He was finally making a move, and she'd been waiting ever so long for him to do just that.

But the more she thought, the more she realized that it had never occurred to her to wonder if she didn't deserve a little bit more from an almost-boyfriend. Which made her start analyzing herself, something she wasn't particularly fond of doing.

As she washed the breakfast dishes and prepared to sterilize the jelly jars, Tiny allowed herself the benefit of self-reflection. Why on earth was she not more intrigued by Luke Yoder? He was handsome, kind, and so steady and sure. He even had his own house—he was a catch indeed. Joel was so very different, and that was putting it mildly.

So, why did he still make her heart race whenever he gave her even the slightest bit of attention? Why did he sometimes make plans and then cancel them because he "suddenly had to work"?

Why had she never questioned that? Was it because she

loved Joel so much . . . or because she was afraid not to love him?

As the answer churned in her mind, she put the kettle on and sat down. She needed to think about this for a moment.

Maybe a long one.

six

• RULE #6 •

*It's okay if you don't have all the answers. That's what the
Internet is for.*

It was their third lesson. But even though they'd barely sat
down in the workroom at the back of the sewing shop, Aaron
was already getting the feeling that something wasn't quite right
with Kayla. She looked pale and seemed a little bit lethargic. He
hoped she wasn't sick.

"Did you have any questions about last week's lessons?"
Kayla asked as she sat down across from him with a sigh, almost
as if she was carrying the weight of the world on her shoulders.

"I don't have any questions."

Her blue eyes sharpened. "Sure?"

"I'm sure. No questions, beyond realizing that there are going to be a great many words on that test that I don't understand," he quipped, trying to make a joke of his lack of knowledge.

Kayla smiled back, but it looked strained. "All right. So, what do you want to work on today? More vocabulary or math?" Just as he opened his mouth to tell her, she flipped through the study booklet and spoke some more. "Or government?" she suggested. "We could talk about the division of power in the federal government." At last she paused and looked up at him. "Do you want to do that?"

Aaron was about as interested in the federal government as he was interested in getting a hole in his head. But since Kayla was acting like that was her preference, he said, "Government is good."

"Okay." Still all business, she flipped through the booklet and pulled out a pencil. "Now, the first thing you need to understand are the checks and balances that are in place." She paused. "You had better write this down."

He opened up his notebook and started writing as quickly as he could in pencil.

After she glanced at his chicken-scratched notes, she continued, speaking at a rapid-fire pace. In minute detail, she went over the legislative, executive, and judicial branches.

All of it was unfamiliar, and little of it made sense. Realizing just how big of a goal he had, Aaron wondered for about the seven hundred twenty-first time if he was stupid for even trying to do something so difficult.

"Aaron?"

"Hmm?"

"Are you, ah, ready now?"

He picked up his pencil again. "Sorry. My mind drifted off, I guess."

"It is a lot." Her expression was sympathetic, but his ineptitude didn't seem to slow her down any. On and on Kayla continued. Every so often, she would pause, waiting for him to keep up before droning on again.

Aaron pretended not to be embarrassed that he was probably misspelling every other one of the words he was writing down.

But his mistakes weren't what had his attention. No, it was that everything about Kayla seemed so different today. So much more distant from the way she'd acted during their first two lessons. He wondered what was going on . . . Then, of course, he started worrying that he'd done something wrong.

"Now that we've gone over the details about veto powers, we can tackle—"

"Kayla, what is going on with you?"

He'd already written seven pages, and his hand was starting to cramp. He no longer wanted to pretend he cared about whether they lived in a democracy or a dictatorship.

She froze. "What do you mean?"

She sounded defensive, but just as he would with Tiny, he wasn't going to back down and pretend nothing was the matter. That never did anyone any good. "You seem really different than you have the last two weeks. It's obvious that something is going on. What is it? Are you sick? Or, are you upset with me? Did I do something to offend you?"

She paused for a moment before shaking her head. "*Nee*, it's nothing to do with you. You don't need to worry about it."

"I might not know the branches of government as well as you do, but I'm not an idiot. If you don't want to tell me what's going on, then don't. But don't tell me not to care. I mean, we're friends now, right?"

She inhaled sharply. "*Jah*. I guess we are." When he raised his eyebrows, she kind of shook herself. "I'm sorry, Aaron. I suppose I have been acting rather distracted and rude. I'll try to be better. Now—"

"*Nee*, Kayla. I'm not complaining about having a grumpy teacher. I'm more concerned about you. You seem . . ." He searched for the appropriate word and wished he knew more of those GED words. Maybe one of them would have described her better. "Preoccupied?"

She leaned back. She was wearing a light blue dress and matching apron, and her dark curly hair was springing in wayward curls around her face. The blue fabric set off her eyes, though he reckoned they were less the color of a winter sky and more the hue of a young blue jay's wing. She would have looked quite fetching . . . if she had been in a better mood.

"Aaron, I'm sorry. You aren't wrong. I am preoccupied. But, don't worry. I'll get better." Flipping a page in the study guide she was following, she said, "Now, what do you think about transition of power? Do you have any questions?"

"*Nee*. But I am curious about your problems."

She shook her head. "It's nothing for you to worry about."

Okay. Well, that put him firmly in his place. He was let down, which didn't make any sense. They hardly knew each other. Tamping down his disappointment, he pointed to the flowchart on the page. "I understand all of this but not so much about the electoral colleges."

She flipped the page again, then launched into an explanation. Aaron tried to understand the ramifications of districting and conventions, but his mind kept drifting. He found himself thinking about how pretty her curly dark brown hair was and how much he liked the way she was so focused on the information that she hardly seemed aware of anything else.

"So, do you understand the differences now?"

"I think so."

Looking up at the clock, she winced. "I guess we're finishing in the nick of time. Our hour is up."

He pulled out a twenty-dollar bill and passed it to her. *"Danke."*

"Thank you, Aaron." Slipping the money into a pocket of her dress, she said, "Would you like to meet again next week?"

He nodded. "Yep. We can finally tackle math." He barely held back a grimace.

"I'll be ready." She pulled on her coat. "Hey, Aaron?"

"Yeah?"

"Do you ever have any doubts about taking the test?"

"I do. Actually, I have second thoughts all the time. I'm pretty sure that even with all your help, there's a good chance I'm still not going to pass this test. And if that happens, I'm fairly sure that it's going to be difficult to deal with. Especially since you're going to be the only other person in the world who knows just how hard I tried."

"Why put yourself through this, then? Especially since you're keeping everything a secret?"

"I guess I figure everybody has to put themselves out there at one time or another. I almost hope I fail, because then it will remind me that the goal was to learn something new and to try, not just succeed. I need to have hope." He smiled, feeling like he was probably sounding like a syrupy-sweet card one found in a drugstore.

"Do you really believe that? That you need to have hope?"

He nodded. "I wouldn't be paying you so much of my money if I didn't."

"I guess not." She smiled softly.

They walked back out into the shop, then straight toward the main entrance. When they were on the sidewalk, she said, "How are you getting home?"

"I'm walking. What about you? Is someone giving you a ride?" He hoped so. It was late and getting dark, and snow was starting to fall again.

"No. No one is picking me up. I guess I'm walking, too." She paused again. "Which way are you headed?"

He pointed to his right. "That way."

"I'm headed that way, too." She didn't move though.

Feeling like she needed someone to talk with, he said, "Do you want to get a cup of coffee or something? We could go to Sacred Grounds. It's close. I have time."

"*Danke,* but I better get home. I told my father I'd make him dinner tonight."

He felt foolish now. Of course she didn't want to sit around and have a coffee date with him. "Oh. Okay. See you."

She smiled at him again and set off without another word.

Aaron forced himself to remember that she was older than him. She had a whole life and probably only thought of him as a kid. In addition, she'd already taken this test, and as far as he could tell, no one had helped her study. She'd simply been smart enough. Unlike him. Even if they could overcome their age difference, it wasn't as if she was suddenly going to like some boy she had to define vocabulary words for.

He shook his head before heading home. But after ten minutes, he saw a familiar face. "Hey, Joel. What brings you out to this side of town?"

"Hiya, Aaron. I'm on my way home. Why?"

"Seems kind of an out-of-way route." Joel's work was on the opposite side of Berlin. At least, Aaron had thought it was.

"Does it?" He shrugged. "I finished work a little early today and have been running a couple of errands. I had some other things to take care of. You know."

But Joel looked guilty and he seemed to be leaving Jane Shultz's property.

Usually Aaron couldn't care less about what plans Joel might have had. But Tiny liked him a lot, and he could tell she was counting on him to step up soon and declare his intentions.

Because of that, he prodded a bit. "Were you just at Jane Shultz's *haus*?"

Joel's posture tensed. "Any reason you're quizzing me, Aaron?"

"Not really, except that I like looking after my sister."

"Tiny?"

The last thing he wanted to do was play another game. "You know that I'm not speaking of Rebecca."

A look of guilt flashed in Joel's eyes. "I don't know what Tiny's been telling you, but she has nothing to worry about. Not that it's any of your business."

Something still didn't seem right about Joel's attitude, but Aaron knew that if he prodded any further, he'd push Joel away. "Good to hear." He smiled. "Sorry. I guess I'm still used to looking out for her. We might be all older, but she's my little sister, after all."

"I understand, though you are right. We're all older now. Tiny certainly doesn't need you watching over her like you used to." After they walked another few steps, Joel said, "Your curiosity has sparked mine. Isn't this rather late for you to be getting off work?"

"It is."

"Want to share what you were doing this afternoon?"

Joel's eyes were shining, and there was a new edge to his tone. Aaron figured he was due for it, too. "Nope. I guess we're both destined to have a couple of secrets to keep."

"Maybe so, Aaron. Maybe so."

The whole conversation had left Aaron with a bad taste in his mouth, like he'd just sipped straight lemon juice when he'd been hoping for lemonade.

But perhaps that was what he deserved. After all, one couldn't always squeeze for information and expect to find only sweetness. Sometimes one got something just as sour and shocking as one deserved.

seven

The moment their plots of land came into view, Joel waved
a hand and told his friend goodbye. Honestly, their departure
couldn't have come fast enough. Aaron, usually the most easygoing person he knew, had suddenly turned into a nosy busybody.

Though, that wasn't really fair, Joel knew. After all, he was
due to come over to see Tiny in just two hours. He wouldn't have
expected her to keep that a secret. Or expected Aaron not to start
looking at him a little bit differently.

But the worst thing in the world would be if the Coblentz
family ever got word of what he was doing. Odd chores around

Jane Shultz's house was definitely not going to be looked at with any favor at all.

Jane was a young Mennonite widow, a woman barely a year older than Aaron and himself. She'd married Wen Shultz, a widower who was not only old enough to be her father, but also in poor health. He'd died before they'd been married for a full year and left her with a large house and, folks said, a mighty sizable bank account.

To make matters even worse for the gossip mill, Jane kept to herself and hardly went to church anymore. More than a couple members of their community—including his own mother—seemed to take great pride in pointing that out to everyone else.

However, when Jane had first called his family's phone shanty and offered him the job, Joel hadn't felt compelled to refuse it. Not that he'd tried too hard anyway. As far as he was concerned, he'd waited long enough to court Tiny Coblentz. Courting her meant that he was financially ready to take on a wife, and because of his own family's situation, he knew he wasn't going to get any funds from them.

When he saw Jane in person for the first time, everything made so much more sense. She had multiple sclerosis and couldn't get around easily on her own.

All he had to do was keep his extra part-time job a secret from as many people as possible. The only person he'd talked about it with was his father, who, though not one to give much credence to folks having nothing better to do than wag their tongues, had agreed that the job was best kept private. Daed had even gone so far as to promise to keep the news from his mother as long as he could.

He was glad of that, though as he looked down at his trousers, he kind of wished that he could announce he had been cleaning Jane's dirty barn for the last four hours. It had been a thankless job, and he'd almost been bit by her horse and kicked by the donkey she'd adopted just weeks after Mr. Shultz's death.

"Joel, at last you're home," his mother called out from the kitchen. "Come here and talk to me. I've been wondering if you'd like me to prepare a basket for you to take over to the Coblentzes' when you go over."

"That's nice of you, Mamm, but I don't think it's necessary."

She poked her head out from the kitchen. "Are you sure? It's just some orange marmalade and sugar cookies."

Seeing that she already had everything ready, he smiled at her. "Oh. *Jah*, Mamm. The Coblentzes will like this a lot," he said as he pulled off his boots. *"Danke."*

"You're welcome. So, when will you—oh, Joel. I'm afraid you smell, son."

"I know. I need to go shower."

"What have you been doing?"

Luckily, he'd already gone over a list of fibs that he could say with his father. "I decided to start taking a few odd jobs here and there for extra cash."

"You have time for that?"

"*Jah*, Mamm. Don't worry. Now, um, I really do need to shower. I *canna* be late for Tiny, you know."

"Of course not. Get on with you now." But as he strode by her, he could practically feel her piercing glare on his back.

This was awful. Beyond awful. There was no telling how long he was going to be able to keep this up. Unfortunately, he was fairly sure that it wasn't going to be long enough.

It seemed that watching Joel Lapp cross the street and walk up the long driveway to their house was more exciting than almost anything else her family had done in quite a while. In fact, the only one who didn't seem all that interested in Joel's progress was Rebecca, and that was only because Mamm had given her a cookie and she was having a grand time smushing it in her palms and smearing it all over her face.

The rest of them, though? Well, Tiny reckoned she should have brought out the popcorn, they were so entertained.

Jack was standing next to their mother and grinning like a factory worker on payday. "He's holding a basket, Tiny. Does that surprise you?"

She knew better than to ask, but she still did. "Should it?"

"If he's bringing you a gift, I guess he's finally courting you in earnest. There's no telling what he'll bring next time. Maybe flowers and candy?"

"I don't expect him to bring me anything. And don't you start acting like you know a thing or two about courting, either, Jack. I've never seen you pick any of Mamm's flowers before you've called on girls."

"I wouldn't have picked Mamm's flowers. There's plenty of places to buy them."

Their mother smiled at him fondly. "And I appreciate that."

Tiny rolled her eyes before looking down at her light blue wool dress, black tights, and black boots. Would Joel find her pleasing? Still?

Or, did Jack's teasing hold a grain of truth? Maybe Joel wasn't coming over to finally declare his intentions. Maybe he was coming over to let her know that he'd found someone else. Feeling nervous now, she nibbled on her bottom lip and stepped farther away from Rebecca, who was now tossing her gummy, wet cookie on the floor. "Mamm, sorry, but Rebecca's making a big mess."

"I know. Don't fret. If she wasn't doing that, she would be making a mess ten other ways."

"Ah, I can see his expression now. He looks intent," Jack announced. "I reckon he has something on his mind, Tiny."

She caught herself from peeking out the window once again. "Stop. You're making me nervous."

"All I'm doing is giving you some information. That's all. It's better to be prepared, you know."

Before she could tell him to go away, Aaron came to her rescue. "Stop making our sister worried when there's nothing to worry about. When was the last time you went calling anyway, Jack?"

"Not lately." When they all started chuckling, he added, "But that doesn't mean I can't tease our sister from time to time."

Joel was now just a few yards away. When he looked up at the house, his pace seemed to slow. *What does that mean?*

"Can't you all go somewhere else?" she asked, not even caring that she sounded as stressed out as she felt. "Joel's going to see you standing there. I'm sure of it."

"So what if he does?"

"He'll probably turn right around, that's what."

Her father spoke up for the first time. "He's not going to do that, dear. But I'll shuttle everyone away and give you two some privacy." He stopped. "But not too much privacy."

"Daed, stop."

Aaron grinned. "Come now. Would you even expect any less?"

"*Nee.*" Had she hoped for it though? Definitely. Putting her hands on her hips, she said, "It's a wonder he's coming over at all, what with the way you all are so overbearing." Not to mention how all of her brothers had threatened him all those years ago. But that was the point, surely. It had been years ago. She was a grown woman now. They needed to realize that and not just use her personal life as reason to *poke fun at her.*

He knocked on the door.

She froze.

Luckily, her mother walked right over to the door and opened it with a gracious smile. "Joel, how nice to see you. It's been far too long."

"*Jah.* I reckon we've all been real busy."

"Indeed. Well, come in now. It's cold out. Let me take your coat, too."

Just as Joel passed it over to her mother, Tiny knew it was time to join them. "Hello, Joel."

He immediately turned to face her. "Hiya, Tiny," he said softly.

There was something new in his expression. Something soft and personal. It was there in his tone, too.

"I've made some *kaffi* and cookies. Would you like to join me in the library?"

"I would. I almost forgot that you all have a library room."

"I'll bring your refreshments out in a few moments, Tiny," Mamm called out.

"*Danke,*" Tiny replied, but to be honest, she hardly heard her mother. Or noticed her brothers standing with their father in the kitchen.

All she was aware of was that Joel had come calling. And, so far, this visit didn't disappoint.

eight

• **RULE #8** •

Keep extra snacks on hand. An extra bottle of water, too.

It had been a terrible walk home. The wind had picked up and seemed determined to freeze Kayla's legs. That was her own fault though. She had only one pair of thick woolen stockings, but she hadn't taken the time to wash them the evening before. So, she'd left the house in thin black tights and had realized within five minutes that she was going to spend the whole day freezing.

But what was one more bother when it had already been a terrible couple of days. She didn't know when things were going to get better, either. Her father's mood had taken a nosedive. After telling Kayla how much he still missed her mother, he'd retreated into his bedroom. He'd barely left for two days, and on the few times he had, he'd been close to uncommunicative.

She didn't know what to do. Not only was she worried about him, but she also knew he was likely going to lose his job, if he hadn't already. And if that happened, she didn't know who else would take him on. Even the Amish-owned businesses, run by kindhearted men and women from their church community, didn't want a worker who couldn't be counted upon.

And if he didn't bring in any income, then they would likely lose their house. She could work all day, seven days a week, and she still wouldn't be able to pay all their bills.

She was so tired.

"Kayla, is that you?"

She turned to find Sarah Anne Miller dressed in jeans, snow boots, and a puffy white coat. She was holding a snow shovel in her gloved hands in front of a cute-looking house that still had Christmas lights on the eaves.

Though she was surprised to see her, Kayla would know the woman's bright eyes anywhere. Some people just seemed to see more than others.

She wasn't in the mood to chat, but she stopped anyway. She owed Sarah Anne so much. Not only did she keep Kayla supplied with books but she'd also recommended Aaron to her. Summoning up a smile, she said, "Hiya, Sarah Anne. I didn't know you lived here."

"It's been my home for thirty years. Are you nearby?"

"I'm just down the road. Maybe a mile?"

"My word. Did you come from work?"

"I did."

"I bet you're freezing. You should come inside for a spell."

"*Danke*, but I ought to be getting on home." She couldn't

help but frown, though. She was in no hurry to take on her father's mood and problems just yet.

"It's only half past five. Are you sure you can't come inside for a little while to warm up your bones? I have chocolate coffee and raspberry scones. Both are freshly made."

"If you've been making scones, you must not have worked today."

"I only went into the main office this morning. It's good to take time from your responsibilities every now and then, don't you agree?"

Kayla thought everything she said made sense . . . and maybe she should heed it, too. "You know what? I would enjoy a cup of coffee and a scone. Thank you."

"I'm so glad. It's been a long day. I could use some girl time." With a quick little turn, Sarah Anne headed to her door. "Come along, then. I promise, I won't keep you too long. Just long enough to thaw out and have a snack." She leaned the shovel against the door, stomped her boots a couple of times, then led the way inside.

When Kayla entered, she was immediately overcome with a feeling of warmth and caring. Antiques, quilts, and comfortable chairs sitting on thick woven rugs greeted her. The scent of lemons and honey filled the air. "Your *haus* is lovely."

"Do you think so? I'm always sure it's a big mess." She toed off her boots and gestured for Kayla to do the same. "Set your coat on one of the pegs, dear, and join me in the kitchen."

After carefully hanging her cloak on a thick silver hook, Kayla paused for a moment at a grouping of pictures encased in bright blue, green, and red frames. The photos were all black and white, but she could see Sarah Anne's bright, inquisitive eyes shining in every one. There was also a handsome man in each photograph. Eager to get a better look, she leaned closer.

"That is Frank. He was my husband," Sarah Anne said. "We were married twenty years."

"It looks like he made you happy."

"He did. He was a good man." A wistful expression filled Sarah Anne's eyes. "Every once in a while, when I first awaken in the morning, I reach over to him. But of course, there's only an empty space."

Though Kayla had never been married, she'd found herself doing almost the same thing. She'd wake up and almost forget that things were so different. Sometimes, she'd even wonder what Levi was doing . . . until she remembered that he'd already found someone new.

Sarah Anne poured coffee into two delicate-looking china cups. "I can never decide if I'm glad to have those few seconds or angry that I do that to myself."

"I've done that myself." With effort, Kayla pulled the bitterness out of her voice. "But life goes on."

"Indeed it does." She cleared her throat. "So . . . do you take cream and sugar?"

"*Jah.*"

"I do, too! You and I are a rare pair, Kayla. Most people try to save their calories."

As Sarah Anne bustled around some more, this time pouring the half-and-half into a pale pink pitcher, Kayla sat down at the wooden table that had been covered with an intricately quilted white-on-white quilt. Unable to help herself, she ran a hand along the worn fabric. "This is lovely."

"It is, isn't it?"

"Did you do all this stitching?"

"Not a bit of it. That is my mother's handiwork, I'm afraid."

"I'd be scared to stain it."

Sarah Anne brought over a small tray holding the two cups, a sugar bowl, the pink pitcher, and a plate of mini scones. "I used to be afraid of that, too." Looking toward the living room, she added, "I kept it neatly folded and encased in plastic. Every so often, I would take it out and show people, then return it to its spot like a fingerprint would ruin it. But then, one time, when I was showing it off to a coworker, I noticed that she wrinkled her nose slightly. It had taken on a plastic smell." She gestured for Kayla to help herself to the sugar and cream and scones. "That's when I realized I was so intent on keeping something precious, I had tainted it."

"You were just trying to preserve it."

"But preserve what? My mother's delicate stitching? Her memory?" She shook her head. "Other people might disagree, but I realized then that my mother didn't spend months of her short life making a beautiful quilt for it to be hidden away and smell old and plasticky, too."

"She'd intended for it to be used."

"She did." Picking up one of the scones, Sarah Anne took a bite. "Oh. This is a good batch, I think."

Kayla had already taken two bites of her own. "They're very good."

"I'm glad you came in. Now, how is young Aaron Coblentz?"

"Aaron?"

"Yes. I mean, you two are still meeting together. Aren't you?"

"We are." Remembering how distant she'd acted toward him during their last lesson, she weighed her words carefully. "I think he is well. I find him confusing, but he might find me the same way as well."

"Truly? He always seems friendly when we visit at the book-mobile."

"He's friendly and seems very kind. To be honest, I don't really understand why he wants to take the test in the first place. He's never come out and told me. I guess it's a secret." After taking a sip of coffee, she thought about how much she tried to hide from the world—Levi's betrayal, the grief for her mother, her confusion and frustration with her father. Even her secret love for books with happy endings. "I'm afraid I have some, too."

"Maybe we all do, yes?" Looking reflective, Sarah Anne mused, "I know I don't always enjoy sharing my bad. I mean, who does?" She chuckled.

"Your bad?" She'd never heard that expression.

"All the things that have marked me over the years. The way I don't always sleep too well at night." Looking down at her hands, she added, "My regrets."

"I suppose you're right."

"I don't know if it matters if I am or not. Not really."

Her almost whimsical way of looking at life caught Kayla's attention. "Perhaps."

"Now, I haven't seen you in the bookmobile lately. Where are you getting your books?"

"I haven't had much time to read lately." That wasn't exactly the truth though. What was wrong was that, for the first time, she wasn't finding as much comfort in her made-up heroes and heroines as she usually did.

"Surely you're joking."

Kayla wasn't sure if Sarah Anne was being serious or not, but she felt a little defensive. "I've got a lot to do."

"Oh. Of course."

"I'm sorry. You've been so kind to me, and here I am, snapping."

"No reason to apologize. It's a librarian's curse, I suppose. We think everyone should have time for books, even if they're busy girls like you."

There was something in the older woman's kindness—her motherliness—that allowed Kayla to lower her shields. "My father isn't doing well," she blurted. "He won't get out of bed, and . . . I think he lost his job."

Sarah Anne's expression went slack. "Oh my word, child! What is wrong? Is he sick?"

"Kind of. But it's not his body that's sick. He still mourns my mother, I think."

"Oh my. Kayla, when did she pass?"

"Three years ago. When I was twenty-three."

"You were so young. That had to be hard."

"I miss her every day. She was a *gut mamm*." She took another sip of coffee. "This might sound bad, but I miss a lot of things that I used to take for granted. My *mamm*, my father smiling and being in charge of everything. Levi."

"Levi?"

"He was my beau. We'd dated for years. I thought we would marry, but we broke up."

Sarah Anne studied her for a long moment. "I'm sorry, Kayla."

"It's okay. Someone once told me that Earth isn't Heaven. Life is supposed to be hard, I think."

"Perhaps, but not all the time, dear. For the record, I'm glad you're living, Kayla. My world would be emptier without you."

Kayla gave Sarah Anne a small smile. "But how do I help my *daed*?"

"It's not my place to say."

Oh, no. She wasn't going to let Sarah Anne off easily now, not when she'd already shared so much. "But if it was?"

"I'd gently remind your father that he is still alive, too. And if that doesn't do the trick, I'd maybe remind him that you are as well. You are too young to raise a father, child."

"He needs me."

"I'm sure he does, but you might need something more than what you have right now, Kayla." She shrugged. "Or, maybe not. Please forgive me, I sometimes have a habit of saying too much. It's a consequence of age, I think."

Kayla's cup was empty, and she'd eaten two mini scones. "I think I had better go. My father is going to be worried about me." That was, if he was out of bed.

"Of course." Sarah Anne popped to her feet. "Go put on your boots, and I'll put a few scones in a bag for you to take home."

"Thank you."

Her mind a clouded mess, she hurried to the entryway and slipped back on her boots and cloak.

"Here you go." Sarah Anne handed her a brown paper tote bag.

Wondering what could be filling up the sack, Kayla found a loaf of bread, a Ziploc bag of scones, and a blue hardcover book. "What is this?"

"Oh. It's . . . Well, it's an old favorite of mine. *Courage to Love.*"

"I haven't heard of it."

"I'd be surprised if you had. It's an old one. A sweet romance, if you will. And, dear, I know you don't have time to read right now, so, don't worry—I won't be quizzing you."

Courage to Love was a lovely book, but a thick one. She reckoned with the way things were going, she likely wouldn't be able to finish it for a couple of months. It didn't sound too interesting to her, either. After all, who would need courage to fall in love?

Thinking like this was no way to repay the woman's kindness. "*Danke*, but I'm afraid I can't accept it. I, um, really don't have much time to read."

"Please, keep it. Enjoy it, or don't. Like I said, I won't be making you give me a book report. Just read it if you have time."

"But that's the problem. I don't have time." Of course, the minute she said it, Kayla wondered if that was exactly the truth. She was beginning to think that she was spending too much time worrying about things she couldn't control.

Sarah Anne pushed aside her comment. "Maybe one day you will, though. In any case, it's yours. A present, if you will. I don't want it back."

"Are you sure?"

"If you went upstairs, you'd see that my hallway is lined with bookshelves." She winked. "Books are good friends, but I probably won't miss it too much."

"I'll take care of it."

"I know you will. And who knows? Perhaps that little book will take care of you from time to time."

Once again, it felt as if Sarah Anne was being cryptic and telling her more than just words.

"*Danke*," Kayla said as she stepped out the door. "It was kind of you to think of me."

"You're welcome, dear."

To Kayla's surprise, Sarah Anne closed the door almost immediately, leaving her alone to walk down the walkway, brown bag in hand. Pushing it out of her mind, she hurried home, working up a sweat and practically race-walking to get away from the cold.

When she opened the door, only silence greeted her. It turned out her father had decided to leave the house, but he hadn't left a note this time.

Staring around the empty room, Kayla almost felt betrayed. Once again, she'd passed up an opportunity to further a relationship in order to help her father. She could have taken Aaron up on his offer for coffee. She could have stayed another few minutes in Sarah Anne's comfortable, cozy home. She could have done so many other things.

Because no one had been waiting for her after all.

nine

Remember to circulate the books that are offered. If, after four months, no one chooses a book, it's time to trade it in for something new.

Aaron had taken to writing his notes in an old-fashioned steno pad that he'd bought to help him wade through the large amount of information he was learning for the test.

After his first tutoring session with Kayla, he'd realized there was a lot he didn't understand in the study guide, not just terms, but even references to the outside world that he wasn't familiar with. Then, there were other areas he thought he understood but needed clarification. He wrote those notes and questions down, often referencing the page numbers and sometimes even starring certain points, essentially prioritizing his concerns since there was no way Kayla could be expected to help him with all of those questions *and* go over new material, too.

Among all those notes and points and questions, he'd also started writing other things. Notes about his dreams. Scribbles of worries about the test, or how he didn't feel too good about keeping so much from his family. But he wrote down thoughts about Tim most of all.

When he was young, he'd idolized his brother. He'd been sure no other person had been as strong, smart, or good-looking at Tim Coblentz. Not that Tim had given him much notice. Instead, he'd kept to himself as much as possible and questioned just about everything their parents said. But, sometimes, late at night, Aaron would peek into his room, and Tim would grin and motion for him to come inside. He'd show Aaron whatever newspaper or magazine he'd gotten ahold of from the outside and talk about things he'd want to do. When Aaron had once confided that he never wanted to live among the *Englisch*, Tim had just laughed. "Of course you don't, *bruder*. You're as perfect here as I am imperfect."

Now, all these years later, Aaron realized that he shouldn't have been so shocked about Tim's departure. It was almost as if Tim had been born to leave and go out on his own—just as it was starting to seem as if he was destined to try so hard to fit in.

Which was really why his quest to take the GED didn't make sense. He wasn't the type of man to disregard his parents' wishes or to keep secrets from the people he loved.

Maybe he wasn't so different from Tim after all?

Or, was there another reason? Lately, he was starting to think that he was spending more time thinking about Kayla than anything else. He was sure writing enough notes to her! No, that wasn't right. They were notes about Kayla, notes he had no intention of her ever seeing. Notes he was embarrassed to even be thinking, let alone putting to paper.

But that didn't seem to stop him from filling up pages with this thoughts and reflections.

Now, sitting on his bed and skimming through his cramped scrawl, he frowned at it all. *What does all this mean?*

I wonder what was wrong today. Did something happen?

How did you end up in the situation you are in? Why did you study for the GED? Had you had college plans? What happened, and why are you living at home?

Does your family know you took the tests, or did you keep it a secret like I've been doing? But, if that's the case, why did you decide to start tutoring me?

Of course, she would never see those notes, just like he would never actually ask her such things. It wasn't proper, and it wasn't any of his business.

But, well, he wished it was.

What he needed to do was rip out those pages and burn them. Then, he could pretend that he hadn't been so nosy and he wouldn't have to worry about his family or Kayla happening upon them.

Yet, he still didn't do that.

Exasperated with himself, he tossed the steno pad in his backpack, along with the study guide and a recent library book, and headed out. He had just enough time to stop by the bookmobile before he began his shift at the furniture store.

After grabbing his lunch and coat, he waved goodbye to his mother and set off toward town. Today, Sarah Anne was going to be near the feed-and-seed store just half a mile away.

He breathed a sigh of relief when he saw that the big vehicle was still parked in the lot, and wonder of wonders, there were hardly any people there.

The moment she saw him, Sarah Anne's eyes lit up. "Aaron, now isn't this a good surprise. I'm glad to see you."

Feeling like he'd just been given a verbal hug, he smiled at her. "I'm glad to see you, too. But did you forget? I told you I'd try to get here this morning."

"I didn't forget. However, I've come to learn over the years that trying and actually doing are two different things. At least it's that way for me."

"For me as well. In any case, I'm glad I got here. For a moment I didn't think I would. My life has gotten busy of late."

"Care to tell me why you've been so busy?" Looking mighty pleased with herself, she prodded, "Could it have anything to do with a certain tutor?"

"It does." He wasn't so sure what he thought about the knowing gleam in her eyes, but he forged ahead. "Kayla has been helpful. She is a good tutor."

"I had the opportunity to visit with her a few days ago. She told me you were a good student. That's high praise, I think."

"That's kind of her to say, but it's not true."

"Oh?"

"I work hard, but learning all of that information doesn't come easily."

"Don't forget that much of what you are learning is unfamiliar. They might not have taught the building blocks in your Amish schoolhouse."

"They didn't."

"See?" Sarah Anne smiled at him encouragingly. "You'll get it.

Kayla believes you will." Though he should have been pleased by the comment, he was disappointed. He had hoped that she was seeing him as something more than just a younger man fumbling through lessons. "She's very smart, and I'm afraid she sometimes doesn't know what to think about my struggles."

"If she has ever thought that, she didn't tell me." Sarah Anne bent down and picked up a pencil that someone had dropped. "She thanked me for giving you her name."

"Ah. Well, I'm glad it's working out." He tried to smile.

She smiled back at him. "Before I forget, I picked up a couple new mysteries for Jack in case you stopped by. Would you like to take them or no?"

"I'll take them. If we waited on Jack to get here, we'd be waiting till the cows came home."

She chuckled. "They're on the bookshelf behind my desk. You'll see three in a stack with your name on it. Go check them out while I help these folks who just came in."

After checking the old-fashioned clock above her desk, Aaron scanned the multiple piles of books and plucked out his stack. There were three new releases, one a thriller set in New York City, one a cozy mystery set in Ireland, and the last looked to be a humorous Amish mystery set in Lancaster County. Liking the idea of Jack fancying a trip to Ireland, at least in his mind, he set the stack on the counter. Then he wandered around and picked up a biography and a children's book on chemistry. He needed all the help he could get!

"Need any help?"

"*Nee. Danke.*" No way did he want Sarah Anne to see his children's book. Quickly, he pulled out his library card and checked out the books on his own. "*Danke*, Sarah Anne."

"Anytime, Aaron. See you next time."

Then, with a quick wave to Sarah Anne, he secured his back-pack, buttoned up his coat, and headed out.

He had a quick fifteen-minute walk to work, and he was grateful for the time to think. And that was what he needed to do, for sure and for certain. He needed to remember his goals and his secrets. He needed to only think about passing that test. That was it.

Then, once he accomplished that tall task and put that piece of paper in a drawer in his desk, he could concentrate on things that mattered. Things like his family and his job.

Yes, those were the things that mattered, things his family valued, things he valued. Furthermore, they were things one could trust and count on. He needed to remember that.

As he approached the store, he reminded himself that Kayla was just a means to achieve his goals. She was not his future. He was her student, a way to make some extra money. That was all. She was never going to be his girlfriend. One day she wouldn't even remember his name.

Yes, that stung, but sometimes reality did sting, and there was nothing wrong with that.

He hoped one day he'd believe that.

ten

"Ma'am? Mrs. Miller?" the mother of the three young hellions called out.

With effort, Sarah Anne bit back that she wasn't a "missus." Well, not anymore. She was in her sixties now. Her marital status didn't matter, did it?

"How can I help you?" she asked instead, trying valiantly not to wince when one of those little boys put his sticky hands all over the four new picture books she had displayed.

"My oldest wants a book that's exciting." She lowered her voice. "It can't be too hard, either. He's a little behind in school."

Hating the way the boy's cheeks had heated, she said, "I can help with that. What's your name?"

"Evan."

"Well, Evan, come with me. I've got a couple of ideas. And if none of these books tickle your fancy, I'll bring some different ones when I come back next week."

As the middle boy systematically pulled out book after book and the youngest started to cry, their mother called out, "Evan, we can't come back next week. Pick something now."

Looking put upon, Evan looked up at Sarah Anne. "Do you have anything with adventure?"

Thanking the good Lord for Percy Jackson, she smiled. "I was just thinking about this book," she said as she picked up the first in the series. "Have you heard of this?"

"Yeah, but I don't know."

She placed it in his hands just as his brother started crying louder. "It's really good." When he continued to appear doubtful, she added, "I'm not the only one who thinks that, either. The stories are exciting from page one. I hope you'll give it a try."

"Evan, get something this minute. We've got to go before your brother turns this whole place inside out!" his mother called out.

Sarah Anne took care not to move. "What do you think?"

Looking like she'd just handed him some cough syrup, the boy shrugged. "I guess I'll give it a try."

"I'm so glad. Now, who has the library card?"

"I do," the mom called out, looking even more frazzled. "We want these three, too."

As another four people walked inside, Sarah reached for both the card and the books and quickly scanned it all . . . then shooed them all out the door in such an efficient way that her old department head would have been proud.

The moment the door closed behind them, one of the ladies who'd come in called her. "Mrs. Miller, could you help me, please?"

"I'd be happy to," she bit out. Boy, some days, she couldn't catch a break!

Two hours later, Sarah Anne pulled into her last stop for the day. It was in the most northern part of her territory and served the smallest number of people. Sometimes, she would only see one or two customers during her two-hour stop.

Actually, of late, she'd been thinking that it was time to take the stop out of her schedule. The person who had originally requested the stop was in Florida for the winter, and the other folks who'd come from time to time hadn't shown up in weeks.

Today, however, she was looking forward to a few hours of solitude. After the craziness in the other parking lot, she felt like everything was disorganized, sticky, and in complete disarray. She also needed to double-check the computer program and make sure that her records were up to date. For a while there, all she'd been doing was checking out books and listening for beeps. She had a big bin of returned books and a slight suspicion that at least a handful of titles left without getting checked out.

After making a cup of tea in her electric kettle, she settled in and got to work. Feeling like she was taking care of her friends, she wiped off books, scanned and sorted them, some going back on the shelves, others in another cabinet to go back into general circulation.

An hour flew by. Pleased to have the time to get so much done, she was startled when the door opened and a man about her age entered. He was wearing a baggy pair of jeans, some well-worn work boots, a green plaid flannel shirt, and a thick fleece. He also had an almost completely bald head and dark brown eyes.

He stood in the doorway, looking around like he'd entered the wrong place.

"May I help you?" she asked.

"Are you open?"

"I am. I'm going to be parked here for one more hour."

He looked at the table covered in books, thanks to the little boys' destruction, and then over at a set of filled bookshelves. "I've never been in here before. How does it work?"

"We have a limited selection of books and DVDs. If there's something here you're interested in, you check it out." She pointed to the two computer terminals set up. "If not, you can look at the main library database and order a book. I'll bring it to you next time I'm here."

"That's it?"

She smiled. "That's it." Getting to her feet, she said, "Did you come in for something in particular?"

"No." He shrugged. "Just was looking for something new to read."

"Well, you came to the right place." Gosh, she hoped she didn't sound as eager as she felt.

"I guess I did. Thanks for your help, Miss . . . ?"

The first person who didn't call her *Mrs.* in weeks! "It's Miss Miller," she said, trying not to grin like it was Christmas Day. "But, please, feel free to call me Sarah Anne. Sarah Anne Miller."

"Pete Canon." He paused, then held out one rugged hand.

Shaking it, Sarah Anne suddenly was really glad she had another reason not to take this stop off her schedule.

"Did I understand correctly that you will be here next week?"

"You did." She handed him her schedule. "Feel free to take a copy of it, if you'd like."

Scanning the neatly organized calendar, he whistled softly. "You cover quite a big area."

"I like to think I do. But that's the purpose of mobile library services, right? I'm here to reach patrons who are unable to get to the brick-and-mortar libraries."

He looked around the small space. "And you do it all alone?"

"I do." She lifted her chin.

"That's a lot on your slim shoulders."

She was pleased he acknowledged just how labor-intensive her job was. She was also vain enough to have caught that he'd called her shoulders slim. *How complimentary*, she thought.

On the other hand, she also didn't like to be thought of as helpless. She was proud of herself for maintaining her schedule and doing the majority of the work by herself. "It is a lot, but it's nothing I can't handle. I'm a fairly capable woman," she added.

He grinned. "Good to know."

He was teasing her, and with good reason, too. *I'm a fairly capable woman*, indeed. She'd sounded so full of herself. "Forget I just said that."

"Not on your life. I'm a fan of capable women." Eyes still shining, he lifted his chin, meeting her gaze. "I'll see you soon, then, Miss Sarah Anne Miller."

She noticed his hands were empty. "Wait a minute. Did you want to check something out?"

"Not today. I'll be back."

"Well, then. I'll see you then."

He chuckled before giving her a salute and turning away.

Only when the door snapped shut behind him did she realize that she'd been half holding her breath. Goodness! Just like a teenage girl!

After opening the door and making sure no one was hurrying over to catch her before she went on her way, Sarah Anne readied the vehicle.

Then, feeling lighter than she had in quite some time, she started the engine and headed back to the main library campus. Usually by this time of day, she would be feeling tired and dreading the hour or so of paperwork and other activities that she'd have to do before she could end her shift.

But today, she was practically humming. Sure, it was silly and fanciful, but she'd had far too few silly and fanciful moments of late. She decided she kind of liked that feeling.

Liked it a lot.

eleven

• **RULE #11** •

It's okay if every day isn't a good one.
What matters is that you woke up.

"Are you sure you ain't too cold?" Joel asked again as they walked along a faint path around the pond on his family's property.

"I'm sure." It was cold, but the air could have been twenty degrees colder and she still wouldn't have noticed. Joel had that effect on her.

He still looked concerned. "I should've given you one of my scarves to wear around your neck."

She laughed. As romantic comments went, it left a lot to be desired. She already had on her white *kapp*, a black bonnet over it, a thick peacock-blue wool dress, black tights, boots, mittens, and her new dark wool cape. She did not need a scarf, too.

Though, if it still held his scent, maybe it would be nice?

Realizing that she needed to move their conversation on or Joel would continue to worry, she said, "Before we know it, we'll be walking around this pond and complaining about thistles."

"Which means, of course, I'll have to help you get those thorns and such out of your tights."

Just imagining him untying a boot and placing her foot in his lap like he used to made her blush. "Surely not."

"I used to do it all the time."

He had. When she was very small, her big brother Tim had been the one to fuss over the little thorns and prickers that would catch against her skin. He'd patiently pull them out and then rub her mother's lotion on her calves. He'd been her hero for doing that, especially since Aaron and Jack would have rather wrestled a swarm of bees than coddle their sister like that.

One day, a couple of weeks after Tim had left, Joel had found her sitting on a bench in between their houses, attempting to pull the briars from her bare skin. She'd been crying, too. He'd known she'd been crying more about Tim being gone than about the thorns. Without a word, he'd sat next to her, placed one of her feet on his thigh, and carefully tended her wounds.

She'd known then that no other boy was ever going to treat her better than Joel Lapp.

"Before we get to spring and summer, there are a couple of things we're going to need to get through first."

"Such as?"

"Groundhog Day."

"We *canna* forget that day, for sure," she joked.

"And Valentine's Day." He glanced down at her. "Surely you won't want to skip that day?"

They'd never celebrated that day. Beyond making some heart-shaped cookies with her *mamm*, Tiny had never celebrated Valentine's Day at all. "I'm not sure what we would do."

"We should plan to do something. I'll think on it."

And, there it was again. A burst of hope, followed on its tails by a burst of wariness. She wanted to be his Valentine . . . but there was a part of her that felt like it was coming out of the blue. "Joel, I'm not sure I understand."

"Not much to understand, I don't think."

He reached for her hand and linked his fingers through hers.

She liked feeling so connected to him. Liked feeling the calluses that had formed on his palms from years of hard work. Liked feeling how strong even his hand was. It was a fanciful image, but she liked feeling that hands like his could help her get through anything.

"Tiny? Did you hear me?"

"I did." Looking down at their connected hands, she murmured, "Sorry, I was just thinking of something else."

He looked down at their hands, too. "It's okay."

"To answer your questions, yes, I do believe it's time we celebrated Valentine's Day. Maybe even with a heart-shaped cake." She smiled up at him, liking the new assuredness she was feeling. After all, he wouldn't have been talking about celebrating such a romantic day if his intentions weren't true. She decided to bring it up. "You know, Joel, until recently, I've been pretty concerned about our . . . friendship."

"Why is that?"

"You know why. We've gone from being friends to hardly ever

talking to each other to you playing hot and cold to, now, holding hands and talking about Valentine's Day."

"All of that wasn't my fault. You know your brothers warned me to stay away from you."

"That was some time ago."

"Maybe I had to grow up."

"I guess that makes sense . . . Though, sometimes it has seemed like you've been busier than usual." Ack. She knew she sounded a bit shrewish, but her mother's comments had stayed near her heart. And, there were a couple of things that Aaron had said that made her wonder if Joel was as ready to settle down as he acted like he was.

"Tiny, I don't know what to say. I'm here now. I'm trying to make plans with you. What else do you want me to say?"

"Nothing."

"I haven't been hiding anything from you."

"Joel, don't be angry with me."

"I'm not angry. I just don't want you thinking things that aren't true."

His whole posture told a different story. "I'm only saying I've missed you and wondered if maybe you've had your eye on someone else."

"I have not." His words were clipped.

"All right. I'm sorry I brought it up." But even to her ears, both his rebuttal and her comments sounded weak. She decided to keep quiet and stop pushing so much. Her hand was nestled in his, and it was a lovely thing. "Perhaps we should start heading back. It's getting late," she added.

"The wind is picking up, too. You're going to get chilled."

After they finished their journey around the pond for the

second time, Joel led her toward the street. They could have simply crossed the small expanse between their two yards, but this gave them a bit more privacy. Tiny took refuge in that. Even when their conversations weren't the best, they still liked being around each other. Maybe that was what love was. Two people who wanted to be together more than they wanted to be apart. She felt her spirits lift. Yes, this was what love really was like. It wasn't all perfect words and grand gestures like in fairy tales. No, real love was filled with flaws and mistakes and regrets, all mixed up with tenderness and loyalty and affection.

"I'm glad we decided to walk this way back to my house," she said at last. "Sometimes, when we say goodbye and rush across the grass, it feels like our time together ends too soon."

"Tiny, I wanted to give us a bit more time together because there's something I've been wanting to talk to you about."

"Oh?" Was he finally going to declare himself?

He squeezed her hand. "*Jah.* You see, you haven't been imagining things. I have been *zeer*—*very* busy of late. But I've had a good reason for it."

This didn't sound good. "What have you been doing?"

"Please, try and listen to me first before you get upset."

"What have you been doing that would make me upset?"

"Let me tell you *why* I've been doing what I've been doing first."

What does that even mean? Testily, she said, "Joel, I'd rather you didn't talk in riddles with me."

"I'm not talking in riddles, Tiny. But if you would just listen first, I'd appreciate it."

She knew he wasn't asking too much. But still, everything about their conversation practically screamed of subterfuge.

Why was he hiding things? And, worse, why was she allowing him to? It hardly seemed fair.

"I'm listening." She glanced his way before gazing out into the distance. Her house was visible now. And though at first she'd hoped their night could last forever, now all she wanted to do was go home and think about their future, and whether there would even be one for the two of them.

"You see, a few months ago . . . I received a call from Jane Shultz."

Tiny didn't even try to hide her dismay. She had no idea why he was bringing up that woman. Everyone knew Jane married her husband for money and didn't even go to church anymore. She flaunted her money, too, by having her groceries delivered so she wouldn't have to mix with the rest of the community. Though Tiny knew it was wrong to gossip, there were some things one simply couldn't deny. "I'm surprised she called you." And even more surprised that he'd answered.

"Well, she had good reason."

"Oh?" Though she was keeping her promise to listen, she couldn't ignore the hot jealousy that ran through her. What could that woman possibly want with Joel? She better not have decided to sink her claws into him.

"*Jah.* You see . . . Jane and I got to talking, and I realized she has been in a difficult spot since her husband passed on to Heaven."

It looked like her worst fears were coming true. Jane was trying to steal Joel. And he . . . well, it looked like he was practically giving her a line to steal him with. Her temper was rising, which probably wasn't a very good thing, but she didn't care. "What do you mean by that?"

"Well, you see, I learned she needed a man around from time to time."

"'She needed a man?'"

He nodded. "Since I had some time, and I felt sorry for her, I decided to help her out."

"You've been going over to her farm?"

"Only chores around the house and such, Tiny. That's all."

Tiny's house was close enough that she could see the kerosene lanterns shining through the windows, and she wished more than anything that she was inside with peppermint tea and a good book rather than out in the icy cold listening to her world fall apart.

"How often have you been going over there?"

"Not often. Only twice a week."

He'd been spending hours alone with Jane at her house. In secret. For weeks now. All the self-righteous anger she'd been feeling free-fell into agony. "Joel, why didn't you tell me about this?"

"I didn't know how." He looked a little sheepish. "I mean, some people might look at all our time together and start jumping to conclusions. To be honest, I was worried you wouldn't understand."

He had been right about that. She didn't. "I don't understand a lot of things about this arrangement of yours."

"Tiny, I'm trying to explain it to you. All you have to do is listen."

"I'm listening, but I'm not understanding." She held up a hand. "And don't you start talking like I'm not capable of understanding things, either. The problem lies with you, not me."

"That's what I'm trying to tell you. There is no problem. I mean, it's not like you and Luke Yoder."

"What do you mean by that?"

"It means that I might have been helping Jane on her farm, but you've been encouraging Luke, even though you knew I wouldn't like it."

"Luke has nothing to do with you."

"That's where you are wrong."

Just as they reached her front yard, Aaron stormed out of the house. He had on boots, dark pants, and a shirt but no coat. "Joel Lapp! We need to talk right this minute."

Looking resigned, he murmured, "Tiny, perhaps you should go inside."

"I don't think so."

"This isn't going to be pleasant."

"Oh, I know."

"Fine." Raising his voice, Joel said, "Perhaps you should explain yourself, Coblentz."

"I will when Tiny goes away."

She placed her hands on her hips. "Tiny isn't going anywhere, Aaron."

"Fine. I wanted to save you the embarrassment, but I'll go ahead anyway. I saw you leaving Jane Shultz's house a week ago."

"I know you saw me. The two of us walked back here together. We talked the whole time."

"We didn't talk all that much. You didn't seem to feel the need to share that you were courting her."

"'Courting'?" Tiny whispered.

"I'm not courting Jane." Leaning toward Tiny, Joel said, "Tiny, you need to trust me. I told you. I've been helping her around the house."

Aaron shook his head. "You might have been doing some chores, but other folks have caught sight of the two of you sitting together. One person even heard the two of you laughing on her back porch."

"I didn't know laughing was a crime."

"Don't play dumb. You know exactly what people heard. You weren't just over there to do work."

"There is nothing wrong with talking and laughing while doing work. There was no harm done. Jane is a lonely woman."

"She ain't eighty years old to your twenty, Joel. Men and women don't spend time together like that without something else going on." When Tiny paused to take a breath, she spied something in Joel's eyes.

And it crushed her.

She was embarrassed to be so disillusioned and to be discussing it all in front of Aaron. "I've been waiting for you for a long time, Joel. I've tried to be patient. I've tried to be understanding. But I'm starting to realize that I've just been stupid."

"Stop it, Tiny. Stop talking as if everything is over."

"I think I'm finally talking as if I'm living in the real world. See, all this time, in my weakest moments in the middle of the night, I would imagine that you'd found someone else. Now, in the light of day, I've realized all my worst fears weren't made up at all. They were simply the truth," she whispered.

"I've been *helping* her," he retorted. "I've been doing some chores around her house for money, Tiny. That's all."

"In secret?" She was naïve, but she'd had more than enough of his confusing excuses. With a sigh, she turned away from the boy she'd sworn to herself she'd love so many years ago. "You're right, Aaron. I should go inside. I don't think I can look at him anymore."

"Tiny, don't walk away from me." His voice sounded pained.

Almost as pained as she felt. But somehow, instead of making her feel hopeful, his plea just made her feel worse. Keeping her back to him, she said, "It seems fairly obvious that one of us has already walked away, Joel. Worse, you walked away some time ago, and I didn't even realize it."

Squaring her shoulders, she started walking. The yard was silent as she made her way inside, making the *click* of the door sound even louder than usual.

Her mother, wearing her favorite sheepskin slippers, padded toward her. "Tiny, I thought I heard raised voices in the front yard. What is going on out there?"

The question was simply too much. "I . . . it's nothing to worry about, Mamm." Feeling like she'd just let her mother down, she muttered, "I'm going to my room for a spell. Please leave me be."

It was a blessing that her mother never followed.

twelve

· RULE #12 ·

*Keep in mind that you are human and
you will make mistakes. Often.*

After watching his sister walk into the house like she'd lost her whole future, Aaron fumed. He'd liked Joel. *Nee*, every member of his family had liked the man, and all of them—especially himself—had been excited for him court Tiny at long last.

If he was honest, he'd often thought about how good it was going to be to have a brother-in-law like Joel. Joel was hardworking, steady, and had never been shy about his interest in Tiny. His sister needed a man like that. She needed someone to dote on her, all of them believed in that.

As good as Joel had been for Tiny, he'd also been good for all of them. He had a wicked good sense of humor, and Jack and

Aaron had often discussed how excited they'd be to have Joel as a brother.

Yes, they'd all thought he would be a good addition to their family.

Well, until Aaron had realized he was sneaking around and his sister was paying the price.

Turning to Joel, Aaron let loose every bit of frustration and anger that had been stewing inside him for days. "I thought I knew you, but I obviously don't. Why didn't you ever tell her what you were doing?"

Joel folded his arms over his chest. "What, exactly, have I been doing?"

"*Nee.* You do *not* get to start playing games with me in my front yard. Especially not when my sister's happiness has been crushed."

"Oh, I haven't crushed anything. You're the one who ruined our fine evening."

"She didn't look that happy when you two arrived."

He raised one eyebrow. "And you know this how?"

"I was watching for you from the window, of course."

Joel gaped at him, then backed up a step. "We're way too old to be monitored like that."

"It's good I was keeping my eye on you."

"You know, I don't have to stand here and take this. I'm just going to go."

The front door opened, and Jack came out, looking just as livid as Aaron was feeling.

"Joel!"

Joel folded his arms over his chest. "Now what?"

"Tiny is inside her room crying, and *mei mamm* said she's upset with you. What did you do to her?"

"I didn't do a thing. It's your brother and his hotheaded temper that you should be concerned about."

"Don't you dare blame this on me," Aaron retorted. "He's been carrying on with that Jane Shultz."

"I haven't been carrying on with anyone. It isn't like that."

Jack marched forward, close enough that his chest was practically touching Joel's. "Tell me Aaron is lying."

Joel lifted his chin. "Fine. Aaron is lying."

Aaron didn't even attempt to keep his voice down. "Jack, I saw them together. I'm not the only one, either. Other people have seen them."

"Like who?" Joel asked.

Since he wasn't denying it, Aaron was only getting madder, but Joel cut him off before he could speak again. "Aaron, I already told you, I've been doing chores for her to earn an extra salary. And, just in case your minds are in the gutter, those chores include yard work, carpentry, fixing drawers that stick and faucets that leak, painting walls, and, when there's nothing else to do . . . cleaning out her grossly overflowing attic!"

Jack blinked. "Truly?"

"*Jah*. I promise, I wouldn't lie to you about that. There were dead mice in that attic."

Something in the way he was talking—and the way he was looking—finally sank in. "You are telling the truth," Aaron said.

"*Jah*. I *am* telling the truth. I am not having an affair with Jane." He wrinkled his nose. "What do you take me for?"

"Why are you doing all those chores? You have a good job," Jack asked.

"You know what? I was going to talk to you both about it, but now I'm not." He turned to Aaron. "I've known you for most of my life. I thought we were good friends. Best friends."

"We are."

"Then you should have trusted me. You should know without a doubt that my intentions toward your sister are true. You should have stood up for me. I'm leaving and going to try to figure out what to do next."

After taking another two steps, he faced them again. "But I'll tell you this. So help me, if you poison Tiny about me any further than you already have, I'm going to make sure you rue that day."

Aaron stood motionless as Joel walked away. But as he faded from view, part of his anger faded as well. And in its place was a burgeoning sense of confusion that made him wonder if everything he thought was true wasn't quite so true after all.

thirteen

• RULE #13 •

*Keep careful records. You never know when you might be
asked to clarify something you did in the past.*

After her mother died, Kayla's father began a tradition of heading to Sarasota from the middle of January until the middle of February. He had a good friend who now lived there year-round with his wife, and for an extremely small fee, he stayed in their converted garage. He would spend his time going for walks, playing cards with friends he'd made over the years, and simply enjoying life in sunny Pinecraft, the Amish community nestled in the heart of Sarasota.

Though he'd insisted that he intended to stay in Berlin this year, Kayla encouraged him to go. She needed some space and she reckoned that he did, too.

Standing next to him today at the front door, Kayla had no idea how he would be able to go for so long with only one suitcase and a carry-on. She looked over her packing list.

"Daed, are you sure you have your prescriptions?"

"I've double-checked."

"What about your money card?" He'd started using a credit card two years ago when he discovered just how difficult it was to get to their bank branch in Sarasota.

He patted his wallet. "I've got it, daughter. I also have snacks, two bottles of water, two books, and my pillow for the bus ride." He folded his arms over the new light green shirt she'd sewn and given to him for Christmas. "Now, what about you? Will you need anything around here that I didn't take care of?"

"I'll be fine. I promise."

Still looking at her worriedly, he added, "Try not to spend too much time alone, Kayla."

"I'll be working, Father. I'm around people all day. You know that."

"I'm talking about in your spare time. You have a bad habit of never taking time for yourself. Think about going to one of your friends' houses for supper or make plans to go walking or somesuch."

"I will." Of course, all she wanted at the moment was some time alone to do and eat whatever she wanted.

"I'm going to hope and pray that you aren't lying to me right now."

"I'm not, Daed." Hearing the crunch of the English driver's tires on the gravel drive, she reached for the door handle. "Now, stop fussing. Bill's here, right on time. That means you've got to go."

Shrugging on his coat, he nodded. "He's a *gut* fella, for sure. Now, give your old father a hug goodbye. I'll miss you, Kay."

"I'll miss you, too. Come home with a tan," she teased, like she always did.

"I'll bring you a seashell," he replied, repeating his standard goodbye as well. Then, without another word, he carried his bag to the car and greeted Bill.

Kayla remained by the door. She already felt his absence, but she didn't want him to see it on her face. Only when Daed looked back at her before Bill turned left did she raise her hand and wave. She continued to stand there as they vanished from sight, allowing herself to feel the twin emotions that always took hold of her—sorrow that she wouldn't see her beloved father for thirty days and the burst of pleasure of being on her own. She liked having the house to herself, but being alone in a dark house made her mood almost as dark.

Being so alone at twenty-six was difficult. She was grown and used to managing a household, but she was still young enough to want more. The truth was that even living with her father, she was lonely. She felt out of sync with her friends and even her cousins. All of them were either settling into married life, having children, or looking for the perfect partner to spend a lifetime with. Sometimes when she was around them, Kayla felt like she wasn't exactly a welcome addition to the group. She was a reminder that sometimes life didn't work out the way one planned. That, sometimes, nothing did.

She knew she was at fault as well. She felt discontented with herself and not sure what she should do to change that. For a time, she'd even considered leaving her faith and walking among the English. She'd needed a change.

She still needed one. Though her tutoring and sewing were good first steps, she had to admit that sometimes, it wasn't enough.

She didn't know what the right decision was. Becoming English might give her more options, but she'd also lose everything that she was. Right now, such a big change didn't seem worth it.

"You need to stop feeling sorry for yourself, Kayla," she said out loud. "Mamm wouldn't like you being in this slump. Not one bit. She'd be telling you right this minute to put your blues away and think of something positive."

Determined to do just that, Kayla did her best to shake off those blues, put the kettle on to boil, and got out her pencil and paper. Then she did what she did best—she planned. Feeling better, she decided to write down four things she wanted to do over the next few days. She wrote down the most obvious first. *Make a peanut butter pie.* Peanuts didn't agree with her father, so she never made anything with them. But she missed some of her most favorite dishes.

Walk two miles every day. She was going to need to get in every step if she was going to eat a whole pie by herself!

Just as she was about to put her pencil to the paper again, the kitchen phone rang.

They might have been New Order and allowed to have a phone, but that didn't mean it rang often. Surprised, she hurried to pick it up. "Hello?"

"Hey, Kayla. I'm glad you answered."

It was Aaron. Forcing herself to keep her tone relaxed and cool, she said, "Is something wrong?"

"*Jah*. Kayla, I'm completely stuck on these word problems. I need your help."

Now she had a reason to spend some time with him today. Her spirits lifted just thinking of how handsome he was, how steady and calm, and the way she sometimes caught him looking at her like he thought she was pretty. "Want to meet at the coffee shop? I'm free this afternoon."

"You don't mind?"

"I don't mind at all. I'm off work today."

"Want to meet at Sacred Grounds in two hours? At three?"

"I can do three. I'll see you there."

"Thanks so much, Kayla. I really appreciate it."

"I'm glad you called. Really."

She walked back to her list, scanned it, and put it to one side. She didn't see any need to worry about that now. No, she had someone to meet instead.

She decided to go put on a fresh dress.

Two hours later, at a back corner table in Sacred Grounds, Aaron was staring at Kayla's caramel latte with misgiving. "That looks like a dessert."

It did. Tina, the waitress, had added an extra helping of whipped cream and then had topped that with a ribbon of caramel. "It probably is closer to a dessert than a simple drink, but I don't care. I love it."

"I've never had one of those." He glanced at his simple cup of black coffee. "I only ever get this."

"If you never stray from that, then you are missing out, Aaron.

These are *wunderbaar*." After taking her first sip, she sighed. "My day has just gotten better."

"And here I thought it was because I called you out of the blue."

She chuckled, pretending as best she could that his comment wasn't right on the money. "Sorry, but I fear this drink is my weakness." She pushed the tall mug toward him. "Take a sip and see what you've been missing."

"I have a feeling I'll regret this, but *nee. Danke.*"

Kayla pulled it back, a little embarrassed that she'd offered him a sip. He probably wasn't used to women being so bold.

When she realized he was staring at her, she felt her cheeks heat. "I'm sorry. I guess I'm making quite a spectacle of myself. Uh, let's get to work."

He pulled out his notebook but didn't open it. "You seem different today. Is it just the caramel coffee?"

"Oh, *nee*. My father left for Pinecraft this morning. He'll be gone for a month. Even though he goes every year, it catches me off guard."

"I reckon it's the change in your schedule."

"*Jah.*" She shrugged. "I *canna* explain it, not really. I encourage him to leave and I've always refused to go down for even a short spell. He and I need our space. But it still saddens me to lose him, if only for a month."

"Is there something more to it? Do you get scared living by yourself?"

After trying that on for size, she shook her head. "*Nee*. It's the quiet that gets to me, I guess." She shook her head. "How are you?"

"Me? I'm fine." He smiled. "No relatives are off to Florida in my *haus*."

"Oh. I only asked because you seem a bit preoccupied as well. Is anything new with you?" She glanced at his face, then picked up her drink again. What was she doing, anyway? He'd contacted her for help, not to chat about life in a coffee shop.

"Besides the usual, nothing is too different. Well, nothing besides the fact that we all thought my sister's beau had finally begun courting, but then it all fell apart, and now the whole house is in a dither."

"What do you mean?"

"I probably shouldn't have said anything, but in a nutshell: Joel, my best friend and the man my sister Tiny's liked forever, finally stepped forward, but then I interfered because I thought he was doing something he shouldn't. And now Tiny's upset, my parents are upset, and I feel justified and embarrassed all at the same time."

"Whoa."

"I know." He shrugged one shoulder. "For the record, I'm not proud of sticking my nose where it doesn't belong . . . But I can't regret looking out for my sister. Tiny's special."

He sounded so dejected that she almost smiled. "Joel who?"

"Joel Lapp. Do you know him?"

"I know the name, but that's all. How old is he?"

"Twenty or so."

"That's why. He's several years younger." And didn't that just make her feel ancient?

"I'm glad you don't know him. Like I said, I shouldn't even be talking about him. Especially not here during our session."

"I don't know about that. I've found that it helps to share problems." Not that she had done all that much of it.

"Maybe it's good that you're so much older than Tiny and Joel. That way everyone is just names." When she raised her eyebrows at that "so much older" phrase, he reddened. "I guess that didn't sound too good, did it?"

She chuckled. "I understood what you meant."

Aaron looked her in the eye. "It feels like our ages don't matter much anyway. Whenever we get together, the last thing I ever think about is our age difference."

"I feel the same way. I'm never sure what age means anymore. Here I am, twenty-six and never been married. I don't have much in common with most girls my age." She paused. Then there was her father. He was twenty years older than her, but Kayla often felt like she was the older and wiser one in the house.

She glanced at Aaron, who was studying her intently. "Actually, sometimes I feel like I have more in common with you than most people."

"Why is that?"

Well, now she just felt foolish. She blurted out the first thing she could think of. "The test, of course."

"Oh. Of course," he added quickly. "I mean it's not like there's a lot of us Amish worrying about particles and vocabulary and integers, are there?"

"I don't believe there is."

"I guess it's good Sarah Anne put us together, then."

"*Jah*. It is *gut*." She smiled, but a part of her felt disappointed that they'd just classified their relationship as merely a working one.

Opening the booklet, Aaron said, "Here's what I can't seem to figure out." He pointed to a long paragraph. "I know I'm supposed to use a formula to solve it, but I'm not sure which one."

"Let's take it step by step." She stole another sip of her coffee, then forced herself to dwell on math and not on the rest of her life. That would be better for the both of them.

"Ready," Aaron said, his pencil poised over his notebook like he was about to begin a race.

She had to smile at that. His excitement and dedication to learning the material echoed so much of what she'd been feeling years ago when she'd prepared for the GED. She embraced that familiarity, finding comfort in it like she did a much-loved sweater. Since there was so much in her world that she wasn't sure about, she treasured the things that made sense.

Pointing to the first problem, she began to explain both the formula and the variables as well as the basic steps. Aaron followed along, gave it a try, and when he got the right answer, grinned.

"*Gut* job. Now, let's tackle the next one."

"I'm on it."

She smiled, loving his English expression, even though it would likely sound funny coming from anyone else in the world.

When he was done, she checked the answer, pointed to the next, and he began again.

They continued in the same slow, methodical way, with her explaining and providing examples and Aaron both copying her work and working on his own portions.

Thirty minutes passed, then forty-five. Their time together was flying by, and things were going real well, too. Aaron was making progress. After those few uncomfortable moments when she'd revealed too much and a new awareness between them had bloomed, the study session had become one of their best.

Well, it was, until Missy and Ramon Troyer entered the coffee shop, gaped at her and Aaron, and made a beeline toward their table.

Kayla's stomach sank. She was fairly sure this was not going to go well.

fourteen

Missy, acting just as smug as she had back when they were teenagers and she was the first in their circle to have a steady beau, greeted Kayla like they were still close friends.

They were not.

"Kayla . . . and Aaron Coblentz. Hello," Missy called out brightly as her husband, Ramon, shook Aaron's hand. "Two people I would have never thought to see together."

"I haven't seen either of you in ages," Aaron said as he closed his notebook. "How have you been?"

"Same as always," Ramon said. "Working."

Watching the interplay between Aaron and Ramon—and Missy's obvious interest in her and Aaron—Kayla felt her mouth go dry. Missy had a habit of sticking her nose in places where it didn't belong and causing trouble. If Kayla wasn't careful, Missy would start asking Aaron all sorts of embarrassing questions, just because she could.

Aaron said, "It's a *gut* day for a cup of hot *kaffi, jah?*"

"It is," Ramon replied. "We've been out walking and decided we needed some sustenance before heading up the hill home. Why, sometimes I feel like this winter will never end."

"It has been a long winter, for sure and for certain," Aaron said.

"What were you two doing when we walked in?" Missy asked. "It looks almost as if you are studying together."

What could she say? Aaron had closed his notebook, but she had a math textbook in full view. "Well . . ."

"We're doing the same thing as you, I suppose," Aaron said with an easy smile. "It's too cold to stay outside without taking breaks indoors to get warm."

Kayla lifted up her mug and took a sip, as if to prove to them that she was enjoying her drink.

"Yes, I guess that's true." She shrugged. "So are you two courting now?"

"Missy, that ain't none of our business," her husband chided.

"If you are, I'm excited for you. I mean, I think it's been years since I've seen you spend time with any man, Kayla. Not since Levi, right?"

"Are you keeping tabs on me?"

"Of course not. I'm just making conversation." Missy smiled, but her cheeks turned red. Obviously when she heard her words, she realized just how bad they sounded. "I'm sorry. Perhaps I shouldn't have brought Levi up. He's probably a sore subject."

"Yet you *did* bring him up," Kayla said.

"I hope you'll forgive me." She laughed lightly. "I didn't mean to offend."

"Oh?" Aaron leaned back and folded his arms across his chest.

"Of course she didn't mean anything disrespectful, Kayla," Ramon said in a rush.

"I'm sure you didn't, Missy," Kayla said.

When neither Kayla nor Aaron said anything more, the silence grew frostier. Taking the hint, Ramon curved a hand around his wife's elbow. "Well, we'd better go get those drinks. Good to see you both." Missy said nothing.

Luckily, there was no one in line, and they were served quickly. Although it looked like Missy wanted to take a seat, her husband shuttled her to the door, probably to save her from embarrassing herself further.

In what had to be one last attempt to gain the upper hand, Missy waved on their way out.

"Enjoy your walk back up the hill," Kayla said with a smile.

Ramon nodded as they exited.

When they were alone again, Aaron grinned. "I guess we just survived our first public outing."

"Indeed." She smiled back at him. "I'm sorry. I should have explained to them that we weren't a couple, but I'm afraid I simply froze. I couldn't figure out how to explain our being together without letting your cat out of the bag."

Aaron saw it differently. In his opinion, the problem wasn't that she had led Missy and Ramon to believe they were a couple; the problem was that he liked the idea of it.

"I could have said something as well, but I chose not to. I guess we're both at fault."

Brightening, she said, "Honestly, you put Missy right in her place for speculating on us. I don't know the last person who did that so well! She looked like she'd swallowed her tongue."

"She deserved it for sounding so smug. I don't know what she was talking about anyway. Nothing we do affects her, or if it does, it would be negligible, right?" He grinned. "How's that for using one of my new vocabulary words?"

"Wonderful-*gut*," she teased. "Truly gold star–worthy."

Aaron laughed. "Kayla, you're one of the nicest women I know."

Her cheeks turned a pretty pink. "You don't have to say that."

"It's true. You've got an attitude and outlook on life that I really admire."

She rolled her eyes. "Now you're going to make my head swell with all these compliments."

"If you're not used to hearing such things, I reckon it's time you did, then. You're smart and kind and . . . one of the most beautiful women I've ever met." Realizing he'd just stepped over the line, he looked down at his hands. "And please forgive me if I've just embarrassed us both."

"You haven't." She chuckled. "Well, maybe a little, *jah*? But, um, since we're being so honest and all, I must admit that I have always thought of you as attractive, too."

She didn't think of him as just a kid. Friendship and desire melded deep inside of him, giving him permission to let her see how he felt about her.

Kayla's eyes darkened before she picked up her cup and took a long sip.

Yes, there was something there between them. It couldn't be denied.

Later that evening, in the safety of her quiet house, Kayla reflected on her conversation with Aaron again.

What had happened? She wasn't sure. One moment, she'd been minding her own business, and the next she'd met Aaron Coblentz and become his tutor. Now? Well, now, she seemed unable to do anything but think about him.

In a relatively short amount of time, she'd gone from being almost happily alone to secretly hoping that something might happen between the two of them.

It didn't make sense. Not one bit.

After taking her cup of hot peppermint tea to her favorite chair in the living room, she lit a vanilla-scented candle and started a fire. And then, with a sigh, she picked up the third book she'd checked out from Sarah Anne. It was time to get lost in a story.

She just hoped this one was better than the other two. She wasn't going to lie. She'd been disappointed in the first stories. She wasn't sure why, either. They had been true to form. Boy met girl. They were both Amish, and the authors got most of the details just right. But the characters had seemed flat. There were no feelings or excitement or, well, anything that she reckoned was a part of being in love. Instead, it felt like the two main characters were simply going through the motions instead of getting swept up in their romance.

She was a little put out. Why wasn't the heroine feeling all tingly and special every time the hero gazed at her with longing?

Didn't the author realize that was what people were looking for when they chose a book?

She sighed and opened the new novel, hoping to get swept away in the words. But for the first time in years, all she wanted to do was let her mind drift to another man, one with blond hair and hazel eyes. One who, in spite of her best intentions, had made her think of things that used to not matter, that honestly *shouldn't* matter . . . but somehow had started to so much more than they ever had before.

What did that mean? Was she falling in love? And if she was, why did it feel so different than how she felt with Levi?

Was it because she'd wanted security and stability from Levi but only wanted happiness and love from Aaron?

Feeling startled by that thought, she got up and wandered around the room . . . then caught sight of Sarah Anne's book. She'd put it on a shelf hours after the librarian had given it to her and then had promptly forgotten all about it.

Sitting back down again, she ran a finger over the raised words on the cover. *Courage to Love.* She'd thought such a thing was foolish when she first read the title. But now that she was beginning to understand just what falling in love might feel like, she realized that it did feel scary. Maybe she did need some courage after all.

So she did the only thing she could. She opened the book to page one and began.

fifteen

• RULE #15 •

Take time every day to read. If you don't do that,
you can't recommend books.

"We should do this more often, Tiny," Luke Yoder said as he threaded two more marshmallows on the end of a wire hanger. "I've missed spending time with you."

They were sitting on a quilt in her family's hearth room, roasting marshmallows in front of a roaring fire. Her mother had made them a pot of hot chocolate and brought out the filled pot along with two big ceramic mugs and a plate of marshmallows. Luke, with his freckles and blue eyes and red hair, was as kind as ever. He'd acted delighted to sit on the floor next to her and sip hot chocolate.

"I've missed you, too. You were gone for a long time."

"Three weeks. As much as I missed you, I can't say I regret my time in Pinecraft. It was warm and sunny. And, of course, my whole family was there."

She now knew Luke well enough to know that every January his whole extended family met in Pinecraft for three weeks. An uncle had a big house just off the beach on Siesta Key and the whole Yoder clan congregated there.

"You're blessed to have such traditions."

He gave her a sideways look. "I am. And every year, it seems, we have more people added to the mix. New babies . . . sometimes new spouses. My cousin Abraham brought his bride this year."

"Did she do all right?" Personally, Tiny couldn't imagine anything worse than being a new bride in such a full house.

"But of course! Oh, I think she got a little tired of Abraham going off with us every morning to fish, but all the women were around. She had lots of company."

"That's good." Noticing her pair of marshmallows was about to burn, she pulled the hanger back from the flames. "These look perfect."

"They do indeed. Now, let me help you." Before she could protest that she was just fine, Luke picked up a fork and carefully slid the treats into her cup. "Here you go."

"*Danke.*"

"Of course. I would hate for you to get burned."

Everything he was saying was proper and sweet. But Tiny couldn't help but feel a bit irritated by his heavy-handedness. She had a feeling that a life with him would be filled with little things like this—Luke taking charge because he knew better and she keeping her mouth shut even though she didn't exactly agree.

It was all so different than with Joel. They sparred and fussed at each other, but then when he did things like try to keep her warm or help remove thorns, she was grateful to him.

Just as she was about to take her first sip of cocoa, Jack came in. "How's it going, Luke? Long time, no see."

Luke stood up. "I'm back from Florida. I was just telling Tiny about my trip."

"I bet she loved hearing about it." He looked down at the pot. "Tiny, did Mamm make you hot chocolate?"

"She did."

"You've got a lot of marshmallows left, too. Mind if I roast a couple?"

"We do." She gave her brother a meaningful glance.

"Fine. I guess I'll have to fend for myself. See ya, Luke."

After her brother disappeared into the kitchen, Luke smiled at her. "Maybe next week you could come to my house."

"Oh?"

"We could sit in front of my stone fireplace there. It would be quieter."

"I don't know if my parents would allow that." Or her brothers.

"I'll talk to your father. I'll point out that there's a good reason for you to see my *haus*." He chuckled. "I'm sure he'll agree that we should spend some more time together." He gazed at her meaningfully. "In private."

She absolutely did not want to be alone with him in his house. For that matter, she was rather sure that she didn't want to see him anymore. Luke was far too full of himself. Nothing like Joel, and that was the truth.

But instead of telling him that, she hedged, "I'm not ready to take that step, Luke."

"Really? I've been coming over here for weeks now."

He was making it sound like she owed him for his time, which kind of made her skin crawl. "I can't help how I feel."

"I think it's because you're so young." He scooted closer to her. "That's why I'm good for you, Tiny. You need someone who is more mature to guide you."

She jumped to her feet. "I'm old enough to know how I feel, Luke. It's time you left."

"Hold on, now." He grabbed at her hand. "You're overreacting. You need to calm down."

"*Nee*. I don't." She'd spoken that loud and clear. And, as she'd hoped, Jack peeked in the room. "Tiny, everything all right?"

"It is fine," Luke said, gripping her hand more tightly.

She pulled out of his sweaty grasp. "It is not fine, Jack. Luke doesn't want to leave."

As she'd hoped, Jack's expression turned dark. "Would you like me to show you to the door?"

"*Nee*. I can find it." Picking up his hat, Luke looked back at her. "I suggest that you speak with your mother about real relationships, Tiny. It's obvious you need some guidance."

"Don't ever speak to my sister like that again," Jack said as he pulled open the front door. "She doesn't need anything beyond you leaving her alone."

Tiny's heart was racing as she followed at a much slower pace behind him. For a moment there, she'd feared that Luke wasn't going to take no for an answer. Joel would've never acted that way to her.

With a grumble under his breath, Jack shoved the door closed. "I know you're sick of me interfering in your love life, but he is not the man for you."

She walked up to him and gave him a hug. "*Danke* for coming to my rescue."

"Anytime," he said, hugging her back. "He didn't hurt you, did he?"

"No. He was just overbearing and rude." She smiled up at him. "And don't worry, I know now that Luke Yoder is definitely not the man for me."

He grinned. "Thank the Lord. I really didn't want to have to see him all the time."

"That's what you're happy about?"

"Well, *jah*. Can you imagine me having to sit across from him every Sunday supper? It would be awful."

She giggled. "It would, indeed, Jack."

sixteen

• RULE #16 •

Never underestimate the value of a good bookmark.

The following day was Tiny's least favorite day of the year. Apple butter day. Looking at the wooden bushel of McIntosh apples, she grimaced. Peeling all those apples was going to take hours. Dicing them and then pulverizing them into a fine paste took even longer. All that was before she even started cooking.

Jack, who'd been walking by the kitchen before heading back to the barn, paused when he saw her mournful expression. "Let me guess, it's apple butter day?"

"*Jah.*" She breathed out a sigh. "I can find joy in making almost anything except apple butter. I hate it so much."

Jack eyed the overflowing basket filled with approximately

a hundred Red Delicious apples. "Maybe you should make a smaller amount. Do you have to make so much of it at once?"

"I do. Otherwise I have to spend more than one day on it and I *canna* do this anymore than is necessary."

Her mother entered the kitchen with a set of towels in her arms. Her impatient glare made it obvious that she'd heard Tiny's complaints. "*Ach*, Tiny. You make too much out of this chore. Stop complaining and get to work."

"I will. Sorry, Mamm." She picked up her paring knife.

"You know how popular your apple butter is, child. Everyone appreciates your hard work."

"I know. I'll get busy right now," Tiny said as she quickly peeled one apple and placed it in a large metal bowl.

"*Gut*," Mamm said as she and Becca headed down to the basement to do laundry.

The moment she was out of sight, Tiny put the knife down again.

Jack gave her a sympathetic smile. "Sorry about your long day."

"*Danke*, but Mamm is right. I shouldn't complain. We get more orders for our apple butter than any of our jams, and making it only takes one day."

"One very long day!" he quipped as he entered the mudroom, put on his boots and heavy coat, then left to work in the barn.

When Tiny heard the door open and shut, she knew she couldn't dally any longer. She slipped on her apron, sat down on their ancient wooden stool, and picked up her paring knife once again.

It was time. Picking up the prettiest red apple, she got to work. Within a few minutes, her hands worked efficiently as her mind drifted to how her mother had painstakingly taught her to do each step when Tiny was only six or seven. For years, Tiny would work by her side, trying her best to emulate her mother's neat, efficient way of peeling and quartering the fruit.

As she continued, she tried to think of the positives instead of her many awful apple butter memories. She wasn't sure how it had happened, but every accident she'd had in the kitchen took place when she'd made this butter. One time, she'd burned herself bad enough to have to bandage her hand. Another time, she'd sliced off part of her thumb with a rather dull paring knife. Then there was the day she had lost track of time, had the stove on too high, and burned the whole batch—and ruined the pot to boot. Her mother had been so put out, she'd made Tiny use her own money to buy a new stewpot. Remembering the moment when she'd had to give most of her savings to the shop clerk at the store still made her wince.

However, her mother was not wrong. Even though she'd had many, many bad apple butter experiences, it was worth it. That counted for a lot.

Yes, she needed to think more positively. Honestly, it was better to be busy than not, especially since she still was mourning the end of her relationship with Joel.

After pausing to make sure no one was around to hear, she talked to God, as was her way. She knew most people preferred quiet, respectful prayers. Not her. She liked to believe the Lord was standing right beside her in whatever room she was in, carefully listening to everything she had to say.

"*Got*, I still *canna* believe my Joel could be so sneaky. Why did he decide to start spending so much time with Jane Shultz? And *jah*, I know I shouldn't be so petty and mean. I realize she has lost her husband and I'm sure that was mighty hard. I'm sure she's been through more than I can imagine. And yes, I promise I'll pray for her and pray for me to be a better person. But, I'm sorry, I'm still not happy about Joel spending so much time with her!"

Of course, she only heard silence, but Tiny kind of, sort of felt His displeasure. She didn't blame Him. She sounded selfish and spiteful. Of course God wanted her to be a better person.

But she wasn't perfect; she was only herself. And if she didn't nurse her disappointment, she feared she was going to dissolve into tears again. That would be so awful.

Sighing, she continued to peel as she attempted to think more positive thoughts. Tried to think about how happy she'd be tomorrow when she'd put up dozens of jars in the cold cellar and the long day of doing her least favorite thing was behind her.

She picked up another apple and peeled away, trying to imagine feeling happy, content, and not angry at Joel. She started thinking about all the other men she knew and attempted to picture herself by one of their sides. Why, more than two eligible men had sought her out. Some weren't even that bad.

No, that wasn't true. Most weren't bad at all . . . except for Caleb. Just remembering the rude way Caleb had cornered her during last year's Christmas gathering made her shiver.

Which caused her to make a good-sized slice on her left palm. Oh, oh why did her mother insist on having such sharp knives?

Running over to the sink, she stuck her hand under the cold running water and tried not to yell, whine, cry, or make things worse. All she seemed to be able to do was bite her bottom lip hard enough to make it bleed, too.

In the middle of her small crisis, she was vaguely aware of a knock at the front door and her mother speaking to whoever was there. Then she heard footsteps.

"Tiny, why are you standing there with your hand under the faucet?" her mother asked. "Oh my word. You did it again!"

"Don't worry. I'll take care of the blood in a minute. It's only on the countertop. The apples are clean."

"You better double-check."

"I will. I promise," she called out as she tried to will her hand to stop bleeding.

"Oh, Tiny," a deeper voice murmured.

She knew that voice! Turning around, she gaped. "Joel, what are you doing here?"

"Helping you patch up your cut, it seems," he said as he walked to her side and turned off the faucet. "Now, let me see," he murmured as he took hold of her hand.

She was too stunned to see Joel to pull her hand away. Feeling out of sorts, she glanced up at her mother hovering in the doorway. For the first time Tiny could ever recall, her mom wasn't spouting off her opinion or cautioning her to be more careful. Instead, she was simply watching the two of them.

He turned to look over his shoulder. "Violet, where are the Band-Aids?"

"There in the drawer next to the pantry. I'll get them."

"*Nee*, that's all right. I can do it."

"That's mighty nice of you. Are you sure?"

"*Jah*. Tiny and me need to have a talk anyway. If she doesn't mind, I'll stay here and help her with this apple butter."

"Tiny?" her mother prompted. "Is that what you want?"

Not really. She was still upset with him and confused by his hot and cold actions. But, on the other hand, she'd known him too long to refuse to hear what he had to say. "Joel staying here is fine. He's right. We do need to talk." And yes, she sounded as if she had just announced that she was getting ready to clean toilets.

After giving them both another searching look, her mother disappeared.

"What do you want to talk to me about?" she asked. Unfortunately, she didn't sound as tough as she'd hoped. That probably had something to do with the fact that her hand was now bleeding well and good all over the bottom of the sink. Just seeing the red stain made her sway on her feet.

"Us. Jane," he said as he easily helped her sit on top of the kitchen counter.

Usually she would have protested the action, but she was rather happy to be off her feet. Instead, she focused on their conversation. "I don't want to talk to you about Jane Shultz."

He frowned. "I don't think we're going to be able to talk about anything until you get your bearings. Close your eyes if you have to, but don't you get all woozy on me."

Ah, but that was typical Joel. He liked to be in control of a situation, even when he wasn't. "I'm fine." Almost.

"You aren't. And you're just as obstinate as ever." He opened several drawers, finally found the first aid kit, and set it on the counter. "Here we go. Let's get your hand clean. Stay still, now."

Another time, another day, she would have slapped his hand away and told him she was perfectly capable of putting a bandage on a cut. But the blood was making her a bit squeamish.

After dabbing her cut with a wet paper towel, Joel raised her hand to his lips and blew out little wisps of air. Watching him purse his lips . . . thinking about how she used to daydream about kissing him . . . well, it made her crumble even more inside.

He stopped. "You're wincing. Am I blowing too hard?"

He smelled so good. And his breath? Well, it was so warm against her skin. *"Nee,"* she answered, her voice strained.

"Are you sure? I don't want to hurt you."

"You aren't. I promise, Joel. It, um, just stings."

He nodded like it made perfect sense to him. And he would have been right, say, if she had been seven instead of seventeen. Now she just felt foolish. She needed to end this little episode and fast. "I'm fine. Please bandage me up."

He didn't smile, but the corners of his eyes crinkled. He was amused. But still, he did as she asked, and before long, her palm was sporting a patch of gauze held in place by some first aid tape. "There. All done." He looked especially pleased with himself.

She'd kept her mouth shut while he'd been patching her up, but now, holding that hand in front of her, she grimaced. "Oh, Joel. I look like I practically got my hand chopped off, you've got so much padding and gauze on it."

"Are you seriously finding fault with my help?"

"I'm sorry. You are right. *Danke.*"

"You are welcome." He held out his hands and helped her hop off the countertop.

She pretended she barely noticed the firm, sure way his hands held her waist. Turning a bit, she started putting everything back in the kit one-handed. "We need to talk about the real reason you stopped by."

"Well, there's two."

"Which are?"

"The first is Jane. She and I only have a business relationship. She is experiencing some health problems and needs help."

"What kind of health problems?"

"I told her I wouldn't talk about them."

Not even to her. "I see. Is there anything else you wanted to tell me?"

"*Jah*, as a matter of fact. What's this I heard about Luke calling on you last night?"

"That's none of your business, Joel."

"You know it is."

She didn't know anything of the sort, which of course, just made her feel even worse about her whole dating situation. "Now that we've talked, you may leave."

He motioned to the bushel of apples. "Don't you want my help?"

"I do not."

"But—"

"I am going to be just fine, Joel!"

"*Jah*, I guess you will be. Goodbye, Tiny."

She held on tight to her anger as he grabbed his jacket and hat and walked out the door. Never even looking back.

And when the door shut behind him, she picked up that paring knife and got to work again. But this time, she pushed all her pain and anger to one side. Instead, she just kept reminding herself that even though her heart was breaking, she was going to be *just fine*.

Perhaps one day she'd actually feel that way, too.

seventeen

· RULE #17 ·

Accept help from volunteers. Actually, accept help from
everyone who offers a helping hand.

Less than one hour after he'd arrived, Joel was striding down the Coblentzes' front walkway. How had all of his good intentions gone so terribly wrong? One minute, he'd been caring for her cut and loving the fact that she was trusting him so sweetly.

And then, what felt like seconds after, they'd begun arguing again. Instead of listening to his reasons for helping Jane, she'd acted peevish. And then she'd had the nerve to defend her interest in Luke Yoder!

Now, he was frustrated, in need of a shower, and wandering outside in the cold.

He was going to need to go home and come up with a plan

B or C. That was obvious. Unfortunately, what wasn't was how he was ever going to get the chance to put any of those alternate plans into action. Tiny now felt further away from being his fiancée than ever before.

Since he had taken the day off from work to call on her, Joel had several more hours before he had to get home. If he did walk inside now, his mother would quiz him, and his younger brother would waste no time in telling him that he should look around for someone else to court.

Since neither option appealed to him, he kept walking. It was cold and snowy but not frigid. Perhaps in the high thirties? Stuffing his hands in his pockets, he continued along the side of the road.

There was something about a crisp winter day. With the fields barren, most animals, except for a stray deer or two, were in shelters of their own making. And because the roads were covered in packed snow, next to no one was traveling. No vehicles, no buggies.

Just Joel.

He liked the peacefulness of it. Craved it, actually. Though he'd never had a problem getting along with other people and enjoyed a wide variety of friends, there were times when his body needed to recharge and simply think. Which was maybe why it was somewhat ironic that out of all the women in his world, he'd set his sights on Tiny. She lit a room up just by walking into it.

And then there was her family. Oh, the whole lot of them couldn't be more unlike his own. His parents were reserved, organized, and sedate. He, his brother, Sam, and his sister, Summer, who was now married, were all cut from the same cloth.

The Coblentz family, on the other hand, was messy, disorganized, busy, and chatty. Something new was always going on, and the first time he'd witnessed them sharing a meal, he'd been reminded of a circus.

Now that things with him and Tiny were in disarray and Aaron and Jack had decided that he'd cheated on Tiny, he doubted he'd ever get to be more than just her friend. But, oh, how he wanted so much more.

He was going to miss the lot of them, for sure. But most especially Tiny.

Walking aimlessly, he took a right on a street he hadn't been on in months. And there, like a beacon he hadn't even known he was looking for, was the bookmobile.

Deciding that the traveling library would be a good break from the cold, Joel headed inside.

Sarah Anne Miller greeted him with a smile. "Joel Lapp, aren't you a sight for sore eyes. How are you?"

"I'm good. I *canna* tell you when the last time we saw each other was. Maybe two months ago?"

"It has to be at least that long. Well, can I help you with anything?"

"*Nee.* I was just out walking and came upon you. I didn't know you drove out this way."

"I don't usually, but we had a request from a lady who is homebound. Her neighbor brought her over when I first got here, but it's been quiet ever since. Winter days are like that, I guess. It's always hard to find a reason to venture out into the cold, even if it's for a new book."

"Ah. Well, I'll just look around."

She pointed to one of those coffee machines with all the pods. "I was just about to make a fresh cup of coffee before I head back in an hour. Would you like a cup, too?" She smiled encouragingly. "It might help you keep warm on your walk back home."

"*Jah. Kaffi* sounds *gut.*"

"Perfect. Coming right up."

He walked over to a foldout table that had about thirty books displayed on it. They all looked shiny and new.

"We've got some real good books just in. There's a few biographies and a couple of historicals, if you've got a mind for one of those."

"*Danke.* I'll look around." But as he picked up the various titles, he found himself not paying as much attention to the books as to his problems with Tiny.

Sarah Anne handed him his cup. "Here you go." She winked. "Whenever I serve coffee to a patron, I always get a little tickled. It makes me feel like I'm working in one of those fancy bookstores in Columbus."

He smiled. "It does feel a bit like that right now." He took an experimental sip and discovered, to his surprise, that it was quite good. "Your machine does a good job. Thank you."

She sipped from her own cup. "I'm glad for the company right now." Glancing at his empty hands, she said, "I've got some mysteries over there if you are interested."

He shrugged. "I mainly came in to get warm, if you want to know the truth. I . . . well, I've got a bit on my mind right now."

"I can understand that. Take your time." She moved over to her desk.

Joel sipped his coffee, enjoying the warmth it brought as much as the jolt of caffeine.

Maybe it was because she wasn't pressing him for information, but he started talking. "I made some mistakes lately with a girl, and I don't know how to make things better without betraying some confidences."

She frowned. "That's a dilemma, indeed."

"Any ideas about what to do?"

"Well, I was married for a long time, and my job used to be in accounting. I'm afraid I don't have too many experiences with rocky relationships."

"You've been blessed, then."

"I have been." A shadow crossed her face. "Sometimes I think I didn't even realize how blessed I was." She looked at him intently. "I know you're young, but do you know what I mean? Have you ever felt that you took things for granted because you didn't know any different?"

It was like she'd read his mind. That was exactly how he was feeling about how things had been with Tiny. He'd appreciated her, but he'd never taken the time to reflect on how truly blessed he'd been to have Tiny's attention, to have the expectation that they would one day court and marry. *"Jah,"* he said, his throat tight. "I have felt like that before." *Nee*, he should probably be more honest if she was being honest with him. "I mean to say, I've been feeling like that today."

"Ah. Well, it looks like you came to the right place, then." She waved a hand. "Books are wonderful things, and I'm hopeful that one of them will help you take your mind off your problems. But if you ever need an ear, come by and visit me. We can chat and catch up. Or, I can even just listen."

Sincerity surrounded her like a wispy cloud, leading him to realize that she meant every word. *"Danke,"* he said simply.

"You're quite welcome."

He finished his coffee, checked out two books at last, and then took his leave. Walking out into the cold again, Joel felt at loose ends. Nothing was going as he'd planned today. Not his visit to see Tiny, not even this walk, as he'd ended up at a bookmobile pouring out his troubles to a retired accountant with a gift for conversation.

It was too cold to simply wander around. The snow was thick, and the sky was filled with the type of low clouds that signaled more snow was on the way. He headed home, lost in thought.

Which was probably why he didn't notice the stray dog until he was upon it. It was a yellow dog. Perhaps part Labrador, maybe part shepherd. More importantly, though, it was baring its teeth and growling at him.

"Hey, now. Don't fret, *hund*. I won't bother you none." He held up a hand as if to prove his point.

But unfortunately, that was the wrong thing to do. Obviously thinking that Joel was about to hit it, the dog bared its teeth and growled again.

In reflex, Joel raised his hand. Not to strike but to fend off an attack.

Immediately, the dog whined and cowered.

"Oh, *hund*," he murmured. "Easy now." Taking a closer look, he realized that the poor thing was next to skin and bones. His heart went out to it. "You've had a time of it, haven't ya?" he asked.

The dog gazed at him for a moment, then limped closer. No doubt, one or more of its paws were injured from all the snow and ice on the ground.

The animal was in pain, scared, and in need of care. But how to go about that, Joel wasn't exactly sure. He'd never had a pet and certainly didn't have the first idea about how to get an injured animal to trust him. "What should we do about you?" he murmured.

The dog's brown eyes blinked. It was as if he was just as surprised as Joel about their present situation. Slowly, he sat down on his haunches. Waiting.

Waiting for Joel. All of his doubts shifted, and all of his worries didn't seem to matter so much anymore. He couldn't ignore the animal or pretend their paths hadn't crossed. Perhaps the Lord had brought them together for a reason? It seemed likely.

"Dog, what do you think? Should you go home with me? I haven't ever had a dog, but I know enough to know you need food, warmth, and care. I'll do my best for you, if you wouldn't mind some mistakes now and then."

The dog scooted three or four inches closer, and its head leaned closer still, almost as if it was waiting for Joel to give more assurances.

And so he did. "Dog, I'm not a violent man. I won't harm you any. And . . . I'll put you on a blanket in my bedroom. You can sleep there. It's nothing fancy, but it's a far sight better than out here. Then, too, I can take a look at your paw and give you some food."

He smiled when the dog scooted several more inches closer and tilted its head to one side, still studying him.

No, still wanting to believe.

In spite of the snow on the ground, Joel crouched down to be at the dog's height. "If I'm going to take you home to be my dog, we should maybe try to be friends, *jah*?" He figured the first step was for the poor animal to know he wouldn't harm him. He held out a hand and waited.

It backed up several inches, but Joel kept his hand outstretched.

Then, ever so slowly, the dog inched forward. "That's right, *hund*. You've got to trust somebody, ain't so? It might as well be me."

A minute later, the dog got to its feet and stepped forward, this time, almost until its black nose reached the tips of Joel's fingers.

Joel's knees were starting to complain, but he stayed put. As the dog seemed to continue to weigh the pros and cons of coming closer, Joel realized that he had no doubts about taking the animal home. It didn't matter if the dog had been abused or abandoned or bit him or didn't trust him. What mattered was that they needed each other. He knew they did. And he didn't even care what his parents were going to think. This dog needed a home, and he was going to provide it. He reckoned Tiny would agree with that wholeheartedly.

He had just started imagining what Tiny would look like when she saw this poor dog when he felt its cold, wet, nose resting against his fingertips.

Joel smiled. "Yellow dog, it is *gut* to meet you. My name's Joel." Ever so slowly, he ran a finger along the dog's head. To his relief, the dog didn't flinch or run away. It just remained staring at him, waiting to see what their next step would be.

And for the first time all day, Joel knew exactly what that would be. "Let's go home, *hund*. I'd pick you up, but even in your state, I fear it would be too heavy a load to carry for a mile." He got to his feet and picked the library books back up.

When he started walking, the dog whined. He patted his thigh. "You, too, yellow *hund*. Come on now."

After a pause, the dog followed him, remaining three or four steps behind.

"That's right. Stay with me. I won't steer you wrong."

It had been a very strange day, full of surprises. He'd doctored Tiny's hand, gotten kicked out of her house, had a heart-to-heart with a librarian, and now had adopted a dog. It seemed his grandfather, his *dawdi*, had been correct all those years ago when he'd declared that one's life had to be shaken up from time to time.

Or, in the dog's case, it simply needed a thread of hope.

eighteen

"I think you should come over for supper soon," Aunt Pat announced to Kayla as they were cleaning up the shop at the end of the day. "You've got to be mighty lonely in that house without your father. And there's no telling what you have been eating. Probably nothing good."

Pat wasn't wrong. She hadn't been eating anything that could be classified as "good." She didn't have a good excuse for it, either. Though her money situation was tight, she did have enough cash on hand to shop for groceries. She was even a fairly decent cook, decent enough to make five or six basic meals. The problem was that she lacked the will to do it. After months of working all day, tutoring, caring for her father in the evenings, and then doing all her regular chores, she had been running on empty. Now that her father was gone and she had the house to herself, all she wanted to do when she got home was collapse. Therefore, her new diet consisted of popcorn, some canned fruit, and a couple of jars of soup. Not that her aunt needed to know that.

"*Danke*, but I've been doing fine. I have been eating plenty."

"How does tomorrow night sound?"

She shook her head in dismay. "Pat, it's like you don't want to hear me."

"If it seems that way, it's because I don't want to listen to any of those lies that you're spouting."

"I'm not lying."

"You might not be technically lying, Kayla, but you're not telling me the truth. I do know that."

They were running in circles. "Aunt Pat, please just listen to me."

Maybe it was the plaintive tone in her voice, but Pat's expression softened. "I'll always listen to you, Kay. Always. However, I also want you to tell me the truth. The real, unvarnished truth—not just the things you think I want to hear."

This was why she loved her aunt so much. Pat forced her to open up and talk about her feelings, even when those feelings weren't all that great. "All right. Pat, the truth is that I'm tired. Too tired to even go to your house for a nice meal. I want to just go home and relax when I get home. It's dark out anyway. You know how nerve-wracking it is to walk or ride a bike on the dark roads."

"You came over last year when your father went down to Florida."

She had. Last year, she'd still been trying to be everything to everyone. She'd kept up the same schedule, and a month later, her father had come home relaxed and happy and she'd gotten sick.

Maybe that was the difference. She wanted to put herself first sometimes. At least for one month out of the twelve. But how did she share any of that with Pat? She acted as if Kayla's father had every right to still be encased in his grief and sometimes even chided Kayla if she complained about his faults too much.

"Kayla, you know I'm only pushing you on this because I love you."

She knew that. She also knew Pat's love was as sweet and unselfish as she could ever hope for a parent's love to be.

"I love you, too. And I appreciate how much you do for me. I really do." When her aunt's eyes softened, Kayla joked, "Can we please drop this subject now?"

"In one minute." She took a deep breath. "Just answer me this. Do your worries have less to do with your father and more to do with Levi's betrayal?"

Kayla felt like she'd just been given a hard push off a very tall horse. "Why are you bringing Levi up? Our breakup doesn't have anything to do with my life now."

"Are you sure? Because I'm starting to wonder if Levi breaking up with you has made you skittish about falling in love again."

Kayla knew she was skittish about relationships. She had trust issues, too. Her mother had died too young, her father seemed to have forgotten that she was only twenty-six and Levi callously breaking up with her because "she had too much going on" had been a terrible betrayal. "Aunt Pat, he has made me skittish about getting in another relationship, but that's beside the point."

"Is it? If you can't forgive and let the past go, I fear you'll never be able to move forward." She lowered her voice. "And that would be a real shame, Kayla. You are a wonderful, giving person. You deserve to be happy."

"I'm sure I'll fall in love again one day. Levi hurt me, but I haven't given up on love."

And just like that, her aunt's entire demeanor brightened. "Does that mean you have been thinking of Aaron, then? Have you decided there really is something special between the two of you?"

Boy, she'd walked right into that trap! Kayla didn't know if there was something there or not. Maybe she *was* afraid to find out? What if she allowed herself to believe Aaron was special but then discovered he wasn't any better than Levi? What if he left her, even knowing that she gave him her heart? What would she do then?

She wasn't sure she would survive that.

"Whatever I've been thinking about Aaron Coblentz is my concern and not yours, Pat." Primly, she added, "I'm sorry, but my life isn't an open book."

Pat propped a hand on her hip. "Is that right? Well, in that case, I hope you know what you're doing. Trouble—and happiness—can come most anywhere and anytime. It's been my experience that both can catch a person by surprise."

Kayla wasn't exactly sure what Pat meant, but she was too tired to try to figure it out. "I'll keep that in mind. But I promise I know what I'm doing."

"Alrighty, then. But until I'm sure of it, I'm going to make sure you're eating well. I'm going to bring you something to take home tomorrow."

"I'll be mighty glad to have that. *Danke*. It's so kind of you."

With a harrumph, Pat turned away, leaving Kayla with her thoughts, but desperate to get out of her head, Kayla practically sprung on the next customers who walked in. "Hiya. May I help you?"

With a blistering sigh, the woman handed her a pattern packet. "I can't make heads or tails of this. Can you help me?"

"That's what I'm here for. I'll be glad to help you as much as I can." Walking to a long workstation table, she said, "Let's see what you've got here."

"It's a mess, that's what it is." She dug in the canvas bag Kayla had only just noticed. "And look at this fabric. I think it's the wrong width."

Smoothing out the light cotton, Kayla had to agree. "This isn't going to work," she said bluntly.

"Are you sure?"

"I'm positive."

"What should I do?"

"You're either going to have to find new fabric to work with the pattern or find a new pattern to go with the fabric."

"Surely not."

Kayla wasn't about to argue with her, but she was tempted to point out that the woman had already realized the same thing before she walked in the door. So, she stood there and waited.

But instead of working with her, the lady turned nasty. "You are completely unhelpful. I cannot believe that more than one person told me to come here. They practically raved about the service here."

"I'm sorry, but I'm only telling you the facts."

"Hmph." She picked up the fabric and started stuffing it into her tote. "I won't be back."

"I'm sorry." But she wasn't. Who would be sorry? The woman was particularly unpleasant. She smiled tightly as the woman roughly folded the pattern all wrong and attempted to stuff it into the bag as well.

Pat rushed over. "Oh my. What is going on?"

"This girl here was just very rude to me. I came here for help, and she would hardly give me the time of day. She acted as if unbending even an inch was going to be too much work."

After giving Kayla a confused look, Aunt Pat adopted a soothing tone. "I'm here now. Please, how may I help you?"

Kayla walked over to the counter as the woman went through her spiel again. She checked out two customers with small purchases as the woman spread out the fabric and patterns again.

"Oh my." Pat gasped. "I'm afraid you are right. It's not going to fit. But let's problem solve, shall we? What do you think about adding a second piece of fabric? One in the same blue but perhaps a sturdier cloth?" She began outlining her ideas, and before her eyes, Kayla could see the woman drop her frustration and begin to work with Pat.

Almost an hour later, the woman bought another fifty dollars of fabric and notions. She even promised Pat she would return with the finished item. As she headed out the door, she paused long enough to glare at Kayla.

Kayla kept her expression blank, but inside she was cringing. For sure and for certain, she had deserved the woman's dark look. People expected kind and personal service when they walked in the door. It was why they came to Pat's instead of driving farther to one of the big box stores. She hadn't been very kind or very helpful.

When the door closed, Aunt Pat turned to her. "Want to tell me what happened?" she asked quietly.

"I think you have a pretty good idea. She needed help, and I didn't give her any."

"And why not?"

The customer had been rude, and that rudeness had grated on her. She never could abide the way some people treated her and Pat like they were beneath them. Kayla was tempted to share that what she told the woman hadn't been wrong. Her project hadn't been fixable.

"I'm sorry," she said at last.

Aunt Pat blinked. "Is Aaron coming for a tutoring session tonight?"

"*Nee.*"

"Then you may go."

Kayla looked at the clock. "But it's only three o'clock." They had two more hours before they closed at five.

"I think we can both agree that you aren't at your best right now. Why don't you go take a little break and relax?"

"All right. I'm sorry, again."

Pat turned to her abruptly. "Kayla, don't you see? I'm not the person you should be apologizing to."

It seemed she couldn't even apologize without messing up. She got her things, put on her cloak, and pulled her purse out of the locked cabinet from the back of the checkout area.

Just as she was about to assure Pat that she would see her tomorrow, the phone rang, taking her aunt's attention.

Kayla settled for walking out the door with a heavy heart.

She was in the middle of some fierce growing pains. She was exhausted, tired of trying so hard to help her father, tired of pretending that Levi's betrayal hadn't damaged the way she looked at relationships. Sometimes she even felt like she'd been covering up how much she still grieved for her mother.

And now, just when the timing couldn't even get worse, she was just about at rock bottom. She wasn't finding comfort in anything. Not work, not her aunt's company, not even her beloved romance stories that allowed her to escape for a couple of hours. She needed a change, and she needed the Lord's help, too. It was obvious that she wasn't going to be able to get better all on her own. *What should I do, Lord?* She silently prayed. *I want to be different. I want to feel hope again. I want to be myself again . . . but I don't even know where to start.*

"Kayla?"

Blinking, she looked up. And saw Aaron walking toward her.

When he smiled at her, Kayla realized her day had suddenly brightened.

It seemed God still answered prayers—and sometimes at lightning speed.

nineteen

Kayla Kauffman had on a gray dress and a black cloak. A black bonnet covered her white *kapp*, and her black stockings and boots looked exactly like those he'd seen on practically every other Amish woman in the area. But the bright red gloves she had on stood out like a cardinal in the middle of winter. They led him to her like she was the only bright thing in a dreary day. And maybe she was?

He was pleased when she smiled at him, though that smile soon faded into doubt. "Had we scheduled a tutoring session and I forgot?"

"Not at all." He shrugged. "Work was slow, so my boss let me leave. What about you? Are you just coming from work?"

"*Jah*. It was time I left for the day as well."

He was surprised, since he thought she usually worked until five. "I guess our meeting on the street like this was meant to be."

Her smiled widened. "I was just thinking the same thing."

Her happiness was contagious. "Would you care to walk home together? I believe I pass your house on the way to mine."

"I live almost two miles away. I'm surprised you're walking farther than me."

"It's bitter cold, and I'm fond of my horse. I'd rather keep her in the barn and wear a good coat."

"Her comfort is my gain, then. I'd love to walk with you."

A warm feeling ran through him as her words registered. Had they finally turned the corner from mere student and tutor? He hoped so. More and more, he found himself thinking about her, but he'd feared the infatuation was one sided. "Let's get on our way, then. The sun is out, but it's still freezing."

As they walked down the street, they passed a few people they knew but didn't stop to chat. Aaron didn't miss the speculative looks that were sent their way, either. In fact, he almost welcomed them. He liked being Kayla's friend. No, he liked the idea of one day being more than just her friend, of one day being the man who got to take her elbow and help her step off a curb or make sure she was warm enough when a cold wind picked up.

Kayla seemed just as at ease. She smiled at him when a buggy stopped beside them and two little boys made faces through the Plexiglas window.

"So, how goes your studying?"

Remembering his attempt to memorize twenty government terms made him grimace. "Not so well, if I'm being honest."

"Oh? What's wrong?"

"Everything," he joked.

"Come now. We both know you aren't doing that badly."

"I haven't been doing that good. I'd like to say it's because I'm overwhelmed from working so hard, but it's rather that I haven't been too motivated of late."

"Why is that?"

He shrugged. "For so long, taking this test was my secret dream. It seemed unattainable, about as hard to reach as the stars in the sky. Because of that, I kept that dream close to my heart." He paused before adding, "I think I was half afraid that if I let someone know about it, it could disappear like a figment of my imagination."

She knew he hadn't told his family about his studies. "Perhaps you should tell your parents, Aaron. At least if they knew, you could be more honest about the stress you've been under."

"They can't know. They wouldn't take the news well. Not at all."

"Really?"

"They are so afraid of me leaving like my brother did, I think they'd do everything in their power to stop me from taking that test." He was actually pretty sure they'd throw out a bunch of ultimatums if he ignored their wishes.

Her eyes widened in surprise. "I see."

"Kayla, I'm not just battling my parents' wishes. I think I'm battling myself, too."

"How so?"

As much as he hated to sound so weak, he forced himself to admit his biggest fear. "Now that I'm so close to taking the test, I'm worried about failing." He was fairly sure he was going to fail, too. He wasn't a great student, and the test covered a lot of material he'd never even heard of. He looked away from her for a moment, in time to notice that the snow on the curb had turned gray and icy. "Careful now," he murmured as he took her elbow and helped her up and down the slippery curb.

When they were back on the dry sidewalk, she said, "I think your fear is perfectly normal. Why, I remember chatting with other people in the exam room before the proctor asked us to take our seats. Every one of us was worried about failing."

"This isn't just pretest jitters, Kayla. I genuinely don't know if I'll pass any of the test."

"Okay. Let's say that you do fail. What will you do then? Will you take it again?"

"I don't know. I might . . . or I might not. Doing all of this over again would be a lot to take on." He paused, then decided to be completely honest. "But I keep thinking that if I don't take the test or don't ever pass it, I'll be giving up a big dream. That would be hard, too."

"I can understand that," she murmured.

He glanced at her again. Kayla looked wistful, or maybe she'd had more challenges passing the test than he'd realized. "You can? Did you really experience doubts like I'm having?"

"A little bit. But I *canna* lie to you, Aaron. I did well in school. Studying and test-taking has always come easy for me."

"You were lucky, then."

"I was lucky, but I've had my other challenges." She chuckled under her breath. "Sometimes I feel it's everything else that's hard."

Aaron knew she'd lost her mother to cancer . . . and she'd alluded to her father's struggles. "What do you mean? I mean, if it's not too personal to share."

"It's not too personal. I . . . Well, I was just thinking about a relationship I was in that ended badly."

"Oh, wow. Was it serious?"

"*Jah*. I mean, I thought it was, but he didn't. Or, perhaps, Levi thought things were too serious. I don't know."

Aaron was confused by her explanation. "I hear it is supposed to snow tonight," he blurted. "Sometimes I feel that winter will never end."

"It always does though, true?"

He nodded. "Where is your *haus*? Are we close?"

"*Jah*." She pointed to the street off to the left. "It's just over the bend. What about you?"

"It's about a mile farther up." He knew his voice was flat, but he wasn't sure what to do about it. He'd taken a chance and opened up to her, and though she had as well, some of that glow that had lit her eyes had faded. Kayla looked just as uncomfortable as he felt. She stuffed her red-mittened hands into her cloak's pockets, covering up the brightness he'd been drawn to in the first place.

"Aaron, when Levi broke up with me, he said a lot of cruel things. He blamed me for things that I had no control over."

"I'm sorry, but he sounds like a jerk. Maybe you're better off without him."

"I am, but that doesn't mean his words didn't hurt." She paused for a moment, seeming to gather her thoughts. "That whole relationship also made me wonder how I could've been so wrong about him. I mean: How was it possible for me to love someone who obviously didn't love me back?"

"I don't think you can put that burden on yourself. It's natural to love other people, right?" When she nodded, he said, "Then you didn't do anything wrong. Levi did."

They had turned onto her street. Sometime during her confession he'd decided that he'd needed to make sure she got home safe.

"That's my house." She pointed to a one-story home with a lovely porch that wrapped around the front to one of the sides. It was all white, except for the black railings and the black frames around the windows.

"It's very pretty."

"*Danke.* I always thought so, too. My mother had wanted a home with a big front porch."

"I'm sorry I was so nosy."

She shook her head. "As bad as this sounds, I'm glad I told you about all of that. It feels good to know it's now out in the open." Kayla's smile faltered as they came upon her neighbor. "Oh, boy. Get ready."

"Hello, Kayla," the woman, who'd obviously gone out to get the mail, called out. "You're home early."

"I am."

"And . . . it looks like you have company today."

"It also looks as if the mail has arrived."

"It has. Two hours late, though." The woman sniffed.

"My word," Aaron murmured.

Kayla's lips twitched. "Well, Mrs. Hershberger, I wish you good day."

The lady merely stared. "Kayla, your father is still gone, isn't he?"

"Yes, he is."

"Hmph," she said, before turning toward her door.

Aaron leaned toward her. "You've got a busybody, *jah*? We've had those."

Some of the pain faded in her eyes. "Yes, I suppose we all have them." She chuckled.

He smiled down at her just as her foot slipped. She reached for the railing, crying out as the wood broke under her weight.

And just like that, she fell with a gasp.

"Kayla!" He knelt by her side, intending to help her.

But then he saw that a thick splinter of wood had embedded itself in her palm and she was bleeding.

Aaron made his decision right then and there. Kayla might have been older, more experienced, and had obviously endured things he couldn't imagine, but today, he was going to be the strong one and help her. It was the least he could do.

"Where's your key, Kayla?"

"It's in the pocket of my purse."

He reached for her purse and scanned the contents. There wasn't much in the center compartments, but the four side pockets looked full. "Which one has your house key?" If Tiny had taught him anything, it was to refrain from digging around in women's purses willy-nilly.

"I don't know. One of the side pockets? Just look until you find it."

He got lucky when he dug into the third pocket. Quickly, he unlocked the door and ushered her into the dark house. "Kerosene or battery lights?"

"I have a kerosene lantern in the kitchen."

Finding a match, he neatly lit the rather large black metal lamp and put it on the table. It cast a warm, pleasing glow in the room, but that wasn't going to be enough to give her any relief. "We need a battery light, too."

She blinked. "Truly?"

"There's a splinter in your hand, *jah*? I'll need good light to tug it out."

She blanched. "Oh. Of course." Pointing to a small, finely made box on the edge of a counter, she said, "There are some in there."

He easily located one and turned it on. As he'd hoped, it cast a bright beam across the room. "One last thing. I need tweezers and a needle. Maybe some alcohol and a Band-Aid, too."

"That would be four things."

He smiled. "You may relax your mind for a second, Kayla."

"There's a first aid box under the bathroom sink. Go down the hall. You'll see it."

He followed her directions, feeling once again like he was invading her privacy as he peeked in two doorways. The first had to be her father's bedroom. It was sparse, with only a blue-and-red patterned quilt on the top of an oak bed. The second was hers. It had pale pink walls, pale maple wood furniture, and a large bookcase filled with paperbacks. There was also a white wicker rocking chair in the corner with a small circular table next to it that was painted white. The whole room smelled faintly of cinnamon and something floral—maybe rose?

The bathroom, in contrast to both bedrooms, was pure white. Underneath was a plastic first aid kit. Grabbing it, he hurried back to her side.

"Did you have trouble finding it?"

"*Nee*. It was right where you said. I wasn't sure which door led to it so I had to look in the rooms."

"Oh."

For some reason, he felt that if he didn't admit he'd seen her room, he would be acting dishonestly. "I like your pink walls."

"You do?"

"You sound surprised," he teased as he opened the kit and pulled out the rubbing alcohol and cotton. "Did you not think a man could appreciate pink?"

Her eyes lit up. "Maybe. My father doesn't care for it. Sometime I fear it's not 'Plain' enough, but I can't seem to find the willpower to paint the walls white again."

Aaron thought Kayla was too hard on herself, but he refrained from saying that. "Are you ready to let me see to your hand now?"

"Yes, of course." She held her hand out. *"Danke."*

There was really no other way to tackle it other than matter-of-factly. "I'll clean it with some alcohol, then try to pull it out with the tweezers."

"All right."

"It's, ah, partially embedded." Was that even the right word? "I might have to use the needle to poke around a bit. I'm sorry, but it will probably hurt."

She grimaced. "Would you mind if you did the deed without describing every step?"

"I can do that." He hid his smile. He rather liked that there was something she didn't do better than him.

"I'm sorry. I'm not good with blood."

"I understand." He didn't think there was going to be much more blood involved, but he refrained from saying anything. Instead, he simply got to work.

He cradled her hand in his own, trying to ignore how small and delicate it felt compared to his. With gentle dabs, he wiped the broken skin, then took hold of the tweezers and carefully gripped the end of the splinter. There was nothing to do but pull it out as gently as he could.

"Oh!" she said, squeezing her eyes shut.

"Almost done." He hoped he was telling the truth.

Seconds later, the little operation was over. He pressed a piece of cotton on the wound. "You can breathe again, Kayla. It's out."

She popped her eyes open again. "Truly?"

"Absolutely." He smiled at her. "I wouldn't lie to you about that."

She blew out a big breath of air. "Aaron, I'm beginning to think you wouldn't lie to me about anything."

"Good, because I wouldn't. I don't plan to, either. I mean, I won't lie if I can help it at all."

"That's a good way to be, right? I mean, even if the truth is hard to say or embarrassing, I'd rather it be out in the open."

Thinking of how much they'd revealed to each other and how much more highly he thought of her than even before, Aaron couldn't agree more. "I think that's a *gut* plan," he said, finally releasing her hand. Once he did, he immediately felt its loss.

twenty

Tiny didn't mean to spy on Joel, but she couldn't seem to help herself. He *just happened* to be around whenever she looked out the window that *just happened* to face his house.

That wasn't quite true, though. The simple fact was that she missed him. Even though they'd argued, even though she was frustrated with his hot and cold courting, she still longed for him. She missed looking forward to his visits, missed anticipating a life by his side. Love was proving to be a very dangerous emotion. Somehow it managed to hurt and soothe her heart . . . all at the same time.

So, whenever Tiny had a spare moment, she walked over to

one of the many windows that faced his house and looked for him. Just to see his face.

To her surprise, Joel wasn't that hard to find. After years of barely seeing him at all, he now seemed to be continually outside in the yard that faced her house.

It was *wunderbaar*! So good that she would have thought it was a little coincidental . . . except that, well, if Tiny wasn't so sure that her eyes were deceiving her, she would have thought she had seen Joel with a very ugly yellow dog. But Joel didn't have a pet. No one in his family did. Honestly, she could have sworn that she'd heard his father once declare that he didn't care for pets. He believed animals were only supposed to be useful.

Now she was beginning to wonder if he'd changed his mind.

Peeking out the window after she'd made and attached labels for her mother's famous chicken stock, Tiny was pleased to see that Joel was outside again. Dressed in a knit stocking cap, black pants, and his usual black wool coat, he looked as handsome as he ever did.

Just . . . happier? Yes, she was pretty sure he was laughing. But at what?

More curious now, Tiny leaned closer to the windowpane and tried to see what Joel was laughing about. Unfortunately, a thicket of trees and bushes impeded her view. It was frustrating. She needed to go outside and investigate.

But what if he saw her? What would happen then? Would he accuse her of spying? She'd have to get all huffy and deny it, but they'd both know she was lying. On the other hand, if she did nothing, she was going to spend yet another day mooning over Joel.

So, it was a dilemma.

"*Hund!*" Rebecca exclaimed as she clapped her hands.

Startled, Tiny turned away from the glass in time to see her little sister and her mother walking in the front door. Bundled up in a thick wool dress, navy cloak, and Tiny's old scarf and mittens, Becca looked as cute as could be. The scarf was wrapped around her *kapp*, and her cheeks were bright pink. Her *mamm* had taken off her simple black cloak and mittens and was stomping her boots.

"What did you say, Becca?"

"*Hund et Joel!*"

"Dog and Joel?"

"Joel got himself a dog, Tiny," her mother explained. "Or rather, it seems to have found him."

They had her full attention now. "What do you mean?"

Her mother blinked. "Just what I said. We were out walking and saw Joel. He's outside with his new *hund*."

Her eyes hadn't deceived her . . . but it still didn't make much sense. "I didn't think his father liked dogs. I'm surprised Joel bought one."

"Oh, he didn't. He was walking home from the bookmobile and spied it wandering around in the cold."

"Really?"

Her mother frowned. "Poor little thing. Joel said it was cold and hungry and had obviously been mistreated. He stayed there for quite a while, coaxing it closer."

"What happened to it?"

"Why, the dog eventually trusted him, dear."

"And then?"

Her mother looked at her strangely. "Well, then Joel took it home, that's what. Now he has a dog."

Tiny was still having a hard time wrapping her head around that. "But Joel has never wanted one. I didn't think he liked dogs."

"*Hund!*" Becca called out again.

Mamm picked up Becca and gave her a little hug. "That's right, dear. Joel has a *hund.*" After putting Becca down, Mamm said, "I believe Joel likes this dog a lot. So, whoever told you that he didn't like dogs was obviously wrong."

No one had told her that. She knew this from a lifetime of watching him. Even though it was foolish, and none of her business, she murmured, "I still find it hard to believe." Of course, what she really meant was that she found it hard to believe Joel could still surprise her.

"Perhaps you should go outside to see for yourself, child. You know, instead of standing in here and spying on him."

"I wasn't spying."

Her mother sighed. "Go meet that animal, Tiny. Even if you don't think Joel likes dogs, we all know that you like them fine."

She lifted her chin. "I think I will do that."

"*Gut.*" Bending down to help Becca take off her cloak, Mamm muttered, "It's about time, too."

Deciding to ignore that, Tiny turned on her heel, walked to the mudroom, and put on her favorite violet mittens and matching scarf before adding a black cloak and her thick soled boots.

Now that she'd made up her mind, Tiny hoped she wasn't going to be too late.

She wasn't. As soon as she rounded the corner of the house, she heard Joel call out. "*Gut* girl, Yellow. You are a mighty fine *hund* indeed."

A happy bark sang through the air in response.

Tiny walked closer and saw Joel toss a thick stick several

yards. She watched the dog run after it, then, to her astonishment, the dog neatly dropped it at his feet, just like they'd been playing the game for months.

Tossing it again, Joel called out, "Go fetch, Yellow!" Then, he stilled as he spied her. "Hiya, Tiny."

Feeling self-conscious, she walked closer. "Hi. *Mei mamm* and Becca just told me you had a dog, but I found that hard to believe."

"So you had to come out to see for yourself?"

His voice was snide. She couldn't say she blamed him for that. She hadn't believed him about Jane, not even when he'd explained that Jane had a reason to be needing help around her house.

"That's not exactly what I was doing," she said.

He raised an eyebrow. "But close enough?"

"*Jah*. I guess so."

She stuffed her mittened hands into her pockets as the dog ran back to Joel and then flopped down at his feet. Joel knelt down and petted her before standing up and facing Tiny again.

"Are you ever going to forgive me for keeping my work for Jane a secret?"

He looked so miserable—as miserable as she felt—that Tiny knew it was time to give him the benefit of the doubt. "I think I had better, hadn't I?" Realizing that she had something else to admit, she added, "I should probably also mention that Luke isn't going to be coming over to my house anymore."

"Why is that?"

"I decided we didn't suit." Remembering his smug manner, she smiled slightly. "At all."

"I guess we're back where we started."

"Perhaps. Though I'd like to think we're in a better place now. I'm trying to be better."

"I'm trying, too, Tiny. And you know what? You're right. We've known each other too long to dwell on disagreements. At least, I feel that way."

"I feel that way as well." She smiled up at him. "Now, will you please talk to me about this *hund*?"

"Her name is Yellow."

"How did you know? Did she have a tag on her collar?" If so, she was going to have to find a gentle way to remind him to return the pet to her owner.

"She didn't have a collar or anything like that. I bought this one a couple of days ago," he said of the bright red collar with a dog bone–shaped tag dangling from it. "I named her Yellow."

"That's a fitting name, indeed. She is quite yellow." Though, she thought "golden" might be a better descriptor.

"*Jah.*" He reached down and gently ran his hand along the dog's coat again. She shivered in happiness. When he smiled down at her again, Yellow wagged her tail.

Tiny thought that was the most precious thing she'd ever seen. The dog adored him, and the feeling was obviously mutual. "The two of you make a good pair."

"I don't know. You know I have no experience owning a pet. But, I'm thinking that maybe Yellow here ain't too used to being one."

"I think the Lord helped you two find each other."

"Maybe so." Lines appeared on his brow. "Oh, Tiny. She looked so sad when I came across her. And her paw was obviously paining her. I think she might have been outside for quite a while."

"In the cold and snow. That's horrible."

"*Jah.*" After another fond look at the dog, he added, "Something about her got to me." He made a fist and planted it in his middle. "I couldn't leave her there on the street or forget I ever saw her, you know? I had to do something."

She had never been in that situation, but she did know how Joel was, and she very well could see him not wanting to leave her. Honestly, she would have been surprised if he had. "I have a feeling that she must have felt the same away about you, Joel. Yellow here could have run away when she saw you, but she didn't."

Joel's expression brightened. "That's true, ain't so?" When she nodded, he smiled. "Maybe me and this dog were meant to be. Maybe we're a *gut* team, *jah?*"

"I think so." With Yellow staying securely by his side, Tiny realized she felt a little jealous. Jealous the dog was getting so much of Joel's attention, and maybe even of the dog's complete adoration of him. It all made her feel a bit like a third wheel, which was silly, especially since just days before she'd been contemplating a life without him.

Belatedly realizing that the dog was still looking at her as if unsure whether she was a friend or a foe, Tiny shook her head to clear it. "Joel, would you please introduce me to Yellow?"

"Of course." He looked at her warily. "She's just learning how I do things, of course. We haven't progressed to manners and such yet."

Joel was already feeling protective of Yellow! Shielding the *hund* from her disdain! "I have no expectations, Joel. I only want to be a friend."

Bending down, he patted the dog. "Yellow, this is Tiny Coblentz. She is a . . . friend."

And, there it was. That pause had been so short, but it symbolized the great shift in their relationship. Or, perhaps it signified so much of what could have been. *Nee,* what should have been. She felt her bottom lip tremble, already grieving for the loss of their romance.

"Tiny?"

"Oh, sorry. I guess my mind went walking." She cleared her throat and held out her hand to the dog. "It is very nice to meet you, Miss Yellow. You're a very pretty girl."

She kept her hand in place as Yellow hesitantly looked up at Joel then back at her. When he nodded, she took two steps closer. Then another. And then, she lifted her nose to Tiny.

Trusting her. It was such a gift. Very gently, Tiny ran one finger along her nose. After a pause, she patted her again. "*Danke,* Yellow. I am glad to be your friend." When the dog thumped her tail, Tiny smiled, feeling like she'd just passed a difficult test.

"I think we're going to be friends now," she said to Joel.

He wasn't smiling, but his eyes were gentle. "I hope so."

Even though it was cold, even though there was snow on the ground, Tiny walked right over and sat on the bottom step of his stoop. Then, just as if they did this all the time, she looked up at him with a bright smile. "Now, tell me everything. Tell me all about how you found her and convinced her to come home with you."

Joel looked like he'd rather be anywhere else. But, still, he complied and went to sit by her side. "It all started when I decided to go for a walk and found the bookmobile."

"You were looking for a book to read?"

"I was." Looking irritated, he added, "I might not read as much as you do, but I do read, Tiny."

"Of course. I'm sorry. That was rude. What happened next?"

Little by little, in halting phrases, he told his story. She listened and reflected and sometimes even forgot that she was cold. She thought about Yellow and how she'd overcome so many obstacles and didn't give up hope. If a dog could do it, then she could, too.

All it was going to take was time and patience. Thank goodness, she had an abundance of both.

twenty-one

"You came back," Sarah Anne said to Pete Canon when he stepped inside. "I wondered if you would."

He looked surprised. "I told you I'd be back in a week. I even took a copy of the schedule."

"That is true. I guess I shouldn't have doubted you."

He smiled. "No reason you should have believed me. We're still practically strangers, aren't we?"

Sarah Anne couldn't disagree, but she was honest enough to hope they could be friends. "Maybe not strangers for long, though. So, how are you this week? Are you having a good one?"

"I'm good enough, and I guess my week is going well enough, too. What about you?"

"Fine. I'm good enough, too." That phrase actually was a good summation of how her week had been. Nothing out of the ordinary had happened—good or bad. But she was hoping that might be about to change.

"Can I help you find something? Or, did you order a book online? If so, I can look . . ." She hadn't thought he had ordered any books to be delivered, but one of the clerks had stocked the reserve cabinet that morning when Sarah Anne had been in a meeting.

"I didn't order anything. I got online a couple of times, fully intending to order something, but it was difficult to make a decision."

She nodded in agreement. "Yes, it is hard to choose a book just by reading a screen."

"Exactly." He grinned. But instead of turning to scan the area for books, he looked at her intently. "So, tell me something interesting that happened to you this week."

He was her "something interesting," but she wasn't going to say that. "Unfortunately, there's nothing worth mentioning." She waved a hand in the air. "People come in, I help them as best I can, and then they go off on their way again."

He smirked, which made a dimple appear in his cheek. "I don't mean here, Sarah Anne. I meant in your life."

Her life. Which meant she was supposed to have something meaningful outside of her career. Drawing a blank, she summoned the first thing she could think of. "I walked on the treadmill."

He chuckled. "And was that a solitary event or a daily occurrence?"

She was so embarrassed. Who even cared about her exercise

habits? She obviously didn't. "Since it was noteworthy, I'm afraid it was a single event." She blushed as she thought about all the parts of her body that could really do with more exercise.

Why hadn't she mentioned something, anything else? "Obviously, it would be better if I made it part of my routine. What about you? Please tell me you lead a more exciting life."

"I don't know if it's all that exciting, but I had a meeting in Chicago and just got back last night."

"Oh? What do you do?"

"I'm in insurance."

She was so surprised that she was pretty sure she gaped at him.

"Ah, do you have something against insurance agents?"

"Oh! No. No, of course not. I just didn't peg you for an insurance type of guy."

One of his eyebrows raised. "No?"

"Not at all. You look like you could be a logger or something."

He laughed. "Don't let the flannel shirts and boots fool you. Underneath this rugged exterior is a computer geek and champion number cruncher."

"Since I'm a former accountant, I won't make that mistake again."

He laughed. "I'm just joking. I work with a lot of big outfits. Ranches, farms, lumber companies. I'm outside almost as much as I sit behind a desk."

"That must be why you look so fit." When he froze, she felt like pressing a hand over her mouth. Honestly, sometimes she thought she was developing her own unique brand of hoof-and-mouth disease, and it was very much a case of inserting her foot in her mouth. "Sorry. Um, sometimes I say things without thinking. I meant to say that you look like you do more than walk on the treadmill occasionally," she said in a rush. "Now, please, look around."

He didn't move. "Hey—"

But whatever he was about to say was cut off because the door flew open, and Jack Coblentz and his little sister Becca blew in.

"Hiya, Miss Sarah Anne!" Becca called out.

"Hiya, Becky," she replied, which, as always, drew a fresh round of giggles.

"It's Becca."

"Oh my stars. Indeed it is." Turning to Pete, she tried to look remorseful. "I'm sorry. I better go help them." She turned away in a hurry. Maybe by the time he was ready to check a book out, he would have forgotten all about her checking him out.

But even as she passed a stack of mysteries to Jack, read *The Night Before Christmas* to little Becca, and then pulled out another two novels for Tiny, Pete never strayed too far from her. Of course, there weren't all that many places he could go. But still, it seemed that he was staying close by.

When the Coblentz kids walked out again with a new stack of books in Jack's backpack, Pete turned to her. "I guess you know them well."

"I do. The Coblentzes are a family of readers, for sure."

"Is that little girl the man's sister or daughter?"

"Sister. Becca's three, and she has the whole family wrapped around her finger, I think."

"She's about the same age as my granddaughter, then. Do you have grandchildren?"

"No. I was never blessed in that way."

"Oh? Children?"

"No. My husband and I didn't have children."

His eyes narrowed. "I didn't see a ring."

"That's because I was widowed some time ago." She figured it was no one's business how long it actually took her to take off that gold ring—placing it in a drawer had felt like losing him all over again. "What about you? Did you marry?" Of course, she was also asking if he was still married.

"I did. Had two kids. After they went off to college, my wife decided her obligations were done and politely asked me if she could go on her way."

"Beg your pardon?"

He grinned, the smile tight. "I had the same reaction, I'm afraid. The kids took it hard, too. We all liked how things were going." He shrugged. "But then, the strangest thing happened. After about two years, I woke up one morning and realized I was happier than I'd been in a long time. Maybe even a decade. So maybe my ex was right and we had needed to break things off."

"Oh." She really had no words. What did one say to that, anyway? That she was happy for him?

He looked uncomfortable as well. "Anyway, that's why I'm not wearing a ring, either. Like the books in here . . . we've all got our own stories."

"I suppose so." She racked her brain, hoping to quickly come up with the right words so Pete would know she felt for him. But she drew a blank.

After a pause, Pete put down the book he'd been holding. "You know, I think I'll be going on my way now. Glad to see you're still doing okay."

Before she could say another word, he walked out, leaving her alone with her questions and confusion. She picked up the book he'd left. *Alive*. An old book about a bunch of survivors in the Andes Mountains. She knew it well. By the time the last person was rescued, he was alive, but just barely. He was changed by his experiences and, yes, even stronger than he'd been before the tragedy had struck.

As the silence settled in around her, she realized she felt much the same way. Alive, but feeling a little battle-worn. Alive, but not completely happy.

Alive, but not completely whole.

She needed to work on that, and then she needed to work on how to patch things up with Mr. Pete Canon, if he ever returned.

twenty-two

"How are you, Kayla?" Rose asked.

"I am fine. *Danke*."

Rose lifted an eyebrow. "Really?"

"*Jah*. Really." Kayla kept her gaze fixed on Rose, all peaches-and-cream complexion and fake concern. At last, Rose looked away.

Kayla inwardly smiled. Yes, she'd sounded rather stiff and distant, but that couldn't be helped. They were sitting next to each other on the bench in the middle of Sunday's service at Rose's parents' house. That meant they were in a rather cramped space next to the metal wall of the building that Amos Byler had built for the express purpose of showing up everyone whenever they came visiting.

Well, that was what Kayla had always thought.

Maybe Rose had, too, since it was, after all, her parents' farm they were sitting in. She'd since gotten married to Dennis and was now expecting their first *boppli*.

It wasn't nice, but sometimes, when Kayla saw Rose—with her wealthy family, doting parents, attentive husband, and now a babe on the way—she practically seethed with jealousy. That emotion embarrassed her. She didn't like being so petty. It wasn't the type of person she wanted to be. But what could one do? She was only human, and a rather flawed one at that.

Rose looked tempted to comment on Kayla's "fineness," but held her tongue. Kayla surmised it was most likely more to do with the fact that Preacher James's usually soothing voice had become suddenly booming as he shared his thoughts about the Pharisees than Rose having a desire to become sympathetic.

Kayla shifted on the bench and stared at the group of men sitting across from them. Memories came rushing back, memories of another time when she had sat on the top two rows and passed notes to her girlfriends when they weren't supposed to. Back then, they used to all stare at the men across the way and dream of being able to claim one of them as their own. And, perhaps, she'd been the one who had looked a bit smug.

It had all been for show, though. Though she'd always been so pleased and proud to have Levi, there had also been the constant mixture of grief for her mother and worry about her *daed*.

Yes, Levi had been an answer to her prayers. *Nee*, she'd *thought* he was an answer to her prayers. But, of course, she soon learned prayers had very little to do with the true state of their relationship.

"I heard your father is in Pinecraft again."

"He is."

Rose leaned closer. "And that you are home alone."

"I am," she whispered back.

"I suppose that can have its advantages." Rose smiled softly. "Ain't so?"

Even though Preacher James continued and two ladies nearby gave them dark stares, Kayla couldn't resist responding. "I don't understand what you are talking about."

"Oh, come now. Many people saw you. At least that's what I heard."

"Saw me do what?" She really was mystified now.

"Invite Aaron Coblentz into your home in the evening for *hours*."

And, yes, she'd emphasized *hours* like that meant something, well, slimy. It set her back on edge and made her temper rise, too. "There was nothing wrong about what we did."

"Are you sure? Two unmarried folks in the house together?"

"I know what we are, Rose."

"Ahem." Preacher James cleared his throat.

She realized then that nearly half the folks in that metal barn were staring at her in shock. Somehow, she managed to procure both a cold sweat and heated cheeks. "I'm sorry," she whispered to the women who were looking at her with disapproval.

Beside her, Rose folded her arms over her chest, almost as if she were attempting to protect herself from Kayla's troubling influence.

Her stomach churned. She looked around the room, trying

to find anything, anything that would take her mind off both the fool she'd just made of herself and the memory of Aaron's visit to her home. But all she found was Aaron himself, staring directly at her.

She knew everyone would be watching her. She knew she should look away. But his hazel eyes, his blond hair, his intense, serious expression . . . all of it was practically a siren's call to her. A pull so strong that she could no longer look away from him, as if she'd been physically tethered to him.

So, she had a choice. She could either concentrate on Rose's insinuations and the interested, nosy eyes surrounding her, or she could pay attention to the one thing that seemed to give her a small measure of comfort.

Suddenly she realized there was no choice. She was tired of worrying about so many things that gave her no happiness. It was time to do something else. Time to give in to what she wanted, even if it was just to share a knowing glance with someone sitting on the other side of a room.

Three hours later, against her better instincts, Kayla had agreed to help take some quilts to a community room that some of the New Order Amish members used. Often, several religious groups in the area would band together to hold an auction or a mud sale. Helping to carry quilts on a sunny winter day hadn't been a problem. Neither had visiting the community center. She had several friends who were New Order.

No, the problem had been the women she was going to be forced to be around for a little while longer. Both Ellen and Frances were older, respected, and seemed to have no problem spouting their opinions about anything and everything. That meant, of course, they would have no problem speaking their mind to her.

At first, they'd only chatted about the weather and how nice it was to see the sun even though the temperature was in the thirties. But then, just after they'd deposited the quilts inside the building, they began their barrage.

"Kayla, you must be more circumspect," one chided. "You were causing a scene today."

"I *wasna* the only person whispering during Preacher James's sermon."

"You were the loudest."

"I was not much louder than Rose." Why couldn't she simply just be quiet? The woman was intent on tearing her down, but Kayla personally had no desire to be pushed around anymore. Why should it matter to her what Kayla did?

"Unfortunately, we're not referring just to today's behavior in church, Kayla. There are rumors that you've been spending a lot of time with men without the benefit of a chaperone."

Oh, that Mrs. Hershberger. She must have told all of Berlin about Aaron's visit to her house. "I haven't done one thing to be ashamed about."

Ellen clicked her tongue on the top of her mouth. "You know, dear, I'm sure you miss your mother. You must think of what she would want."

No. No, she wasn't going to do this again. "My mother passed on to Heaven three years ago."

"She's still watching you, though," Frances said.

"I reckon she is. But I don't choose to worry about what she thinks."

"That's what we're talking about, child. You should. You want her to be proud of you, *jah*?"

"What makes you think she isn't proud of me?"

Ellen blinked. "Now, you know what I mean." She glanced at the other woman. "We're only speaking to you out of concern."

Perhaps her mother was the voice in her ear, warning her to simply smile. Perhaps it was her conscience. Either way, she was ignoring it. "I still don't understand to what you are referring. And why are you not asking me about my father?"

"Pardon?"

"My *daed* is alive and well. However, it doesn't seem like you are concerned about me disappointing him. Why is that?"

As she'd hoped, they gaped at her.

As she feared, she felt good about that.

Just as she was wondering what to do next, she spied Aaron walking toward her. "Kayla, it is you," Aaron said as he approached. "What a nice surprise."

Though she was aware of the two ladies listening to every word, she beamed at him. "We were just delivering quilts."

"Are you free now?"

"I am."

"*Gut.*" Smiling at the two women, he said, "I'm sorry to interrupt your conversation, but I don't think I can let this opportunity slip away." Holding out his elbow, he smiled. "Ready?"

"Beyond ready," she said as she took his arm. "Good day, Ellen and Frances."

"Good day, Kayla," Frances replied. Ellen said nothing. No doubt she was glaring at Kayla's back. But she didn't care one bit. Aaron had rescued her, and she was now holding on to his arm like they were a true courting couple. Right now, at this moment, nothing else mattered.

By now, Kayla thought she knew Aaron Coblentz fairly well. She knew his goals, she knew what came easy for him and what didn't. She knew he favored sandwiches and didn't like peanut butter or ice cream. She knew he was a little shy and didn't like to spout off about things unless he'd thought of the consequences.

Actually, Kayla thought there was little Aaron could do that would surprise her.

She was wrong.

He was currently a man of mystery, as confusing to her as the time she'd watched *Star Trek* with an English friend and had no idea who the creatures on the screen were.

Furthermore, now, he was walking beside her, all confidence and assurance. She, on the other hand, was simply trying to catch her breath.

After another minute or two, she let go of his arm so she could walk at a slower pace. Immediately, he slowed down, too. "Sorry, Kay. I'll slow down."

She wasn't sure if she should take his arm again and decided against it. But she did want to know what he was thinking. "Aaron, what just happened?"

"That, Kayla, was me helping you out."

"'Helping'?"

"*Jah*. And now you may say thank you."

She chuckled. "Thank you. I couldn't believe it when I saw you. It was like you appeared out of the blue."

"I felt the same way when I spied you." He grinned. "And

thank goodness I did, too. It didn't look like your conversation with those women was going very well."

"It wasn't. They're catty busybodies." Thinking back to how ornery she'd been, she added, "I'm afraid I wasn't being very nice, either."

"Now I'm really glad that God thrust us together this afternoon."

She was, too. "Not that it matters, but I have no idea where we're going."

"That's because I haven't told you."

"You're certainly being rather cryptic."

He chuckled. "Thanks to you, I actually know what that means." Looking mischievous, he added, "For the record, I'm not being cryptic." He turned toward a wooded path. "I wasn't sure where to take you. Until I saw this trail."

Their steps were slower now, and the air felt a little chillier, now that much of the sunlight was blocked by branches. She looked around. It was pretty, to be sure. But that said, Kayla couldn't imagine why he wanted to take her there. "Do you walk over here often?" she asked. Maybe there was a special rock or something he wanted to show her?

"*Nee*. I haven't walked here in years." He lifted up a scraggly branch so she could crouch underneath it. "It looks about how I remember it."

"And how is that?"

"Private." He stopped suddenly. "I'm starting to feel like there's not many places in Berlin for us to be completely alone. Your aunt Pat's workroom, your house . . . and here."

There was a new look in his eyes. A warmth that she'd used to pretend she saw in Levi's but probably never actually had.

Feeling tentative, she said, "Is there a reason you need privacy right now?"

"Oh, yes. You see, I've decided to not wait any longer for this."

She stood dumbly as he turned to her, pulled her up against him, and kissed her. He placed his hands on her cheeks, turned her jaw slightly, and then proceeded to kiss her like he was a starving man and she was a double-decker club sandwich.

All she seemed to be able to do was hold on to his shoulders and kiss him back. She wasn't aware of anything else. She could even say he kissed her senseless. But since she felt as if every one of her five senses was on fire, that was far from true.

She'd now kissed two men. Levi and Aaron. And if she had known what a kiss could truly be like? Well, she might not have been so crushed about Levi's departure all those years ago. Some things were simply beyond compare.

twenty-three

Sometimes Sunday supper went on far too long. Tonight, surrounded by his nosy family and all of their knowing glances, Aaron decided this was one of the longest suppers he'd had in years.

It didn't help that the meal was Hawaiian Chicken with rice and stir-fried broccoli. He wasn't a fan of the dish at all. In his mind, chicken should only be grilled, fried, or baked. Not sautéed in a sweet sauce with a bunch of pineapple and green peppers thrown in.

"Aaron, is there any specific reason why you're glaring at your plate?" Mamm asked. "The rest of us are almost done, but you've hardly eaten a bite."

He was just going to say it. "I don't care for this meal."

Tiny looked affronted, which was probably because she'd made half of it. "Why not?"

"I don't know. There's something about the sauce that doesn't sit well with me." And since he was spouting off his opinions, he added, "I'm sorry, but I've never liked this meal."

"I like it," Jack said. "I think it's fine."

"*Danke*, Jack," Mamm said.

Aaron glared when his brother grinned at him. Jack was a constant burr on his side, that was for sure.

"You should have told me about your feelings, Aaron," Mamm said. "I wouldn't have made you eat it all this time."

"*Jah*, you wouldn't have had to suffer through it for years and years," Tiny added, like he had intentionally tried to upset her.

"Of course I wasn't going to say anything. I'm grateful for the meal." He looked over at his sister. "And for the hands that made it."

Tiny rolled her eyes.

"You might be grateful, but you've hardly eaten a bit of it," Mamm said. "You are wasting food."

Great. This was exactly what he got for spouting off opinions. "Fine. I'll eat more of it." He was twenty-one years old. Why was he having to defend himself, anyway? He glanced at his father, half expecting him to reprimand him for speaking his mind. But instead, Daed only looked amused.

"Why are you smiling, Thomas?" Mamm asked.

"No reason, Violet." He picked up his fork. "I'm eating my food. I promise."

"Argh." Turning to his little sister and softening her tone, Mamm said, "At least you're eating, Becca. You're being a *gut* girl."

Becca picked up a piece of broccoli and popped it in her mouth.

Aaron speared a piece of chicken and chewed.

"I happen to think that the real problem isn't this supper at all," Tiny said. "I think it has to do with Kayla Kauffman."

"We do not need to bring Kayla into this conversation just because you wish I was eating your sweet yet spicy chicken."

"My chicken is *gut*, but even if it was bad, it wouldn't have made you so grumpy. I think that has something to do with a certain someone who you were walking with today."

If he were fifteen years younger, he'd seriously think about kicking Tiny's shin so she'd be quiet. "Again, do not bring up Kayla."

"Why not?" Jack asked. "I mean, everyone saw you walking with her. You were gone for a long time, too. What did the two of you do?"

"That is none of your business."

"I'm in the dark. Who is Kayla Kauffman, and how do you two know each other?" their mother asked.

Both Tiny and Jack looked at Aaron and smiled.

"Kayla works at the sewing store on Main. We've ah, struck up a friendship. That's all."

"Her name sounds familiar." Mamm tapped a finger on the table. "Oh, I remember now. Her mother had a terrible cancer. She died just a few months after being diagnosed. The ladies in our church district brought her father a quilt."

"*Jah*, she told me about her mother's death."

"That must mean you've gotten close."

"We have. I mean, we're friends and all."

"So, you're close friends."

Only his mother could make those four words sound like so much more. *"Jah."*

"Kayla is Aaron's special close friend, Mamm," Jack quipped, reaching over to Aaron's plate to spear his largely untouched chicken breast.

Aaron gritted his teeth. "Can we talk about something else now?"

"I suppose we could, but I prefer to hear what's going on," Mamm said. "Aaron, are you courting her?"

If he said no, he'd have to make sure they didn't find out about his tutoring. If he said yes, they'd wonder why they didn't know. Suddenly, the memory of the way Kayla had felt in his arms rushed forth. He'd kissed her. He'd kissed her, and it had been wonderful.

"Yes, I'm courting her. Kind of."

"Why haven't you told us about this before now?" Daed asked. "She is Amish, right?"

"Jah, she's Amish."

"Good, because I don't want you around the English any more than you already are at the furniture store."

Which was his father's veiled reference to Tim. "Kayla is not English. She's New Order Amish."

"Why have you been keeping her a secret?" Tiny said. "Is something wrong with her?"

"Nee. She's fine. Perfect."

"If you want to go courting, you should call on Beth," Jack said. "She's always liked you."

"I don't know how I feel about you courting a girl we've never met," Mamm murmured. "Your father and I would feel better if we knew her."

"I am not a boy. I'm a grown man and should be able to do what I want, within reason. And there is nothing wrong with Kayla Kauffman. She's pretty, very kind, and smart. I would be blessed, indeed, if she liked me as much as I admire her."

And with that, the whole table grew silent. Even Jack put his fork down. Why had he leapt to her defense like he that?

Daed pressed a napkin to his mouth. "She sounds like a wonderful girl—ah, woman. I hope we'll all get a chance to meet her soon."

"I hope so, too," Mamm added. "And, Aaron, you are right. It was wrong of me to pass judgment on a woman I hardly know. It was also wrong of us to tell you how to live your life or who you should fall in love with. It's been my experience that love is a personal thing." She looked down the table at Tiny. "Wouldn't you say, Tiny?"

"*Jah.*"

"Speaking of Tiny, does anyone think we should ask her how Joel and his new *hund* is?" Jack asked.

"*Nee,*" both Tiny and Aaron said at the same time.

Jack held up his hands. "Sorry, I just thought I'd move the conversation along."

Just as Aaron was going to put Jack in his place, their father spoke. "Jack, you are a *gut* son, but you have a way of needling people that is going to get you into trouble one day. Mark my words, one day you are going to fall in love, and it's going to change everything."

"Love won't be like that for me."

"It will, Jack," Mamm murmured. "I must admit that there's a part of me that looks forward to the moment that happens, too."

"Me as well," Tiny said. "I can't wait to see what girl wraps you around her finger."

"When I do fall in love, I can promise that there aren't going to be lots of surprises. Everything is going to go according to plan."

The whole table burst into laughter. Their parents, Aaron, Tiny . . . even Becca, who looked delighted to be a part of all the fun.

The only family member not laughing was Jack. He simply looked befuddled.

"Aaron, go to the kitchen and make yourself a sandwich," Mamm said.

"*Nee*, it's okay."

"It is not." With a small smile, she waved her hands. "Go on, now. Otherwise, you'll be hungry all night, and there ain't no reason for that."

"*Danke*," he said as he got up and took his plate into the kitchen.

When he opened the refrigerator and started hunting for turkey, the other members of his family started chatting again, and he realized that even though none of them was perfect, he didn't ever want to be anywhere else.

twenty-four

He was living his dream. Well, perhaps not his dream, exactly, but Aaron couldn't deny that he was feeling a good amount of satisfaction as he looked around Zeiset's Furniture. Everything was displayed neatly, the customers were being taken care of by Paul and Judy, and Mr. Zeiset was snug and warm in Pinecraft, Florida.

For all intents and purposes, he was in charge and he hadn't even had to take the GED test. He'd been so pleased when Mr. Zeiset had asked to speak to him first thing the other morning. After saying how pleased he was with Aaron's work ethic and conscientious nature, Mr. Zeiset had told him he was going to be in charge of the store for the next month.

It had been a wonderful conversation. Truly, something he'd been hoping and praying about for a long time. Now, he just had to run everything perfectly so Mr. Zeiset would give him that promotion.

"Aaron, can you come over here?" Paul called out.

Getting his head back on track and out of the clouds, he walked to the dining room area. "*Jah*, Paul?"

"Aaron, Mr. Villas here is hoping to get this table to his house in Medina by the end of the week, but it looks like we are out of stock in the store." Paul tapped both the SOLD sign and the price tag, obviously hoping Aaron noticed it was their most expensive table. "Do you think that's possible?"

"I can't think of a reason why not." Flipping through the pages on his clipboard, he scanned the inventory list for the warehouse. "Ah, here we are. Yes, we do have another table in stock. Delivery should be no problem."

The older man looked pleased as punch. "Really? That's terrific. My wife is going to be so happy. Her whole family is coming to town this weekend. If you couldn't get that table delivered, I would've had to go someplace else." He ran a hand along the smooth wood. "I didn't want to do that, though. You sell quality furniture here. Every piece is a work of art."

"Since many of our vendors are Amish, I can tell you that they treat each piece like a work of art, too. We're proud to sell them at Zeiset's."

Mr. Villas pulled out his cell phone. "I'm going to text my wife that our table situation is solved." He paused. "That's if you're sure you can get that table to our house?"

"I'm sure. You'll be eating your supper on it Friday night."

"Excellent." Mr. Villas beamed. "Thank you so much . . . Aaron, is it?"

"Yes, sir. Aaron Coblentz."

Mr. Villas gave him a hardy handshake. "Good doing business with you, young man."

When the gentleman walked a few steps away and started texting, Paul edged closer. "Um, are you sure about this, Aaron? I didn't think we had another table—"

"I'm very sure. Go ahead and place the order and put Mr. Villas on the delivery schedule for Friday." When Paul still looked hesitant, Aaron adopted a firmer tone. "*Danke*, Paul."

Paul nodded at last. "Let's go sit down and fill out the order and set up a delivery time, Mr. Villas."

The next four hours passed like the wind. Aaron helped customers, unloaded boxes, and began scheduling the deliveries for the end of the week. In and out of the warehouse he went, checking orders, examining the delivery map, and tagging furniture for routes and days of delivery.

At five o'clock, he told Judy and Paul goodbye, assuring them he'd be right behind them. And he had no doubt he would be able to stick to that goal. He was right on time, too, until he couldn't find the table Mr. Villas had ordered. After walking through the entire freezing warehouse twice, he went back into his office and retrieved the clipboard that had the inventory sheets attached.

With a pencil in hand, he scanned the items but couldn't find the number. Had Paul filled out the form wrong? Mentally berating him, Aaron strode out to the showroom and checked the table's item number with the one he'd found on his sheet.

After another fifteen minutes, he'd found the discrepancy, and it wasn't Paul's mistake at all. No, it had been his. He'd transposed two numbers. There was no other table in stock or on the way. It was no wonder Paul had been looking at him so strangely.

Obviously, he'd been wanting him to call the manufacturer to see if a table could be rushed. Now it was too late to call, and he didn't know what he was going to do, besides the obvious, which was to call Mr. Villas and admit his mistake.

Already dreading it, he fished around for the order form. There was nothing to do but tell the truth, apologize for his mistake, and take whatever criticism the customer was going to dish out.

Just as he was about to pick up the phone, it rang.

"Zeiset's Furniture, may I help you?" he said.

"Yes, you can tell me why you're working so late," his boss joked.

"Just trying to keep everything running like you do, sir. How is Florida?"

"As sunny and warm as ever. Every year, I tell my wife we need to stay another week longer next time. We've already been to the beach two times!"

"That's real nice, sir. I'm happy for ya."

"Uh-oh. I know that tone of voice. What happened?"

Though there was a big part of him that didn't want to ruin his boss's day and share what he'd done, Aaron knew there was no getting out of the truth. "I'm sorry to say that I made a big mistake today, sir."

"You'd best tell me what happened, then."

Feeling even worse, Aaron forced himself to tell the whole story, even the part where Paul tried to stop him from making such a big error.

"What were you going to do before I called?"

"I was about to call Mr. Villas and admit my mistake."

"Scott Villas has been a good customer over the years. He's a good man, but he's not going to take this lightly."

"I kind of figured that."

His boss paused. "Okay, I just got a pencil and paper. Give me the order number and the name of the table again. Then, I want the phone number of the manufacturer. It's Higgens, yes?"

"*Jah,*" Aaron replied as he opened a file and read the company's contact information to his boss.

"I'll give them a call and see what I can do."

"But, sir, it's already after six."

"There's an extension I can use to get Brian Higgens's cell phone. Don't worry, we'll find that table."

"I hope so. I am real sorry about this, Mr. Zeiset."

"Mistakes happen, Aaron."

"Yes, but I really wanted to prove myself to you." Then, because he couldn't seem to stop himself, he added, "For the last six or seven months, I've had a new goal, and that was to make a good impression so I can one day be assistant manager or manager for you. I've even been trying to study for the GED. But now I feel like I've been a fool."

"Why the GED?"

"Well, I figure you need someone with more education than I've got."

"You've been working for me since you were fourteen, Aaron. You've gotten a lot of education here over the last seven years."

"Obviously not enough."

"Aaron, I can't tell you if getting your GED will help you or not. Maybe that's something you feel you need to pursue, but I will tell you that I don't think knowing more math or science or whatever would have helped you today. Only experience can do that."

"Yes, sir."

"I should also remind you that I already believe in you. If I didn't, I wouldn't have put you in charge."

"Yes, sir. Thank you."

Mr. Zeiset chuckled. "No reason to thank me. You're a good employee, son. But I feel like I should remind you that as bad as this mistake might seem, you are going to make a worse one, one day. That's not the issue. What does matter is how you handle the mistake."

"I'll remember that. *Danke.*"

"I hope you will, son. Now, go home, but check your shanty's phone for messages later, okay? I'll be calling you with some answers."

"I'll pick up. I promise I will."

"Good," Mr. Zeiset blurted before he hung up, leaving Aaron holding the phone and realizing that today's roller-coaster ride might have ended up being one of the best days in a very long time. It had certainly given him a lot to think about.

twenty-five

Kayla didn't know where her father was. He hadn't come back on his scheduled Pioneer Trails bus and he hadn't been on today's bus, either. The only thing that kept her from worrying herself sick was the fact that she'd talked to several people who'd recently returned from Pinecraft. They'd relayed that her father had seemed just fine. One had even mentioned that he had said he wasn't sure when he would return.

So, he was fine. He just hadn't elected to contact her.

Her heart was sick. She hated that he didn't think of her in times like this. She knew him well enough to realize that he wasn't trying to be difficult, it just hadn't occurred to him to let her know about his change of plans.

But honestly, she would have been more hurt if she wasn't so mad. They had bills to pay and little to no money in savings. To make matters worse, she'd run into his boss while she'd been out walking yesterday, and he'd given her a mouthful. It had been awful, getting berated for her father's problems in the middle of the street.

Now, here she was again, walking home while stewing about her father's faults. She was so tired, tired of worrying, tired of working, tired of complaining about things that didn't change.

When she saw the bookmobile in the distance, her heart lifted. She didn't really need a new book, but seeing Sarah Anne's kind face and being surrounded by some of her favorite things could surely lift her spirits.

There were two buggies parked nearby and a bicycle, too. Pushing aside her disappointment that she wouldn't be the only patron today, she pinned a smile to her face and headed inside.

Only to be surrounded by chaos.

There were at least four children chattering, arguing, and crying. It created a terrible din. There was a woman yelling at Sarah Anne and a young English man standing in front of the lone computer terminal, moving the mouse around and clicking it over and over and muttering under his breath.

She would have turned back around if it hadn't been for the pleading look on Sarah Anne's face. It was obvious the woman was silently begging Kayla to stay.

She couldn't say no to that.

After wondering what to do for a moment, she came to the conclusion that the only thing to do was to help all these people so they'd leave as soon as possible. Even though it was selfish, it was a nice thought.

With that in mind, she marched up to the mother of at least some of the *kinner*. "I noticed your *kinner* might need some help. Since Sarah Anne is busy, can I help?"

The lady nodded wearily. "If you could, I'd be very grateful. I promised each of them they could have one book, but they're arguing over them all."

Noticing the pile of books and an assortment of gum wrappers, Kayla inwardly grimaced. They were also making a mess.

Concerned that the mother wasn't being more involved, Kayla looked at her more closely and noticed she had dark circles under her eyes.

"I have the flu," she said. "I think I'm over the worst of it, but I'm so tired."

And . . . the situation had just become worse. The mother had the flu and was in the bookmobile, touching everything. Kayla swallowed hard. "I'd be happy to help your children."

"Danke." The woman sat right down with a sigh.

Before she could back out on her promise, Kayla picked up the books from the pile the small hooligans had tossed on the floor. "These are wonderful books," she exclaimed. "Why, they're some of my favorites."

As she'd hoped, the children turned to see what books she was talking about.

"Which one?" the oldest boy asked.

"I think you will like Hero's story." She handed him a short storybook about a boy exploring the woods.

"What about me?" his sister asked.

"You need this little book about Hans the polar bear, I think." The little girl smiled as she held it to her chest.

And so it continued. Kayla passed over two more books to the siblings, then, after obtaining their mother's library card, she helped each child scan their book and get a receipt.

By the time the last child was done, their mother had all of them lined up with their coats and cloaks securely buttoned. *"Danke,"* she said.

"It was my pleasure," Kayla replied.

As she watched them leave, she realized it actually had been her pleasure to give a helping hand. Seeing that mother who had clearly needed a tiny break had been a good reminder to her. Everyone had problems. Kayla might have a wayward father, but she wasn't sick with four children in need of her help.

She noticed then that the bookmobile had cleared out and it was only her and Sarah Anne there.

"Boy, that was fast! I can't believe how quickly everyone cleared out."

Sarah Anne opened a drawer and pulled out a can of Lysol. "Well, my dear, you took care of five of the people in here, and I took care of everyone else."

There was something in Sarah Anne's tone that was worrisome. As she watched the librarian spray practically every surface, Kayla said, "I hope you're not upset with me for stepping in."

"Not at all, dear. Believe me, I'm grateful." She picked up a stack of books and set them on a counter. "I was getting a little harried, for sure."

"Is it like this often?"

"Not at all. Usually everything goes as well as I could expect it to." Picking up a scrap of paper, she added, "But there are times when I wish I had an assistant, and you were an answer to a prayer!"

Kayla picked up the gum wrappers and tossed them in a trash can. "If I was an answer for you, I feel like that woman and her kids were an answer to mine."

"How so?"

"I was feeling a little overwhelmed before I came in, and if I'm being honest, I was feeling a little bit sorry for myself as well. Being around that poor mom reminded me that I'm not the only person who is having a difficult day."

"Would you like to talk about what's been troubling you?"

Kayla actually had come for just that reason, but now she realized that wasn't what she wanted to do. "I'll be okay," she said simply. "It's nothing I can't handle."

Sarah Anne looked at her for a long moment, then nodded. "I understand."

"Danke."

"Did you come for books?"

"Kind of. I wanted to see what was on the shelves, though I still have two books at home to read."

Sarah Anne snapped her fingers. "Oh! I almost forgot. Look what I have for you." Bending down, she opened a cabinet and pulled out a new romance. "Look what just arrived, hot off the press."

It was the newest book by her favorite author, and it looked brand-new. "Am I going to be the first person to check it out?"

"You are." She smiled brightly. "I thought it might be fitting, since you like her books so much."

"Danke." This book did make her happy. She would probably read it in one sitting. But there was a part of her that wondered if maybe she was too old for such novels.

"What's wrong?"

"Oh, I'm just wondering if I need to graduate to different types of books."

Sarah Anne frowned. "What do you mean? They aren't for teenagers, they're adult romances."

"Yes, but everything in their lives works out so perfectly. That's not really how life works, is it?"

To Kayla's surprise, Sarah Anne didn't reply immediately. Instead, she seemed to ponder that question for a moment before finally replying.

"I'm sorry, but I have to say that is exactly how life works. Oh, we don't all eventually experience perfect romances." She chuckled softly. "Honestly, I don't know too many people who would say they do. Even good marriages aren't always perfect every minute of every day." She inhaled. "But, dear, I feel I must remind you that we're not in charge. Our Lord makes sure everything does work out well. Sometimes it's just on His timing, not ours."

"I guess you're right." She still wasn't sure, though. She believed in God and knew He looked out for her, but she thought He was pretty busy. Surely He wasn't going to worry about all of her problems.

In any case, the Lord's concern didn't always translate into novels. In all of her favorite books love conquered all. But how could love conquer her father not coming home to do his job or help her pay the bills?

"Kayla, it's okay if you don't want to read this book. It's even okay if you don't agree with me. You're entitled to your own opinion. I promise, I am not trying to make you believe something you don't."

"You're not being pushy. I guess you're just giving me a lot to think about."

"If that's the case, I'm glad about that." Sarah Anne sat back down and picked up her glasses. "Now, I guess I better organize these books before I get on my way back to the district parking lot."

Kayla realized then that she was still holding the book—and that her views on romance and falling in love had recently started to change. Maybe she didn't just believe in romance novels; maybe she believed in real-life romance, too. "Wait. I . . . Well, I'd like to check this out."

Sarah Anne smiled and held out her hand. "Hand me your library card, and we'll get you taken care of, dear."

Twenty minutes later, as she neared her house, Kayla realized her spirits were lifted. Yes, it was cold and she probably had a mailbox full of bills and she was going to have to eat canned soup for supper, but that was going to be just fine. No matter what else was waiting for her at home, she had a new book to read.

Giving in to temptation, she sat down on her front stoop and opened the novel Sarah Anne had saved for her. She flipped to the first page and skimmed the first three paragraphs. It seemed an Amish girl named Lucy in Missouri had not one but two beaus courting her. Kayla laughed when Lucy's mother proclaimed that her social life was wearing the whole family out.

Minutes later, she'd reached the end of the chapter. Suddenly, she was aware of a pair of cardinals in a nearby tree and the way the sun was glinting on the roof of the house across the street. When she walked inside her house, it was obvious nothing was any different . . . but her world did seem a little brighter. She was grateful for that.

twenty-six

• RULE #26 •

Don't be afraid to recommend something new
from time to time.

Joel and Tiny had come to an agreement of sorts. She was no longer going to question his work at Jane's, and he was going to limit his hours at her house. Tiny hadn't asked him to do that, but he didn't want to push his luck. He knew that she might understand his efforts, but she wasn't exactly comfortable with him spending so much time with Jane. He also knew that she wasn't in any hurry to have to discuss it with her brothers.

Joel didn't blame her about that. Though he couldn't fault Jack and Aaron's need to protect their sister, it was obvious that they were overreacting. Plus, as far as he was concerned, his actions had nothing to do with Jack and Aaron Coblentz.

They should be worried about themselves and not what he was doing.

Especially since he was doing nothing wrong.

After more than a bit of struggle and prayer, Joel knew it was time to stop worrying about himself and Tiny. The fact of the matter was that Jane needed the help, and he needed the money.

After all, he'd started it all with one goal in mind, and that was to buy a house for him and Tiny. Though his parents had hinted that he and Tiny could live with them for a year or two after they married, Joel didn't want to start his marriage in his parents' house. And his parents were young, too young, he thought, to be delegated to a *dawdi haus*.

Besides, they already lived next to both of their families. As far as he was concerned, couples needed a place of their own, and he aimed to give them just that.

All that was going through his mind as he finished his work for Jane. He was pretty proud of himself, too. Today he had attached rails in her main bathroom as well as the hallway powder room. All were sturdy and straight. More importantly, they would give her peace of mind.

He'd just swept the floor and thrown the trash in the garbage can in the back when she came out of the living room.

"You're done already? I tell you, Joel, you're a wonder."

"Hardly that. You know I'm always glad to help ya." That was the truth, too.

She studied him for a long moment before walking forward on her braces. Though he sometimes wanted to simply go to her so she wouldn't have to exert so much energy, Joel was beginning to learn that Miss Jane needed her independence. Well, as much as she could have, considering she was having such a hard time with her MS these days.

He kept his expression calm and steady as she approached. "Looks like your new braces are working out."

"The *doktah* told me the same thing." She rolled her eyes. "I can't say I feel the same way."

"Oh?"

"They've been a challenge, for sure and for certain." She held up a wrist. "I even got some good bruises from them."

"Is that normal?"

"I don't know. Maybe. The doctor and nurses didn't seem too concerned about them. Actually, all they keep saying was that using them won't get easier if I don't use them at all."

"Sorry, but that does sound like pretty good advice."

"I can't disagree." She let go of one of her braces, reached in the pocket of her apron, and pulled out a check. "Here's today's payment. Thank you again."

"I'll be back in a couple of days."

"Oh. Not tomorrow?"

He was too afraid to be seen coming out of her house so often. "I'm sorry. I, uh, can't come over every day. I've got some other work to do." He inwardly winced. Even to his ears, his excuse didn't sound believable.

"Oh. Of course." She smiled. "Plus, I'm sure you want to see Tiny."

"I do. My *daed* always says courting a woman is a commitment, and I reckon he's right."

"My husband used to tell me that it wasn't time wasted, though."

"I agree." He smiled, hoping he looked more carefree than he felt.

He wasn't sure why everything was so complicated. He didn't want to have so many secrets between him and Tiny. He didn't want to have to explain his schedule Jane. He didn't want to have to defend himself to Tiny's brothers. But if he had learned anything in his life, it was that not everyone thought like he did or wanted to always hear the truth. He'd learned that some people simply liked to pretend everything was just fine and that nothing ever changed, even when change was likely the only thing one could count on.

"Well, I'll be seeing ya, Jane. I wish you a good evening."

"For you as well. *Danke* for all of your help. I don't know what I'd do if you weren't here."

"I can't help but believe that you'd get on just fine. You're a strong person, Jane."

"I don't know if that's true, but thank you for saying it."

"Don't forget to lock up."

He heard her laugh as he closed the door and made himself keep walking instead of lingering to hear the bolt set in place. He needed to make sure no one thought he was doing anything other than simply a job, if they thought anything about him being there at all.

twenty-seven

Once a year, take inventory. It's amazing the things you'll find
that have suddenly appeared. Or have suddenly gone missing.

Tiny realized her decision to visit Joel on the spur of the moment wasn't like her. Not at all. Honestly, she wasn't sure what had instigated the idea in the first place. One minute, she'd been staring out the window, looking for signs of Joel and Yellow. And the next? The next, she was slipping on her cloak, putting three of her prettiest jam jars in a basket, and heading over to Joel's house.

But later, when she found herself standing in the parlor of the Lapp house, holding a basket of jam with no Joel or Yellow in sight, she felt impulsive, awkward, and more than a little foolish. It really was time she started thinking about the consequences of her actions more often.

Mrs. Lapp, however, seemed delighted she had stopped by without an invitation. "This is such a nice surprise, Tiny. I don't know how many times I've told Joel that I wish you stopped by more often."

By "more often," she probably meant *ever*. Tiny couldn't think of the last time she'd been in the Lapp house. "I felt the same way," she said. "Plus, I thought you might enjoy some jam."

Mrs. Lapp took the basket and set it on the table. "I will, indeed." She clasped her hands in front of her. "Guess what? Your visit is perfect timing. I just took some poppy seed bread out of the oven and I have hot water for tea. Would you share some with me?"

"Of course. *Danke*." Mrs. Lapp started toward the kitchen. "May I help you?"

"Of course not," she said with a smile. "If you've been making jam today, you've been on your feet a lot. Rest, and I'll be right back."

Instead of sitting, Tiny wandered around the room, looking at the stack of books on the coffee table, the basket of knitting near the fireplace, the finely made wedding ring quilt carefully draped over a chair. Though it had been years since she'd sat in this parlor, she reckoned it hadn't changed much at all, except maybe the light sheers on the windows? Perhaps the glider rocker in the back corner? Or the braided rug underneath the coffee table?

Tiny supposed it didn't matter. All anyone would really notice was that the Lapp home was as different from the Coblentz home as could be. Everything in this room was spotlessly dusted and clean. The wooden floor looked freshly swept, and there was even a fresh, clean scent that clung to the blissfully silent air.

In contrast, the Coblentz house was a mixed-up mess.

Mrs. Lapp paused when she returned with a tray of tea and neatly sliced poppy seed bread. "Tiny, is everything all right?"

Tiny rushed back to the sofa and sat, just like a child who'd been caught stealing cookies. "Yes, of course. I was just looking around at everything."

"Oh." Looking a little uneasy, Mrs. Lapp said, "I haven't washed the walls in months. I'm sure they're due for a good scrubbing."

"I wasn't thinking that at all. I was actually reflecting on how peaceful and pleasant it is here. I mean, in comparison to my house."

Mrs. Lapp laughed softly as she handed Tiny a cup and a small plate with bread on it. "I suppose it would seem quieter. There are only the four of us here, not six."

Joel's sister, Summer, had married two years ago and now lived over in Charm. So it was just Joel, Sam, and their parents. But, it was more than that, too. "It's not that I'm complaining about mine. It just feels like a nice change," she added. Why had she even said anything? She sounded like a complainer!

Mrs. Lapp sipped her tea. "Funny, Joel sometimes says he enjoys the excitement around your house. I enjoy hearing the stories he shares about all of your goings-on, too. It sounds like there's never a dull moment."

Thinking about some of their crazy dinner conversations, Tiny felt her cheeks heat. "That's one way of putting it. I'm afraid all of us have opinions that we feel the need to share a bit too often. It can get rather loud."

"It sounds fun—though, perhaps, exhausting," Mrs. Lapp said with a chuckle. "I fear I'm quiet by nature."

"I imagine every household is different."

"I would agree. When I first got married, I was so worried about trying to run my home as well as my mother ran ours when I was growing up. *Mei mamm* finally took me aside and said there was no right way to raise a family or run a house. The Lord put a variety of people on the earth for a reason." She smiled softly. "I've always remembered that."

"It's good advice." Taking a bite of the bread, Tiny nearly moaned. The poppy seed bread was moist and tasted faintly of almond, and the glaze on the outside was a mixture of vanilla and cream. "This is delicious."

"I'm glad you like it. I'll send some home with you, Tiny."

"Danke." Tiny smiled and took another bite before realizing Mrs. Lapp was no doubt waiting for her to state her reason for coming over. "Mrs. Lapp, I came over to see you but also to see Joel. Is he around?"

"He was out in the barn when you arrived. I think he's washing up now. He'll be in to join us in a few minutes."

"How is Yellow?"

"Oh, that dog is something else!"

Tiny braced herself, waiting for a litany of complaints. But Mrs. Lapp just smiled.

"I'm afraid she's become the center of our world."

"Even Mr. Lapp's?" Tiny asked before minding her tongue.

"Especially Mr. Lapp's! He greets her before he greets the rest of us."

"I'm surprised."

"I am, too. Neither of us ever wanted a pet, as I think you know. But there's something about that sweet yellow dog that has taken our hearts. Maybe it's because it's obvious someone was cruel to her. Or because she's just so sweet. Whatever the reason, we already love her dearly. Last Sunday afternoon, she sat next to me on this here sofa while I knitted."

"Joel seems happy with her, too."

"He is, though that might be an understatement— Oh! Hello, Joel. We were just discussing Yellow."

Tiny turned to Joel, who had just walked in with Yellow by his side, and was struck, as always, by how handsome he was. Today his cheeks were bright pink, either from the cold outside or the scrubbing he must have just done. His dark hair was damp, his shirt was untucked, and he even had bare feet.

She got up. "Joel, put a pair of socks on. You'll catch your death."

He laughed. "Hello to you, too, Tiny."

"Sorry, but really, you need to get warm. Your hair is damp, too."

Though his gaze was warm, he shrugged off her worries. "It's nothing. That's what happens when one washes in the stationary tub in the barn. Water gets everywhere. But a little bit of water never hurt anyone." He bent down to Yellow. "Right, girl?"

The dog, giving him a look of adoration, wagged her tail. It was very sweet.

But still, Joel had to be freezing.

"I swear, you need a keeper!" Walking over to him, she grabbed his hand and pulled him to the fireplace. "Stand here a minute."

Linking his fingers with hers, he let her tug him into place. For a few seconds they stared at each other, almost like each was attempting to fit into their new type of relationship. Tiny held her breath.

"Is this what our life is going to be like, Tiny?" he asked at last. "Years of me getting bossed around by you?"

His warm expression compelled her to smile up at him. "Only when it's obvious that someone needs to take care of you."

Mrs. Lapp laughed.

Tiny was startled, only then remembering they weren't alone—and she'd been mighty heavy-handed with him . . . All while holding his hand! Right in front of his mother!

Embarrassed, she dropped Joel's hand like it was on fire. "I'm sorry. I didn't mean to sound so . . ." But her words drifted off, because there was really no way for her to explain what she'd been doing.

Joel stepped closer, into her space. "Tiny, there's nothing to apologize for. I'm glad you care."

It was true. She did care about him. Very much. She always had, even when she didn't want to. She blinked and simply gazed into his eyes.

His mother got to her feet. "Oh my word!" She pressed a hand to her chest. " I *canna* believe it, but I completely forgot to cut up the vegetables for tonight's supper. Yellow, would you like to help? There might be a carrot in the kitchen for you."

"Mamm, it's all right," Joel murmured. "You don't have to leave."

"All the same, I think I will," she said as she turned away. "Come on, Yellow."

Watching Yellow follow Mrs. Lapp out of the room, Tiny pressed her palms to her cheeks. "I hadn't thought it could happen, but I think I made even more of a fool of myself in front of you than usual."

He reached for her hands. "You didn't make a fool of yourself. You never do."

"It certainly feels like it's been a common occurrence." Especially of late.

"It hasn't. I like how you act. I don't want you to change a thing."

"*Danke.*"

"May I ask why you came over today?"

How much could she tell him? How much could she share without making herself completely vulnerable?

She already knew the answer, of course. If she wanted a real relationship with Joel, a relationship that led to a long and happy marriage and life together, she needed to be brave enough to allow him to know what she was feeling.

"I came over because I was tired of waiting."

"'Waiting'?"

"Waiting to spy you outside. Waiting for you to come over. Waiting for everything to be perfect between us."

"Tiny, it already is perfect."

She shook her head. "*Nee,* it's not. I got upset and jealous about Jane. You got upset at me for not believing you. We've been circling each other for years, both hinting at our feelings but never admitting what is in our hearts. That's not perfect at all."

"But don't you see that is what love is like, Tiny? It's not about being perfect for each other. It's about accepting and loving each other's imperfections. It's about wanting to be happy instead of wanting what is flawless." He squeezed her hands gently. "It's about what truly matters."

"Like us."

"*Jah,* like us." A small glint appeared in his eyes. "I mean, it is like us . . . if that means you feel something in your heart for me?"

"You know I do." She wanted to tell him that she loved him, too, but she was still too afraid.

"*Gut.*" He bent down and pressed his lips to her brow. "I'm glad you came calling today, Tiny."

"Me, too."

With a pleased-sounding sigh, Joel gathered her in his arms and held her, right there in his bare feet in the front parlor of his house. And Tiny realized that this hug was exactly what he'd been talking about. It was surprising and a little funny and a bit unfamiliar.

It was absolutely perfect.

twenty-eight

• RULE #28 •

You can't change everyone's life, but you might be able to make a difference. Don't forget that.

Kayla had been pleasantly surprised when Aaron had stopped by Aunt Pat's store during lunch. He hadn't stayed long, just long enough to ask if they could meet at Zeiset's Furniture instead of in the back of Pat's shop. It seemed he had a lot of work to do and not enough time to do it.

Kayla had agreed immediately. Meeting at the furniture store meant that Pat could lock up whenever she wanted. Though she didn't stay for Kayla's tutoring sessions with Aaron anymore, Pat had admitted that leaving the shop without locking up everything herself had weighed on her mind. So, Kayla was happy to give her aunt a break. But more importantly, Kayla was looking forward to spending some time with Aaron. It had been such a terrible week. As each day passed without hearing a word from her father, her stress mounted. She was worried about him, mad at his actions, and stressed about how she was going to pay their bills.

In addition to worrying herself sick and working at the sewing shop, she'd also taken on another tutoring job. This one was with a difficult eleven-year-old girl. So the only bright spot was her scheduled time with Aaron. It might have been wrong, but Kayla was coming to realize that she needed to see him. There was something special between them, she was sure of it. She couldn't wait to see where their relationship went.

She'd arrived at Zeiset's a few minutes late since she'd had a bit of work to take care of before seeing Aaron, both at the shop and with herself. It had been foolish, but she had fussed with her hair and appearance. She wanted to look her best for Aaron now.

He made her feel young and hopeful for the first time in years, and she savored that feeling, especially since she'd felt so forgettable after the way Levi had left her without hardly a backward glance. She welcomed the giddiness, too. For so long, she'd felt so burdened by life, she'd begun to wonder if she'd ever feel hopeful again.

"Hello?" Feeling a bit like she was breaking and entering, Kayla slowly opened the empty furniture store's front door. The whole sales floor was empty, and only one set of lights was on. "Aaron?" she called out. "Are you here?"

"*Jah!* Sorry, I'm in the back. I'll be right there. Go have a seat if you want."

There were about two dozen places to sit. "Where would you like to have our study session?"

He popped his head out of a doorway. "There's a table toward the back. It looks like a conference table. It's nothing fancy. You'll see my study guide on it."

"Okay."

He smiled at her, warming her insides. "I've got to head to the break room. Want a cup of coffee? I just made a fresh pot."

A cup of fresh coffee sounded like heaven. "Sure. *Danke.*"

"No problem." He smiled at her again. "I'll be there in five."

Though he'd been smiling, Kayla thought he sounded harried. "Take your time. I'm going to look around."

When he didn't reply, she smiled. She was learning enough about Aaron to know that he was considerate to a fault—but that he also took on too much. She hoped he finished with whatever he needed to get done. Otherwise, he'd be half thinking about that instead of his upcoming test.

Glad to have a few moments to herself, Kayla wandered around the store, enjoying the rich scent of furniture polish, wood, and beeswax. A gas fireplace was lit along the back wall, and it threw off enough of a glow to cast a pretty shine to the furniture nearby, as well as a good amount of heat.

Pulling off her cloak, mittens, and black bonnet, she set them carefully on a table and stood in front of the flames. Last night the wind had howled, and they'd gotten three inches of snow. She'd been so cold in her room that she'd ended up bringing her pillows and blankets to the living room and sleeping on the couch. Because of that, she'd had both a crick in her neck and a lingering chill in her bones that didn't seem to want to leave.

How much longer she was going to be able to pretend she wasn't in a dire financial situation, she didn't know. Well, at least she was going to get her tutoring money today. As soon as she left the store, she was going to go straight to the market. She could hardly wait to make something fresh for supper.

"Here's the coffee," Aaron announced as he returned to the showroom. "Sorry about the wait. It took me a moment to find two clean cups."

"I needed that moment to warm up." Joining him at the table, she tried to get right to work. "I went ahead and brought you the dates and locations for the next tests. Which one do you want to register for?"

"Well, about that." He picked up a pencil and rolled it around in his hands. "Kayla, I don't think I'm ready for that test. I don't know when I'm going to be able to take it."

"Really? But I thought you were in a hurry to take it so you could get a promotion."

"I was. But I'm afraid if I take it and fail, it will just make me look worse." Wrapping his hands around his cup, he said, "The fact is, Kayla, I'm just not sure if I'm ever going to be able to pass that test."

She was shocked, but she reminded herself that even though they were in a relationship, he was still as insecure as any of her other students. He needed some encouragement. "I think you're letting your self-doubts get the best of you. I believe in you, and you need to believe in yourself, too. You need to be positive." He still looked torn, so she added, "I think you're solid on the math and science section. We just need to bump up your English skills. But, we'll get there. I know we will."

"I don't know." He sighed. "See, something happened this week. I made a big mistake on an order and I had to talk to Mr. Zeiset about it. I was so *neahfich*. Kayla, I thought I was going to get fired."

"But you didn't."

"No, I didn't. But what happened really surprised me. I told him how disappointed I was in myself, and I even shared how I've been studying for the test so I could one day achieve my big dream of getting a promotion."

Kayla was impressed. "What did he say?"

"He reminded me that I've been learning a lot of things about the business during the many years I've worked here. He said a piece of paper wasn't going to make much difference because he already feels ready to give me more responsibilities."

She could tell from the way that Aaron's voice deepened that he'd been very touched. "That's wonderful. Truly."

"It was incredible, that's what it was. I went from being sure I was going to get fired to standing in the middle of the office gaping like a codfish."

She giggled. "Goodness."

"I'm not exaggerating. Well, not much," he said with a grin. "I was so floored I could barely talk. I just about had tears in my eyes."

She was so pleased for him. He was a good person. A really wonderful man. "I'm so glad Mr. Zeiset told you all that."

"Me, too." He sipped his coffee and took a deep breath. "But I have to face the truth."

"What truth is that?"

"That I might never be able to pass the GED, Kayla."

She shook her head. "*Nee*. That's not true. I'm a *gut* tutor, Aaron. I promise, you'll pass."

"*Nee*, that's not what I meant." He leaned toward her. "Kayla, what I'm trying to say is that I think I'm going to give up that dream for a while. Maybe forever."

"You don't want to study for the test at all? You're not interested in taking it anymore?" She honestly couldn't believe it. They had spent hours working on various formulas in math and dozens of vocabulary words. Plus, when he'd started, he'd seemed so earnest.

"Not at all." Waving a hand around the shop, he added, "Like I said, since my boss is on vacation and he put me in charge, that test isn't necessary anymore."

"Because you've achieved your goal." Kayla knew her voice was flat, but she didn't think it could be helped. Though his reasoning made sense, there'd been a part of her that had really thought he had also been hoping to pass the test for himself. She'd thought they were kindred spirits in that regard.

Obviously, she'd been wrong.

Aaron was still smiling and talking quickly. "To be honest, I've had some challenges—maybe more than a few—but I'm working through them. So I decided to stop trying to do something I'm never going to be able to accomplish. That's why I wanted to meet today."

It took her a second, but she finally realized what he was telling her in such a roundabout fashion. "You wanted to meet today in order to tell me that we're done."

His hazel eyes widened. "You're making it sound so permanent! *Nee*, we're not *done*, Kayla. All we're done with is this tutoring." While she gaped at him, he stood up, obviously signaling that the meeting was done. "There's a silver lining to be found now, too."

"Which is?"

"Well, now you don't have to spend the next hour hammering me about grammar and punctuation or whatever else we were going to work on. Now we don't have to only talk about this test every time we see each other." His expression warmed. "We can concentrate on other things."

Those were the sweetest words, words she would usually be so grateful to hear. Just not today. Until he started calling on her, she wasn't going to have a reason to see him anymore.

And today, she wasn't going to get the extra money she'd been counting on. Things were going to be stretched even tighter now.

He was still acting like he'd just told her the best news in the world. "Sorry to rush you out of here, but I still need to finish a couple of things."

"Of course. That's no problem at all." She stood up and slipped on her cloak, but didn't move. For some reason, her feet seemed glued to the same spot.

Aaron cleared his throat. "Kayla, that's all right, yes? I mean, I thought you would be happy to go right home and relax. You've been working so hard. You can take the night off. Ah, put your feet up."

Feeling a bit like she'd been kicked in the stomach, she reached for her bonnet and rested it over her *kapp*. "*Jah*. Indeed I can do that." She smiled tightly. "I'll get out of your way now." Anxious to get to the door now, she quickened her pace.

He followed her. "Hey, I thought you'd be happier about this."

"I am happy for you." It was almost as good. She tried to smile. "*Gut naught*."

He reached for her arm. "No, wait. Kayla, you seem upset. I know we've been working hard, but it's not your fault I decided not to take the test. Surely you understand why I made this choice. I mean, you can see my point of view . . . right?"

"I do. I do see your point of view." She sounded ridiculous, but she couldn't help it.

"Then cheer up! Everything is going to be great."

She wanted to be happy for him, she really did. However, she wasn't a perfect person. Right this moment, she was disappointed and so stressed about everything that she wasn't able to hide it. And she really, really wanted him to stop telling her to be happy, to relax, and to cheer up!

"It doesn't really matter what I feel, Aaron. After all, this was your dream, not mine." She carefully tied the ribbons on her bonnet so the wind wouldn't blow it off.

"I don't understand why you're being like this."

"Like what? I'm fine."

He shook his head. "You are not fine."

"Okay, how about this? There's nothing for you to worry about." She shrugged as she fastened her cloak around her shoulders. "I was simply your tutor, ain't so? And you were just one of my students. Life goes on."

"Wait. There's more to us than you being my tutor. You know that. I know that." He reached for her arm. "We have a relationship. That isn't going to stop. I mean, I don't want it to stop."

She didn't, either.

After pulling on her gloves and picking up her tote bag, she met his gaze. It was moments like this when he seemed so young. It was as if it hadn't occurred to him that she also had dreams and goals and pressures.

"Aaron, if it's all the same to you, I think it might be a good idea to keep our relationship as merely friends."

"All because I changed my mind about that test?"

"No. There are other reasons."

"Is it the kiss?"

"*Nee*. Of course not."

"Is it our age difference?"

"Partly." She walked to the door.

"No, wait. I'm grasping at straws here. What else is the problem? And don't say I don't have a right to know, because I think I do."

His statement, though she was sure he meant well, hit her wrong. Turning to face him again, she said, "It may come as a surprise to you, but I have a life as well. I have things I'm working on and problems I'm trying to solve."

"I never thought you didn't." He held out a hand. "Why don't you sit down? We can talk."

"It's not that easy."

"Sure it is. We have a lot in common, Kayla. I know we do."

"We also have some differences we might not be able to overcome."

"I disagree."

"Aaron, you are living with a loving family yet still struggling to share something as basic as your desire to take a test. I'm trying to figure out how to keep my home. I have grown-up problems, Aaron. And you? Well, right now it feels like you're still trying to grow up."

His expression was filled with shock and hurt. "That's not fair. I have a good reason for not talking to my parents about that test. My older brother, Tim, left the order after getting baptized. He's been essentially shunned. Just because I hadn't shared all of that with you doesn't mean it didn't hurt."

She was stunned by the news. On another day, Kayla knew she would react with more compassion, but at the moment, all she could seem to focus on were her own problems. "I wish you would have trusted me enough to tell me about Tim when we talked on Sunday."

"Just because I didn't tell you about Tim doesn't mean we didn't share a lot. You're acting as if that time together wasn't special."

It had been special, but maybe that was the problem. Everything the other day had been so wonderful that it now felt like a tease, like she'd gotten a hint of what their life could be like together, but now it seemed like they were going backward again.

"I had better go." She walked out and tried to ignore her growling stomach.

It turned out that wasn't too hard to do, because the guilt she felt for saying such things was weighing just as heavy on her mind.

twenty-nine

• RULE #29 •

Don't forget that librarians are excellent mystery and problem solvers. If you encounter something mysterious in your midst, aim to fix it.

Zeiset's boasted a really good front door. It was solid, kept out the air, and always closed with a satisfying *thunk*. Aaron had often thought of it as a metaphor for the business itself. But from now on, Aaron was fairly sure he was always going to think of that door as a symbol of just how much had gotten away from him that he wasn't able to stop.

Like Kayla.

He stood with his back to the fire, staring at the closed door, and kept reviewing their conversation. It hadn't gone anything like he'd hoped. Honestly, he'd been so embarrassed about his lack of success in the studying department that he had thought Kayla would be happy he was finally coming to his senses.

Instead, she'd just seemed upset.

Just as disturbing had been her comments about how he was not the only person with problems. He hadn't liked thinking that he'd been so self-centered. Had he really only talked about himself during their many conversations?

And, what had she meant when she'd said she was trying to keep a roof over her head? He knew it was just her and her father in their house, but surely her father made good money? Good enough to take care of their bills?

Then it hit him. Of course he had no idea what her father did or if he had a good job . . . because he'd never asked. No, he'd been far more worried about himself and what she thought of him than to wonder more about her.

So now he was feeling like he'd completely ruined their last conversation and maybe even their relationship. Worse, he had no idea what to do, which felt just as bad.

Two raps on the door jerked him out of his musings. Glancing at the clock, he saw that they'd been closed for almost forty-five minutes. He knew he should just ignore it.

But then he saw it was Sarah Anne Miller and . . . the widow Jane Shultz.

He hadn't realized that his bookmobiling librarian and Jane knew each other, though why he had thought he knew who everyone was friends with, he didn't know. Then, right on the heels of that realization, he noticed that Jane was holding herself up with braces and that Sarah Anne was supporting her. Surprise, mixed with a good dose of shame, coursed through him. Joel had been telling truth. Jane Shultz was struggling and needed help.

Of course she needed help. But he'd been so worried about reputations and rumors that he'd never even wondered how he could lend her a hand as well.

Quickly, he opened the door and ushered them in. "Hello, ladies. We're closed, but it's awfully cold out there. Would you like to come in and rest for a moment?"

"Oh, thank you, Aaron," Sarah Anne said in her usual, breezy way. "That wind came up out of nowhere, and it's a tough one. I felt it all the way to my bones. Some of the roads out here are getting bad, too. I had to cut short my day because the roads were becoming covered with ice."

"So, therefore you went out shopping?"

"That's my fault, I'm afraid," Jane said. "I needed some medicine and Jo—I mean, the person who has been helping me with some of my errands and such couldn't come in for the next few days." Looking fondly at Sarah Anne, she said, "Sarah Anne here was so kind to offer to take me to the pharmacy."

"It was no trouble." She sighed. "Though, I have to tell you, Aaron, I was hoping you might be open late tonight."

"Do you need a piece of furniture?"

"Again, I'm afraid that is me," Jane said. Looking down at her braces, she added, "My uh, MS has gotten worse, I'm afraid. The doctors gave me a good talking to about pretending that it wasn't."

"She needs a new chair that she can get in and out of easily," Sarah Anne added. "I know it's late, but could Jane look at chairs now? It's hard for her to get around when the store is crowded."

And there was yet another reminder of how self-centered he'd been. Instead of judging Joel's actions, Aaron should have been judging his own. Even if he hadn't known Jane needed a chair, he could have, at the very least, mentioned she was in need to some women in his church district who reached out to people in their community who could use some help.

Realizing the two ladies were still waiting for him to reply, Aaron brought himself back to the present. "Of course. Let me go turn on some more lights so you two can look around."

"*Danke*, Aaron," said Jane.

He smiled at her before walking to the back of the store to turn on the main set of lights, grateful that the store was owned by a Mennonite family. Sometimes conveniences like electricity became a necessity.

"Oh! This is much better!" exclaimed Sarah Anne.

Jane didn't say too much, just slowly walked over to the row of comfortable easy chairs.

Aaron was enough of an experienced salesman to know to stay to one side. The ladies would likely want to touch the fabric, try out the chairs, discuss features, and then signal him when they had questions. He was grateful for the reprieve anyway, because he couldn't help but think of all the mistakes he'd made with Joel of late.

It was evident now that he was guilty of listening to idle gossip and being judgmental. Obviously Jane needed assistance, and Joel had been helping her. Instead of being caring and understanding, Aaron had tried to twist it into something that it wasn't.

"Aaron? Aaron?" Sarah Anne called out. "Are you all right?"

He rushed forward. "I'm sorry. I guess my mind had gone walking."

"I'm the one who should be apologizing. I'm sure you're tired and more than ready to go home. It was wrong to just show up. At the very least, I could have called the store and asked when we could stop by."

"A call might have helped on another day, but I was here anyway tonight. Now, how can I help?"

Jane patted two chairs, one of which was top of the line and made by a well-known manufacturer and another which cost far less but was still good quality. "I'm not sure which chair to choose. Can you help me decide?"

"That's what I'm here for." Carefully, he outlined the pros and cons of each.

"Which would you choose?" Sarah Anne asked.

"Honestly, I would pick this one." He patted the less expensive model. "It's comfortable, well built, and not as hard on the bank account."

"Someone can deliver it, yes?"

"Of course. I'd have to look at the delivery schedule, but I'm confident we can get it to your house within the next couple of days, Jane."

Jane smiled. "I guess the decision is made, then. I'd like that chair, please." She reached for her purse, which was over her shoulder, but she wobbled a bit.

"Please, sit down, won't ya?"

"*Danke.*" She gripped the arm of a chair to help her maneuver. "It's times like this that I wish my body worked like it used to." She smiled, but even in the dim light, Aaron could tell Jane was embarrassed.

He stepped back. "I'll be right back with the bill."

"Take your time."

As he clicked buttons on the computer, he could hear Sarah Anne speaking to Jane.

"Here, dear," Sarah Anne said, "give me your check, and I'll fill it out for you. Then all you'll have to do it sign it."

After she got Jane's checkbook, Sarah Anne met him at his desk.

"All of this was very nice of you, Aaron. Truly kind."

"What did I do that was so special? Stay open to make a sale? Don't thank me for that." Especially since he'd certainly done a lot more to be embarrassed about in regard to Jane Shultz.

"You know what I mean," she murmured. "You didn't have to be so helpful. You certainly didn't have to encourage Jane to buy the lesser priced item."

Aaron was offended that Sarah Anne had even considered that he might have acted any other way. "This is my job, but selling furniture is not who I am." Standing up straighter, he added, "Besides, I can promise you Mr. Zeiset would have done the same thing."

"Oh. Of course. I'm sorry I offended you."

"You didn't. I mean, you did a bit, but I overreacted. I . . . Well, there are some other things on my mind, I'm afraid." He shrugged. "Perhaps I'm not at my best right now."

She relaxed. "I've had days like that."

"I'm sorry to say I've had more than a few recently." After carefully double-checking his math, he told Sarah Anne the price.

While she filled out the check and walked it to Jane, he checked the schedule.

"It looks like my men could deliver your new chair tomorrow, Jane. Will that be convenient?"

"So soon?"

"You live nearby, and it's just a chair. We can load it on the truck without a problem."

"Then, yes! Yes, of course tomorrow is fine," she said with a little laugh. "I'm so glad we came tonight, Aaron."

"I am, too." Both Jane and Sarah Anne had given him a reminder of what was important in life. Being decent mattered so much more than a reputation . . . or listening to idle gossip. "Now, let me help you ladies out to the car."

Sarah Anne held the door open while Aaron stayed by Jane's side, keeping a hand out in case she slipped on the slick, wet sidewalk.

Jane stayed quiet, and he wondered if it was her natural reticence or if it had something to do with the community's treatment of her in general. Or, maybe it was more personal, maybe she'd heard he thought there was something wrong with Joel spending time at her house. But, of course, there was no way for him to ask without making things even more awkward.

After helping her into the car, he smiled at them both. "Well, I'll be seeing ya."

"Goodbye, Aaron. Thank you again for your help," Jane said very properly.

He bowed slightly. "You are very welcome."

"And I will see you at the library," Sarah Anne said.

He laughed. "That you will. Good night."

Grinning, Sarah Anne rolled up her window then drove off. Aaron watched her vehicle disappear into the night and thought about the many difficult conversations he'd had lately. He wondered what God was wanting from him. Did He want him to stop hiding behind his insecurities and become his own man? Or, was this the Lord's attempt to get him to think of others instead of just himself? If that was the case, then He had succeeded indeed. Now all he had to do was start praying for things to finally settle down.

Walking back inside to turn down the kerosene lamp, Aaron wondered if he even wanted things to settle down. He felt more alive and fresher than he had in months.

He didn't know if it was due to his new goals, this recent visit with Jane . . . or Kayla. Or, maybe he was finally growing up and thinking about other people besides himself?

If that was the case, he knew what he needed to do. He needed to stop by Kayla's house on the way home and check on her. If she needed him, he wanted to be there for her.

thirty

• RULE #30 •

Give thanks for Presidents' Day, Martin Luther King, Jr.,
Day, and Labor Day. Everyone needs a day off.

Kayla had seen Aaron's flashlight before she'd recognized the man himself. By the time she did, she rushed to open the door and shuttle him inside. It was far too nasty an evening out for him to be visiting houses. "My stars! Aaron, come in and get warm!" She opened the door and ushered him in before thinking the better of it.

"*Danke,* Kayla. My fingers were starting to feel numb."

It was only when he was inside that she became aware of how dark it was. Snow was starting to fall, and it was altogether inappropriate for them to be completely alone in her house. Gossips' tongues would be wagging for sure.

She clasped her hands in front of her middle. "It's late, Aaron. What brings you by?"

He looked as if he felt as awkward as she did. "I could say I just happened to be in the neighborhood . . ."

"Which would be a lie, of course."

He nodded. "How about the truth, then? I didn't like the way things stood between us after our conversation. I was worried about you."

She sighed. "Oh, Aaron. Take off your coat and come stand in front of the fire."

He immediately complied and stood so his back was facing the flames. After a minute, he smiled. "Thanks. It really is cold out."

She noticed his boots were damp. "Do you want to take off your boots, too? Let them dry a bit?"

"Ah, no. I don't think I'd better take off too much more. But, you can tell me what is going on with you."

"I am fine."

He rolled his eyes. "Not that again. You mentioned you were worried about keeping a roof over your head. What did you mean by that? And, come to think of it . . . Where is your father?"

Kayla was too tired—and they'd already said too much—to put up a front or make up a story. "My father is still in Pinecraft. I think."

"You think?"

"*Jah*. He, uh, was supposed to come back several days ago, but he didn't get on the Pioneer Trails bus."

"I'm so sorry. Is he sick? Did something happen to him?"

That was the problem, wasn't it? Part of her wished he was hurt or sick because then she could understand why he hadn't come back when promised. "*Nee*. He just doesn't want to come back." Her lip trembled, but she tried to hide it.

Concern lit his expression. "Come here," he murmured, reaching for her hand and leading her to the sofa.

She didn't protest. Honestly, the last couple of days had taken such a toll that she appreciated someone taking charge of her, if only to make her sit down for a few minutes. Realizing just how alone she'd felt, tears pricked her eyes. Worried he was going to see her cry, she turned her face. But he reached out with one hand and directed her eyes toward him again.

"Kayla. Talk to me. What do you think is going on? Are . . . are you afraid something has happened to him?"

"I was worried at first, but the two times I met the bus, I talked to some acquaintances who had seen him in Pinecraft, alive and well."

"That doesn't make sense."

Looking at Aaron's strong jaw, knowing how good he was, how much he tried, she realized that, of course, he didn't understand her father's way of thinking. He had no experience with such things. But, she reminded herself, Aaron was no stranger to pain. Tim's departure and his parents' shunning of him had been traumatic, indeed. It was obvious that Aaron still missed his brother and likely always would. If anyone would understand how hard it was to love someone but not necessarily agree with his actions, it was Aaron.

She pursed her lips, then decided that nothing good was going to come from hiding her father's problems anymore. "Aaron, my *daed* is a good man, but he's a selfish one, too. He's also impulsive and doesn't think of the repercussions of that. I fear that this is simply another time when he doesn't want to think about his responsibilities."

"Doesn't he have a job?"

She appreciated that his tone was hesitant and not filled with accusations. "He does. My father works at an RV factory in Millersburg." Thinking of how irritated the driver had seemed yesterday when he'd come over only to find out her father still hadn't come home, she winced. "Well, he did."

"Kayla, are you saying he lost his job?"

"I'm not positive, but I believe so. He's been gone a week longer than anticipated and never told anyone, not me or his boss, Mr. Edmonds. The English driver who came over to pick him up said he would tell Mr. Edmonds about my father and that he wasn't going to be pleased."

Aaron winced. "Oh, Kayla. I'm sorry."

She lifted her chin in a weak effort not to seem quite so pitiful. "I am, too. But if I've learned anything, it's that nothing gets better if I sit around and feel sorry for myself."

"But is everything okay?"

"I hope so. I'm trying to figure out how to pay our rent and the rest of our bills."

"I can help with that. How much do you need?" He stood up before she could say a word, started fishing through his trouser pockets. "I have some extra money here."

"*Nee*, Aaron. I don't want your money."

"Kayla, I want to help you." He sat back down but kept his wallet in his hand. "You're not alone, you know."

But that was the problem. In many ways, she was. Besides, what would she do if she allowed herself to depend on Aaron and then he changed his mind about her? Gathering her wits, she said, "I appreciate you saying that, but there's nothing you need to do. I'll be all right."

After studying her for a moment, Aaron stood up and walked to the kitchen. "It just occurred to me that it's getting dark out. What are you having for supper?"

"Aaron! Come sit down."

He opened up the refrigerator and stared inside. She knew what he was seeing, of course. Fairly bare shelves. There were some condiments, a couple of eggs, a quart of milk, and a lone pair of oranges inside. After looking his fill, he closed the door and turned to her again. "Kayla, be honest with me. Have you eaten supper already?"

"*Nee.*"

"What were you going to eat?"

She shrugged. "Some scrambled eggs, I guess."

His voice hardened. "What about tomorrow?"

"I'll figure that out then."

"Kayla, you know I can't handle hearing that."

Hurt, she folded her arms across her chest. "I don't know what you expect me to say, Aaron. You don't want me to lie and you don't want to hear the truth."

"I want you to say you'll come home with me tonight."

She couldn't have been more shocked if he'd asked her to start doing jumping jacks right there in the kitchen. "What? Of course not."

"Don't say no. Listen, I'm not asking you to do anything inappropriate. There's tons of room in my house." He waved a hand. "You can share a room with Tiny, or I'll sleep on the couch and you can have my bed. You can eat supper with us, and breakfast, too. If there's anything we have a lot of, it's food." He laughed. "Well, food and noise."

Aaron was making it sound like her problems were so easily

taken care of that she almost started laughing. "I cannot go over just like that, Aaron."

"Why not?"

"Because I'm twenty-six years old. I'm a grown woman and I don't need to have a sleepover." And certainly not in his bed! "I'll be fine."

"If you're worried about what my family will say, they'll be glad to have you."

"It's not that. It's that I need to be here. For me."

"So you won't take money and you won't come home with me. You'd rather sit here and eat eggs."

"You make it sound like that's a bad thing. It's not. Eggs are perfectly healthy."

Aaron raised his brows. "Next, I suppose you're going to tell me that oranges are a good breakfast?"

She was about to say that, so she switched gears. "*Nee,* Aaron. What I was going to tell you is that while I appreciate your concern, my diet is none of your business."

"Will you do me a favor, then?"

"What?"

"When you do decide that my concern for you *is* my business, let me know. You need help, Kayla, and I want to be here for you."

"I don't think you know what you're saying."

He stepped closer. "That's where you're completely wrong. Kayla, I know exactly what I'm saying. I want to be a part of your life. I want to be around you all the time. I want there to be something so special between us that you don't hesitate to come to me first with your problems."

"But that sounds . . ." Her voice drifted off. She was too afraid to say what it sounded like.

Aaron didn't seem to have that worry, though. Reaching for her hands, he gripped them lightly. "I know what it sounds like. It sounds like I like you. " He lowered his voice. "It sounds like I'm serious about the two of us, Kayla."

She might have been older. She might have been more experienced in many things, but she still gaped at him.

And then Aaron, looking oh-so-smug, reached down, kissed her lightly on the lips, and then walked outside. "Don't forget to lock the door, Kayla. Good night."

She closed the door, bolted it, and then said to the empty room, *"Gut naught."*

And just for a second, she imagined saying that to Aaron when he was sleeping on the other side of her bed.

thirty-one

Tiny was in the living room with the rest of the family, attempting to finish up the thousand-piece puzzle they'd gotten for Christmas, when Aaron burst inside with a blast of cold air.

"I need everyone's help," he called out.

Tiny shared a confused look with Jack as their father asked, "With what? And close that door, son. The wind just blew a puzzle piece on the floor."

"Fine. It's closed," he said as he strode forward. "Now, everyone, you need to listen. Kayla needs help."

Practically as one, the whole family turned to stare at him.

"Kayla needs help from all of us?" Jack asked. "Aaron, what did you do?"

Daed stood up. "And while you're talking, you can share where you've been. It's almost eight o'clock, son."

"I had to stay late at work and then I decided to visit Kayla."

Mamm stood up, too. "At her house?"

"Obviously. And, just so we all remember, I'm twenty-one years old. You're talking to me like I'm a teenager."

"There's no need to speak so snippily. I promise, I haven't forgotten your age," Mamm said. "Now, go take off your coat and get some supper. We'll talk after that."

Aaron took off his coat but stayed in the middle of the living room. "My supper is part of what is wrong."

"You are being as clear as mud, son," Daed said. "What, exactly, has gotten you so spun up?"

"Kayla's father is missing, and she doesn't have any food in her house."

Well, that brought every one of them up short. Even Becca stopped playing with her blocks and stared up at Aaron in wonder.

Tiny walked over to his side. "Aaron, I'm sorry, but you are going to need to back up a few paces. Why did you feel the need to visit Kayla tonight, and what do you mean her father is missing?"

"Do we need to go over there now?" Jack asked. "The snow's gotten bad, but we could make it."

"Again, let's take things one step at a time," Daed said. "Aaron, your mother has left food out for you to eat. Go hang up your coat, take off the wet boots, and come to the table. We can sit with you while you eat."

"Fine." They all relocated to the dining room as Aaron did as their father asked. After briefly closing his eyes in prayer, he said, "I think I need to backtrack a bit so you all can understand why I went over to see Kayla tonight."

"Then start at the beginning, dear," Mamm murmured.

"Okay. It all started when Sarah Anne Miller and Jane Shultz came into the store after hours."

Jack grunted. "One would have thought our favorite librarian would be picking better women to be hanging out with."

"That's awfully harsh, Jack," Tiny said.

He looked at Tiny and Aaron. "What? I'm sure you were thinking the same thing. That woman has a bad reputation. We all know that."

"Jack, we'll have none of that talk," their mother chided. "You should be ashamed of yourself."

"Sorry," he said, looking Tiny's way.

She knew Jack was on her side, but she also felt like they were being too hard on Jane. "Why were they there so late?"

"It turns out that Jane has MS. You know, multiple sclerosis. Did any of you know that?" Aaron asked as he started motioning for everyone to pass plates around so he could get his fill.

"I knew she had some health problems, but I didn't know what, exactly," Tiny admitted as she passed him the steamed broccoli. "Is she all right?"

"I think so . . . up to a point. She has to use braces to get around. Sarah Anne drove her to the shop in the hopes that I would help them after hours. It seems big crowds upset Jane, and she gets worried about being jostled."

"What does this have to do with you visiting Kayla?"

"Well, it made me realize that Jane's had a pretty big secret that she's been reluctant to share, which of course made me think of mine."

Their father picked up a spare roll then passed the breadbasket to Aaron. "What is this secret, son?"

"It's a pretty big one, I'm afraid," he hedged. "I don't think you're going to like it."

Jack looked at him intently. "And it has to do with Kayla?"

"*Jah.*"

Their mother looked worried. "Uh-oh. Maybe you should discuss this with just Daed and me. In private."

"No way," Jack said. "Tiny and I are invested now."

Tiny couldn't disagree. She nodded.

A whole parade of emotions crossed Aaron's face before he put his fork down and spoke again. "I've been secretly studying for the GED."

Knots formed in Tiny's stomach as she waited for her parents to explode. Instead, it was like the whole room took a collective sigh.

"That's it?" Jack asked.

"Well, yeah. I've been paying Kayla to tutor me."

"Because?" Daed asked.

Tiny noticed that their father was holding his tongue, but barely.

Aaron must have noticed, too. Quickly, he blurted, "Before any of you gets worried, I don't want to leave our faith."

"Are you sure, Aaron?" Mamm asked.

He nodded. "I wanted to take the GED because I wanted to get a promotion at work. And to prove to myself I could do it."

"Didn't Kayla take it years ago?" Mamm asked. "I seem to remember hearing something about that."

"She did. She passed it easily about four years ago."

"Why did she take it?" Jack asked.

"It's not my place to say," Aaron murmured.

Tiny studied her older brother. His expression was carefully blank, and it was obvious that he, like she, had grown up a lot during the last couple of weeks.

"Well, tell us how your sessions are progressing, son," Daed said. "Are you finding it difficult?"

"And do tell us when you plan to take the test," Mamm added. "Is it soon? If so, I'll make a cake to celebrate."

Aaron looked so puzzled that Tiny covered her mouth with her hand so she wouldn't burst into laughter. "If you could see your expression, Aaron. It's priceless."

"It's also justified. I'm amazed at how well all of you are taking the news. I thought everyone was going to be shocked."

"Well, I am surprised, of course. But . . . not that shocked," Mamm said. "I have noticed that some of the books you've been reading had to do with science and math."

"I'm surprised, but now that I think about it, I guess it makes sense," Daed said. "I figured something had to be going on with you and Kayla. She went from being a stranger to someone you seem to be spending all your time with. Your friendship seemed to spring up out of nowhere."

"She is my tutor," Aaron said. "But we're more than that now." He shook his head. "Sorry, I'm still trying to come to terms with all of you taking my news so calmly."

"What they're trying to say is that Kayla being in a family way would be a lot more shocking," Jack said with a wink in Tiny's direction.

Tiny covered her mouth again. This family was goofy. And

what was Jack doing, speaking about Kayla being in a "family way"? None of them were that prudish. "Jack, honestly. Just say what you mean. You thought Aaron and Kayla had been fooling around."

"Fine. Aaron, if you and Kayla had been doing more than k-i-s-s-i-n-g, we'd all be a lot more shocked."

"Sorry, but I'm feeling kind of shocked right now. I'm trying to tell you all about something serious, and you are making jokes."

Becca giggled.

"Jack," Daed warned. "Enough of that."

"I'm sorry. I'll stop."

Tiny turned to Aaron. "*Anyway* . . ."

He sat up straighter. "*Anyway*, earlier today I'd told Kayla about how I wasn't going to take the test anymore because Mr. Zeiset had already hinted that I was going to get a promotion. But for some reason she looked sad about that."

"Because she was going to miss spending time with you?"

"That's what I thought. But now I realize it was because she needed the money. Her father isn't very responsible. He's on vacation in Pinecraft now, and she's trying to pay their rent. I think she's hungry, too."

"My word."

Tiny looked around the long, sturdy oak table that her grandfather had built for her grandmother. It was imperfect, full of flaws and nicks, but it was a thing of beauty. It was also still holding enough food for another three people, at the very least. "Maybe we should bring her some of our supper?" she suggested. "I'm with Jack. It's snowy, but we could walk over there without a problem. We've got lots of flashlights."

"We're just going to show up with tonight's leftovers?" Jack asked. "Oh, I'm sure that will make her feel special."

"Hey, it was a *gut* supper," Tiny said, especially since she had made most of it.

Just as Jack opened his mouth to spout off another comment, Aaron cut him off. "I already invited her here for supper. I said she could have my room, and I'd sleep on the couch tonight."

"You offered her your bed?" Tiny asked.

"What, would you want Kayla to sleep on the couch?"

"*Nee*, but—"

Their father interrupted. "Since she's not here, I'm guessing that she didn't take you up on the offer."

"No, she didn't." A line formed between Aaron's brows. "I didn't feel like I could argue with her about that, so I dropped it. But that doesn't mean I don't feel bad for her." He put his fork down. "Daed, what do you think I should do?"

"About the test, your tutoring, your secrets, or Kayla?"

Ouch. Tiny hated when her father made so much sense. It always made her wish she thought things through better. There was something even more striking about her brother being put into his place though. Aaron was the responsible one. The steady, kind one. Even though she'd guessed about his test taking, it still made her feel uneasy to see him having to face her parents that way.

"How about we only focus on Kayla right now," Aaron said in a dry tone.

Her parents shared a look. "First of all, it's too late to go back out there. The weather is bad, and Kayla could be asleep. Tomorrow is soon enough," Mamm said.

Daed nodded. "I agree. Aaron, you're going to have to pay Kayla another visit tomorrow. But I think you should bring Tiny."

"Why do I have to bring my sister?"

"Yes, why do I need to go?" she asked.

"You can bring a casserole you made," Mamm said with a smile. "Plus, Kayla might be more receptive to the food if it comes from Tiny and not her, ah, special friend, Aaron."

Tiny slowly nodded, though of course she had not made any casserole to take to Kayla. "All right."

Aaron blushed but nodded as well. "Okay. That's what we'll do, then."

"I am not done, son. There is more."

"Yes?"

"I want you, Tiny, and Jack to pay a visit to the widow Jane tomorrow as well."

"Why do we need to call on her?" Jack asked. "And why me? I haven't talked to the woman in ages."

Their father's expression hardened. "Because you have been very busy sticking your nose into other people's business, Jack. You got mad at Joel for working at her house, interfered with him calling on Tiny, and even spoke disparagingly about Jane tonight."

"I didn't know she was sick," Jack said.

"That's no excuse. It's time to offer to help Jane Shultz with a couple of chores around her house." Daed turned to Tiny. "And, Tiny, you may bring Jane a cake."

She was going to be cooking all morning. "*Jah*, Daed."

"*Gut.*" Their father folded his arms across his chest. "As far as I'm concerned, I think this test taking, gossiping, worrying about Kayla, and spying on Joel Lapp and his new dog is the Lord's way of helping the lot of you do some growing up." While Tiny gasped, Daed said, "Tiny, you have a fine young man who is working hard to provide for you. It's time you worked that chip of jealousy off your shoulder and thought of someone else besides yourself."

She looked down into her lap. "All right."

Daed placed his napkin neatly on the table before eyeing Aaron over the rims of his glasses. "And you, son? Well, you have a good job, a good life, and a good heart. It's obvious there's more connecting you and Kayla than study skills. I'm pleased that you've stopped worrying about your differences and have begun focusing on what the two of you do have in common."

"I agree." Looking serious, Aaron added, "Kayla is a fine woman. I love her, and I'd be blessed to have her as my wife one day."

Looking pleased, their father stood up. "This was a fine supper, Violet. *Danke*. And, now that Aaron is all done and we have tomorrow decided, I'm going to take Becca here into the other room." He helped her out of her booster chair and grasped her hand.

Their mother looked mystified. "All right . . . but what are you going to do with Becca?"

"We are going to play blocks."

"Blocks?" Jack grinned.

"I do know how to play blocks, son. It wasn't all that long ago that I sat on the floor, doing the same thing with Tim."

Aaron barely stopped himself from gasping. He couldn't remember the last time his father had mentioned Tim without one of them bringing up his name first.

Maybe Daed, too, was changing a bit.

After he and Becca walked into the living room, Tiny and her brothers turned to their mother. She was wearing a small smile. "Now, the three of you may work on the dishes."

Then she stood up, too, and went into the living room.

"What just happened?" Jack asked.

"I think we just got put in our places," Tiny murmured.

"I didn't even know I was so out of place," Jack said. "Did you, Aaron?"

"Right now I don't know what I know . . . and what I don't," Aaron said.

All Tiny knew was that she was going to be cooking a whole lot in less than twelve hours. "I do. Well, come on, boys, start helping me bring everything into the kitchen. I'd like to get this over with as soon as possible since I'll be working in the early morning, making cakes and casseroles."

Jack and Aaron both stood up and each picked up a serving dish. Tiny was grateful for that as she led the way into the kitchen.

thirty-two

• RULE #32 •

Keep a step stool on hand. You never know when someone is going to need a little boost.

Aaron was sitting on his bed in a pair of flannel pajama bottoms and a sweatshirt when there was a light tap on his door. He almost ignored it, but figured he would simply tell Jack or Tiny to go away in person. The last thing he wanted to do was hear more of their opinions about how to run his life.

Seeing his mother on the other side of the door drew him up short. "Mamm?"

She walked right in. "Aaron, I know it's late, but we need to talk."

"About what?"

"About a few things," she said crisply as she sat down on the chair at his desk. "Close the door, please. The last thing we need is for Jack and Tiny to wander in, too."

He closed it and sat on the edge of his bed. "Mamm, what is going on?"

She took a deep breath. "You need to take that test, Aaron."

"I promise, Mr. Zeiset said he doesn't think it's necessary."

"I'm not talking about work, son. I think you need to do this for you." Gazing at him intently, she added, "I fear if you don't follow through and take the GED, you're going to always wonder what would have happened."

"I never expected you to support my taking it." No, he wasn't going to tiptoe around Tim anymore. "I thought you would worry I was going to leave, too."

"I know you're not your brother." A shadow entered her eyes, but she continued, "But even if you did want to leave, that would be your choice, not ours. Your father and I have a lot of regrets about the way we handled things with Tim."

"You do?"

"Oh, *jah*. How could we not? He was always independent. He always wanted to do things *his* way, even when he was a little boy." She looked down at her clenched hands. "But I never gave him the support he needed, Aaron. I never actually followed through on the things I said were important. I told Tim over and over that our Lord was in charge and that He was there to help each of us . . . but then, I went right back and acted as if I knew better." Her bottom lip trembled. "And then he left, and your father and I made it so that he could never come back."

"Tim knew what would happen if he left."

She nodded. "He probably did . . . And we might have even

done the right thing. But that doesn't change the fact that I miss him every day."

"I miss him, too." Tim's departure had left a hole in his life. He was always going to miss him, would always wonder what happened to him and if he was all right. When he spoke again, he knew his voice was thick with emotion. "There's a good chance I won't pass the test."

"But it seems to me if there's a chance you won't pass, there's also a chance you might." She smiled suddenly. "All that is certain is that you will never know what happens if you don't take it."

She was right. "What about Daed? Does he feel the same way?"

She nodded as she got to her feet. "We've both learned the hard way that fear for what might happen isn't a very good companion. Just like in love, we reckon it's better to take a chance."

Aaron hugged her. "*Danke,* Mamm. You've given me a lot to think about."

"I just wanted to make sure you knew that perfection is over-rated. No one needs you to score perfectly or even to always be happy. Only that you give life a try."

"I'll do that."

Placing one cool palm on his cheek, she looked up into his eyes and nodded, then walked out without another word.

Aaron reckoned that nothing else needed to be said.

After much discussion, Jack, Tiny, and Aaron made a plan for the day ahead. First, they walked to Kayla's house to drop off a picnic basket filled with fresh scones, fried chicken, a jar of apple butter, and about a dozen other small items.

Standing to one side with Jack, Tiny watched Aaron knock on Kayla's door. When Kayla answered, she smiled warmly at Aaron. "What brings you here so early?"

Aaron gestured to Tiny and Jack. "We wanted to bring this by to you."

Her eyes widened. "That's a big basket."

"It's just filled with some odds and ends," Jack called out. Tiny felt like rolling her eyes, since of course Jack had nothing to do with it.

Ignoring them both, Aaron stepped closer to Kayla. "I hate the thought of you going hungry," he murmured softly.

"Oh, Aaron." Looking tentative, Kayla glanced at Tiny and Jack again. "Would all of you like to come in?"

"I'm sorry, we can't. We have another errand to run," Aaron said as he lifted the heavy basket and placed it inside her door. "I'll be thinking of you, though."

And then right there, in front of the whole world, Aaron kissed Kayla on the lips. "Eat now," he said before turning away.

"*Danke!*" Kayla called out.

"Anytime, Kayla!" Jack called out.

After Kayla shut her door, Aaron threw an arm around Jack. "You can never keep your mouth closed, can you?"

"Not where you're concerned, brother. But don't worry, I won't tell anyone that you've taken to kissing Kayla in broad daylight."

Aaron groaned, but Tiny couldn't help but giggle as the three of them headed over to see Jane Shultz.

Since none of them knew Jane well, they figured it would be

awkward at best, but like bad-tasting medicine, over relatively quickly. They walked together with Tiny in between her older brothers and holding her Mississippi Mud Cake. Easy to make and always appreciated.

Unless, of course, one didn't like chocolate, marshmallows, or pecans.

"Do you think she'll like the cake?"

"Of course. It's a mud cake," Jack said.

"Yes, but some people don't like chocolate. Or, she may count her calories." Low-sugar and low-fat, it was not.

"We're bringing her a gift. She'll be pleased about it," Jack said.

"What do you think, Aaron?"

"I think she's shy and self-conscious about the toll this disease has taken on her body. I don't think she's even going to want us to come inside."

"But we'll sure try, won't we?" Jack asked.

"I guess. I'm twenty-one years old, and it still doesn't occur to me to tell our parents I don't agree with their 'good' idea."

"You're not alone in that."

"All this complaining and neither of you even helped me make this cake this morning," Tiny said. "I had to get up at four-thirty to get the casserole, this cake, and all my chores done."

"You know I was in the barn," Jack said.

Tiny turned to Aaron. "What about you? What's your excuse?"

He shrugged. "I couldn't make that cake if you handed me all the ingredients." They stopped at the foot of the path leading to the front door. "Are we ready to get this over with?"

"*Jah,*" Tiny said. "This cake is getting heavy."

With Jack leading the way, they walked up the path, then

Tiny and Aaron stood to one side while their brother knocked on the door.

The three of them gaped when Joel opened it.

"Tiny!" he blurted before visibly composing himself. "I mean, hello, Aaron, Jack, and Tiny. What are you doing here?"

Eager to prove that she really had changed, she smiled at him. "I baked Jane a cake."

Joel's eyes widened. "Why?"

"Because it's time I stopped just listening and actually did something. Don't you agree?"

"I . . . I don't know what to say."

"Then, how about this . . . May we come in? It's cold out here, and my cake is heavy."

"Oh. Um, sure."

Standing in the entryway and looking at the assortment of tools and building materials on the ground, it was obvious to all of them what Joel had been doing. He'd been putting railing on the wall for Jane to hold on to when she walked up and down the stairs.

"Looks like you could use some help," Aaron said.

"Don't worry about it. I can handle it."

"Jack and I will help you."

"Why?" Joel asked.

Jack had already taken off his coat and tossed it on a chair in the front sitting room. "Because it's time we helped," he said simply.

"Joel?" Jane called out as she slowly walked out of one of the back rooms and into the foyer. "Is someone . . . oh! Well, um, hello there, Aaron." Her smile was strained. "And, Jack and Tiny, too. I'm sorry, do you all need Joel? If so, feel free—"

"*Nee.* We came here to visit you," Aaron interrupted. "I mean, after seeing you last night, I realized that a visit is overdue."

"I agreed," Jack said.

Tiny knew she had a lot to talk to Joel about, but first she was more than ready to try to make things right between her and Jane.

"I brought you a cake, Jane," Tiny said. "I hope you like chocolate."

Jane looked at all of them. "I'm sorry, I don't understand."

"I could give you a story, but the truth is I didn't know you had MS until I saw you last night. I feel bad that you are living here on your own and wished I would have done something earlier," Aaron said.

"And since we know Joel has been helping out from time to time, we thought maybe you would accept our help today as well," Jack added.

"I am not helpless."

"Of course not. But since we're here, how about we give Joel a hand?"

"I could use it, Jane," Joel said. "Otherwise, it's liable to be the most crooked bannister in town, or you're going to get a dozen extra holes in your wall."

"Well, of course. Thank you." She looked at Tiny helplessly.

"Maybe we could have some cake and catch up?" Tiny asked hesitantly. "Or, um, maybe get to know each other?"

"I could put on coffee."

"I love coffee. Lead the way."

Tiny followed Jane into the kitchen and saw many signs of just how hard the easiest tasks had begun to be for Jane. The counters were cluttered, and some of the upper cabinets had a film on them. The floor had been swept, but Tiny could tell it was in need of a good mopping.

Jane paused before carefully walking the percolator to the sink. "I want to apologize for the state of my kitchen," she said as she rinsed out the carafe. "I'm afraid it's gotten the best of me."

"Please don't apologize. We came over without being invited. It was rude for us to show up without warning." Pointing to the cake, she said, "My only defense is that I came bearing a gift."

"It's been a long time since I've had something that looks so yummy. Perhaps you would like to do the honors while the coffee sets to brew?"

"Of course." While Jane measured the coffee grounds and set the percolator on the stove, Tiny got out plates and silverware and cut them each a generous slice. By the time she had carried them to the table, Jane was filling up a little glass jar with milk.

Tiny couldn't help but reflect that their motions felt as familiar as pinning up her hair in the mornings. The comfortable silence seemed to cut through the awkwardness between them and put them on even ground.

When the coffee was done, Jane looked at Tiny apologetically. "I'm afraid my hands aren't as steady as they used to be. Would you mind pouring and carrying over our cups?"

"Of course not." She set the two cups, the jar, and the sugar bowl on a tray Jane had set out and brought it to the table. "Look at us. I can't remember the last time I've spent the morning having cake and *kaffi* with a friend."

Jane wrapped a hand around her mug. "Is that what we are, Tiny?"

No. No, they weren't. In her world, friends spoke to each other at church. Friends reached out to each other and lent a hand during difficult times. Friends definitely didn't believe—or repeat—malicious rumors.

"I guess we're not," she said hesitantly. "But I'd like to change that."

"Why? Because of my disease? Is it pity?"

Was it?

"No, I think I just want to be a better person," she said at last. "Jane, I used to think we had nothing in common. You were married and living in this beautiful house in town, and I was just a teenager."

"That is true." She smiled softly. "We might only be five years apart in age, but in some ways we've had a lifetime of different experiences."

Tiny nodded. "I was very sad for you when your husband died. I mean that sincerely. But I would be lying if I didn't also mention that, of late, I've been a bit jealous of you."

"Of me?"

"You are poised, slim, and very beautiful."

"Hardly any of that."

"You are. Then, when I learned Joel was spending so much time here, I assumed the worst, which is something I'm not proud of."

"You thought there was something between him and me?"

"*Jah.* I was jealous."

"Tiny, I promise that you have nothing to be jealous of. He talks about you all the time, and I still miss my husband."

"I'm ashamed of my behavior, Jane." Though she was no doubt stumbling over words and probably not making a lick of sense, Tiny forced herself to continue, "I'm so sorry. I guess this proves I have a lot to learn, ain't so?"

"Maybe we all do."

"Does this mean you'll allow me to at least try to be your friend?"

Jane picked up the fork and speared a section of cake. "Only if you'll allow me to try, too. I *canna* make cake anymore, but . . . I'll always be happy to serve you coffee."

Tiny giggled. "That's enough. More than enough."

Joel popped his head in. "The banister's up. I thought I heard laughter in here."

"You did," Jane replied. "We've been talking about cake and coffee."

"Ah." When Jack and Aaron appeared by his side, they all exchanged confused looks.

Jane smiled again. "Perhaps you men would like some cake as well?"

"I'm in," Jack announced. "It smelled up the whole house, and Tiny wouldn't let any of us sneak a bite."

"I'm not going to refuse, either," Aaron said. "Okay if I get out some plates, Jane?"

"Of course. They're in the cabinet to the left of the oven."

Aaron looked over at his shoulder. "Joel, what about you?" After a pause, he asked again. "Ah, Joel?"

"Good luck getting his attention," Jack muttered.

"I heard ya. Don't be rude," Joel said, still not taking his eyes off of Tiny and Jane.

"You still haven't answered, though. Do you want a plate?"

"*Jah. Danke.* If Tiny made it, I know it's going to be wonderful-*gut.*"

"It is," Jane said.

Joel walked to the table and sat down beside Tiny. "I wouldn't expect anything less."

"Danke," Tiny whispered.

"Do you see what I meant now, Tiny?" Jane asked.

"Oh, yes," she whispered, staring right back at Joel.

Her brothers started snickering, but when Joel smiled at her, it seemed as if everything else faded away. At last, it felt like everything she'd ever hoped for between her and Joel was happening at last.

She was so glad about that.

thirty-three

It felt like Christmas, her birthday, and payday all at the same time. Try as she might, Kayla couldn't think of another way to describe how amazingly wonderful her basket was. Right after Aaron, Tiny, and Jack left, she'd unpacked the goodies and arranged them all on the counter. There was a chicken and broccoli casserole, a package of bacon, six fresh eggs, a loaf of bread, some canned vegetables, and even a tin filled with oatmeal raisin cookies. Every bit of it looked delicious.

After deciding to bake the casserole that evening, she put the eggs and bacon away, then plucked three cookies from the tin. After she set the kettle on to boil, she took a bite. As she'd expected, the treat was as delicious as it looked. She was so grateful to the Coblentzes for the gift . . . and so very grateful to Aaron for caring so much about her in the first place.

That gratitude made her think of something she hadn't thought about in far too long: her mother's daily devotional books. Taking one from the bookshelf, she held it close . . . hugging the memories to her heart.

Her *mamm* had loved those books. Daed used to buy her one every year on Mother's Day. She'd fuss and say she didn't need a gift to celebrate being a mother . . . and then would beam.

Every morning before she even woke Kayla up, her mother would take a few minutes to read the daily devotion and pray. Sometimes, when Kayla was nine or ten, she'd ask her mother to tell her the scripture verse that she'd read that morning. Mamm would do so with a pleased smile.

Everything eventually changed, of course. Her mother became tired and was eventually diagnosed with cancer. Daed started working more and therefore began to ask more of Kayla. And Kayla? Well, she'd entered a challenging period of her life. She'd been besieged by mercurial emotions. Happiness would suffuse her, only to be followed by depression and then anger. The last thing she'd thought she had time for was devotionals.

After making tea and gathering her cookies, Kayla sat down at the kitchen table and opened the front cover. She'd never asked her mother how she picked a devotional to read. Maybe she started on page one and worked through the year? Maybe she flipped through the topics until she found one that spoke to her? Deciding the Lord didn't have a preference, she simply opened the book in the middle and read.

Love bears all things, believes all things, hopes all
things, and endures all things. 1 Corinthians 13:7.

The scripture verse was so perfect, so . . . needed, she could hardly believe it. She read it again, this time out loud, letting the perfect words caress her ears as much as her eyes. "'Love bears all things, believes all things, hopes all things, and endures all things.'"

Only then did she read the devotional author's words about the verse. The woman described love as both the romantic kind and the perfect love of Jesus. Kayla thought about that for a moment and realized it could also be applied to her father. She loved her *daed*, so much. But she was also disappointed and frustrated with him. She wasn't his parent, and she resented being thrust into the role of his caretaker. She loved being his daughter, yes, but did that mean she had to become the responsible one while he lived carelessly?

She didn't think so.

As she read the verse a third time, Kayla realized there was more there than just love. There was belief and hope and endurance. Yes, love was all of those things. When her mother was suffering through the last stages of cancer, they'd all loved and believed in her, hoped for strength and peace . . . and they'd endured.

If she could get through that with her mother, and survive Levi's heartbreak, she could get through this period with her father as well.

Feeling more at peace than she had in weeks, Kayla closed her eyes and prayed. She prayed for her father, for herself, and even for Aaron. Most of all, she gave thanks for this moment of clarity.

Minutes later, when the ringing phone called her back to the day, Kayla felt as if she could tackle almost anything now.

Getting to her feet, she hurried to the kitchen and was able to pick it up on the third ring. "Hello?"

"Kayla, it's me."

Her father. She almost sagged in relief. "Daed! Daed, I'm so glad to hear from you."

"Are you all right? What were you doing just now? The phone has been ringing and ringing."

"I was praying. I got out one of Mamm's old devotionals and read one."

"Oh."

He sounded taken aback, and she was a little glad about that. Maybe he would realize that he also needed to take some time to think about the life he'd been living.

Until then, she decided to get some answers for herself. "Why haven't you come back?"

He hesitated. "We can talk about that when I get home, Kayla."

It sounded like he was hiding something. "Why do we have to wait? What's wrong with right now?"

"I'm afraid it might take a while and there's a line of people waiting to use the phone. I only wanted to let you know that I am coming home on the bus tomorrow. I'm going to need some help bringing everything home. Would you be able to hire a driver and meet me?"

She closed her eyes. He hadn't called to check on her or to make sure she was okay. No, he'd only called to ask for her help. Once again, he seemed oblivious to their bills and the fact that she'd been working nonstop so she could pay them.

It was obvious that the cycle would continue if she didn't finally stand up for herself. Gathering her strength, she said, "I'm sorry, but I won't be able to hire a driver or meet you at the bus."

"Why not?"

"I don't have the money to pay the driver, Daed. Plus, I'm working at the store."

"Are things really that tight?"

"You know they are."

He paused, then blurted, "Well, just ask Pat to give you a loan. She'll do that, I'm sure."

Kayla was sure Pat would because she'd loaned him money in the past. But Kayla wanted to do everything she could to avoid leaning on her aunt yet again. "I'm not going to do that. Sorry."

Again, there was a lengthy pause on his end of the phone. "I don't understand what's come over you. Nothing you're saying makes sense."

"I think you know it does," she said softly. "We can't keep going on like this. I need to start living my life and you need to start living yours."

"Kayla, you don't understand."

She knew what he was about to say next. He would start telling her how difficult his life was and how much he missed her mother. Then, he would even hint that it was a good thing that Levi had broken things off because he needed her. "Things have been really hard for me here. I sure hope you will be able to get more hours at the factory."

"I won't be able to get any more hours because Mr. Edmonds gave my job to someone else. I could hardly believe it."

So, her worst fears had come true . . . and once again, he was blaming other people instead of himself. "I believe he did that since you never came back and the driver came here two days in a row." It was all she could do not to add that his actions weren't very loyal at all.

"You couldn't have called the factory and explained everything?"

This was the last straw. "Explained what, Daed?" Ready to get off the phone, she blurted, "I love you and I want to be there for you, but I don't think that means I should have to keep the house, cook the meals, and pay most of the bills all by myself while you go to Pinecraft . . . I need to find my own place to live."

"You *canna* leave me." His voice was heavy with indignation.

But instead of making her feel more sympathy for him, she was disappointed. Didn't he realize how much she had given up for him? Didn't he remember she'd lost a mother, too? Didn't he realize he'd been taking advantage of her for years?

She was just so tired. Of the juggling and the battles and being ignored. "I'll hope and pray that you have a safe journey home. I'll see you tomorrow when you get back."

"I'm disappointed in you."

Though it was tempting to hold her tongue, she decided what was in her heart also had to be said. "I'm disappointed in you, too, Daed. And I'm sorry, but if Mamm were here, I know she'd tell you the same thing. Goodbye." She hung up before he had a chance to respond.

In the sudden silence of the kitchen, she could hear her heartbeat pounding in her ears. She felt as if she'd just run a mile, she was so out of breath. After pacing the length of the kitchen for a few moments, she at last got ahold of herself.

At least her father had called and he was now coming back to Ohio soon. That was a good thing. She'd been so worried about him. And she was glad she'd spoken her mind at last. With some surprise, she realized she didn't regret any of the things she'd told her father. She'd needed to share how she'd felt and she'd needed to be heard.

After turning on the kettle for another cup of tea, she retrieved her mother's devotional and thought about the verse she'd read three times. It had been the right message at the right time.

Feeling more optimistic than she had in years, Kayla pulled out a sheet of paper and a pencil and decided to make a list. But not of things she needed to do. This one was about things she *wanted* to do. Her dreams, her goals, her wishes.

Picking up the pencil, she considered all her choices. But in the end, it wasn't hard to choose what she wanted to write down at all.

1. Start making decisions that are good for me.

That made sense.

The second? Well, it took her by surprise, but she was just as excited by it.

2. Give Aaron a chance. Give love a chance. They are worth it.

thirty-four

Since Tiny and Joel had seemed smitten with each other and Jack had said he was going to help Jane straighten up a few things before going home, Aaron walked to the closest library branch and asked the clerk to help him sign up for the GED. To his relief, the woman didn't mind helping him in the least. Less than fifteen minutes later, it was done.

Feeling pleased with his success, Aaron returned to Kayla's house. Though he knew his *mamm* might be upset he didn't bring Tiny along to play chaperone, he didn't think Kayla would mind one bit. He sure didn't. He wanted to let her know as soon as possible that he'd not only changed his mind about the test but had also already signed up for it.

But even more important than that test was Kayla herself.

He was now more determined than ever to show Kayla just how much she meant to him. Yes, work was important, and that promotion was, too. But now he realized that nothing was going to mean much if he and Kayla weren't okay. He needed her in his life.

Aaron knocked on her door, hoping and praying she would be open to another impromptu visit from him.

When she did appear, she had on a different dress than she'd been wearing earlier that day. Now her dress was light gray. It should have drained the color from her cheeks but instead made her look even more beautiful.

At least, he thought so.

Realizing they'd been staring at each other for several seconds, he tipped his hat. "Hiya, Kayla."

"Aaron. You're back."

"I guess I couldn't stay away," he teased.

Her pretty blue eyes were full of confusion. "But . . . we just saw each other a couple of hours ago."

Even though Aaron knew he was being a mite overbearing, he gently moved around her and walked inside. After carefully closing the door behind him, he turned to face her. "You're right. We did see each other. And we did talk—and not just this morning. But I don't think I said enough."

"Oh?" She folded her hands in front of her waist. "I thought we discussed a lot of things."

"We did. But I realize now that even though I told you about my dreams and goals and regrets, we never actually talked about what really mattered."

"And that is what?"

"You." He exhaled. "Me. Us."

A smile played on her lips before she firmly regained her composure. "'Us'?"

Reaching out, he took her hand and linked his fingers through hers. "Kayla, I'm not smart like you. As much as I try, I'm never going to have all those fancy words in my head to convey my thoughts like you do."

"You're giving me too much credit, Aaron."

"*Nee*, listen. What I'm trying to say is that it doesn't matter. See, I don't want to be *like* you. I want to be *with* you."

Her hand went slack in his own. "Pardon me?"

Ah, if only he could grab hold of one of those romance books she liked so much and borrow some of the hero's lines. Maybe then he'd be able to convey what was in his heart in a pretty way, a way that was worthy of how he felt for her.

But because that wasn't possible, Aaron forged on ahead. "Kayla, I love you. I love you and I want to be by your side every day." Hearing those clumsy words, he shook his head. "Let me try this again. Kayla, I want to be by your side all the time. For now and forever."

"Forever," she murmured.

Why had she repeated that? Had he been too high-handed? Did Kayla think she didn't have any options?

He started talking faster, hoping that something, anything, he said would be enough for her to give him a chance. Or at least not throw him out.

"Listen, you don't have to feel the same way. It's okay if you feel that I'm rushing you too fast or that I need to prove myself to you or that you're simply not ready for an engagement or marriage. All I ask is that you don't say no."

"'Don't say no'?" The muscles in her throat worked as she swallowed. Then, in a strained voice, she asked, "Aaron, are you asking me to marry you?"

"Kind of." When her eyebrows rose, he inwardly cringed. He really should have practiced what he was going to say.

"Aaron?"

It was obviously now or never. "Kayla, yes, I'm asking you to marry me—I mean, what I'm doing is asking you to give me a chance to prove myself to you, to give me some time to become the person you want to have in your life, to be married to you . . . ah, one day. Will you do that?"

Kayla stared at him a long moment before walking into the living room and sitting down. Then, she pressed her hands on her cheeks and took a deep breath.

He'd done this all wrong. But honestly, he didn't have much more to offer her than he already had. He didn't have much else besides his heart, his promises, and a respect for her time.

Worried she was crying, he walked to her side, his heart firmly lodged in his throat. Feeling annoyed with himself, Aaron sat down beside her. Though he yearned to wrap his arms around her and apologize for making her so upset, he knew he had to give her the time she needed.

After a minute passed, she turned to him and smiled. "Oh, Aaron, I'm sorry, but I just needed a moment. You wouldn't believe the day I've had!"

She wasn't crying. She didn't look mad. But now he was the one who was confused. "Ah, what happened?" he asked slowly.

"Well, after your surprise visit this morning, I was reading one of my mother's devotionals to find some clarity, which was wonderful. But then, on its heels, came a phone call from my father."

"At last." Well, now her reaction made a lot of sense.

"*Jah*. At last." She smiled.

"Did it go all right?"

"Oh my goodness. *Nee!*" She shook her head in dismay. "Somehow, it went from him telling me he was finally coming home to me telling him I was moving out. And then, he had the nerve to tell me I had to stop thinking only of myself."

"Oh. My. Word." Aaron was tempted to tell her a dozen other things about how he really felt about her father, but he didn't dare. Every one of them was not very kind and way too honest. "How did the phone call end?"

"Not well." She bit her bottom lip. "I . . . well, I essentially hung up on him, Aaron. And I don't even feel bad about it."

He took her hand because he couldn't go without touching her any longer. "I'm glad you don't feel bad. You shouldn't. He crossed the line when he didn't come home."

She exhaled. "I finished that call just a few minutes before you knocked on the door again. I was actually sitting at my table writing a list of wishes for me. And . . ." She stood up, hurried to the table, and brought back a sheet of paper. "Look what my second goal is."

Taking the sheet, he read it. Then, yes, he read it again. "'Give Aaron a chance.'" He searched her face. "Why?"

"Because I love you, too." She smiled then.

It was so sweet, so very darling that he did the only thing that was fitting. He pressed his hands on either side of her jaw, leaned close, and kissed her. And when she relaxed against him and linked her hands around his shoulders, he knew he'd done the right thing.

This? Well, this was what life was for. Loving and laughing and living. And baring one's soul and then hearing everything he'd never known he wanted or needed spoken. And because of that, his world had become complete.

thirty-five

• **RULE #35** •

*Encourage lifelong reading. And when the circumstances allow
it, maybe encourage lifelong kindness, too.*

ONE WEEK LATER

Joel had been teaching Yellow to sit and stay when Tiny had
come over. Again.

He couldn't believe that Tiny, the woman he had loved for
most of his life, had taken to courting *him* now. His parents were
mighty amused at the switch in roles, but he didn't mind that
she had the need to take some control in their relationship. He
thought it was cute, especially after she'd confided how she'd
been waiting on him to come calling for years. Because of that,

he'd decided to let her determine the pace. Tiny now came call-ing every two or three days.

When she did, he greeted her with a kiss on her cheek. And yes, sometimes, he even served her cookies and tea just like she would have served him at her house.

"Hiya, Tiny," he said as she approached. "It's good to see you today."

"It's *gut* to see you, too." After bending down to give the dog a pet, she looked up at him and smiled. "It seems you and Yellow are having another lesson."

"We are, though I think Yellow is more interested in the sunny day than learning." As was their custom now, he gave her a quick hug and a very chaste peck on the cheek. "I'm glad you came out to join us."

"Me, too."

He was just about to flirt with her a little when she said, "I've got some news to share, Joel. You better prepare yourself."

"This sounds serious. What's it about?"

Her hazel eyes lit with amusement. "It's nothing bad, I promise. But I did just come from Jane's *haus*."

"And?"

"And . . . Jack was already over there doing chores!"

He was glad Jane was getting help, but he wasn't sure why Jack helping her was news. "And this is noteworthy because . . ."

After glancing around, obviously to make sure no one else heard, she said, "Because I think Jack likes her. When I got there, they'd been having tea at her kitchen table."

"Tea?"

"I know! Can you even imagine? My brother is a lot of things, but a man who sits at a table and sips tea is not one of them."

She was right. As straight and stalwart as Aaron was, Jack was brash and boyish. "I reckon you might be onto something."

"I think so, especially since they looked so very cute together."

He laughed. Jane, with her auburn hair, and Jack, all charm and blond good looks, probably did make a good pair. He hoped the best for both of them. He took Tiny's hand and squeezed it lightly. "This was good news. I'll do my best to keep it a secret."

"I will, too." Her expression faltered. "Ah, Joel, I still feel bad about how I handled your secret with Jane."

"You shouldn't. As much as I'd like to say I would've handled everything better if the situation had been reversed, I don't know that I would have," he admitted. "It's one thing to say I would understand you spending time alone with another man, but I don't know if I would have been very nice about it."

"No?"

"I wouldn't have been jealous, too."

She smiled slightly. "Is it wrong of me to be glad about that?"

"Of course not. I don't want you to be perfect, Tiny. I just want you to be yourself."

"I don't want you to change a thing about yourself, either," she said. "I like you just the way you are."

He led her to the porch where it was more secluded. "Really?"

"Well, of course, I don't know all your faults yet." Looking up at him, she pretended to look worried. "Hmm. Do you snore?"

"*Nee*, though I *canna* be sure. I sleep alone, you know. Do you snore?"

As he had hoped, she looked appalled. "I certainly do not."

"Are you sure?" he teased, pretending to look concerned. "Has anyone ever shared a room with you?"

"*Nee*, but my brothers would have said something, especially since Jack snores terribly."

"All right, then. I guess I'll believe you."

She took a breath. "Hmm. Do you have annoying habits like forgetting to put the cap back on the toothpaste?"

"It's always on, and I always put it away in the drawer." Liking the way her eyes had lit up, he continued to quiz her. "What chores do you hate to do? Beyond making apple butter, of course."

"That's easy. Gathering eggs."

"Truly?"

"The hens sense that I'm afraid of them and peck at me. Every morning, I give thanks for Jack. He gets up early, feeds the horses, and gathers eggs." Her eyes widened. "Oh, dear. Please don't tell me you are afraid of hens as well."

"I'm not afraid of them. You won't have to worry about ornery hens when you're my *frau*." He just about slapped a hand over his mouth when he realized what had just slipped out. Maybe she wouldn't notice . . .

She froze. "Joel?"

Standing on his porch, out of sight from the street and her house, and away from any windows, Joel figured this was as private a moment as he was likely to get, but it was probably far from the romantic, intimate moment he was sure Tiny had dreamed about. Surely it would be better to wait until night, so he could propose under the stars or in candlelight or something pretty to make this moment truly special.

He frowned. "Tiny, I'm sorry. This sure wasn't how I wanted to do this."

She blinked. "To do what?"

"Ask you to marry me."

"Joel." She blinked. Tears sprang to her eyes.

Uh-oh. Was she disappointed that he didn't have candy and flowers? "Tiny, listen. Can we talk about this another day?"

"*Nee.*"

"No?"

"I've waited half my life for you to propose. There's no way I'm going to wait another couple of days."

"But I was going to get on one knee and ask you properly, after I spoke with your parents, of course."

She put a hand on her hip. "Oh, Joel. You don't need to speak to my parents. They know your intentions. Everyone knows your intentions."

She had a point. He'd been hinting about his plans for a long time. "I guess that is true."

"You know . . . you could kneel right here."

"Where?"

"Here. I think there's plenty of room."

"But—"

She folded her arms across her chest. "Of course, if you don't think I deserve such a gesture . . . I guess we could wait awhile and see what I say when you finally decide to ask me."

Finally? Before he lost his nerve, he knelt down in front of her. Hoping and praying that she would say yes quickly and that his mother didn't decide to open the door and start hanging quilts over the porch railing, he said, "Tiny—I mean, Elizabeth?"

"*Jah?*"

"I think I loved you from the moment you ran after me and your brothers and demanded we let you play hide-and-seek with us. I know I loved you when we were in school together and you never made fun of me for always making the lowest score on spelling tests. And I knew I was going to love you forever when we went to our first Singing and you never left my side. Will you marry me?"

"*Jah*, Joel. I will marry you and be your wife."

Gingerly, he got to his feet, reached for her hands, and kissed her sweetly. It wasn't quite the kiss he wished for, but there were limits to what he was willing to do on his front porch in broad daylight.

When he stepped back and she smiled at him, he grinned. "I guess, at long last, we did it. We are going to get married."

"We are indeed," Tiny said with a laugh.

Her face was so happy, so beautifully perfect that he pulled Tiny into his arms and kissed her properly.

After all, it really was the perfect time.

They were all on pins and needles. When Aaron had taken the test, he'd given Sarah Anne Miller's email as his contact information. It seemed they sent the scores through the Internet instead of through the mail. Sarah Anne had warned him about that and had kindly volunteered to lend him her email address. Whenever she received his scores, she would call Kayla's house and then Kayla would contact him.

All that meant he needed to be patient and to have faith that everything would happen in God's time. But that didn't mean it was easy.

He was sitting in the family room halfheartedly reading *The Budget* but really trying to imagine how he would react to whatever news Kayla brought to him. Would he be disappointed to discover that he hadn't passed a single component or simply resigned? No matter what the news was, Aaron wanted to make sure he didn't take it out on Kayla. After all, she was only going to be the messenger.

From across the room, Tiny sighed. "Aaron, didn't the proctor say the scores would be sent today?"

"That's what he said, but that could have changed."

"I certainly hope not."

"No need to sound so indignant, Tiny," Joel teased.

She looked like she was about to argue but chuckled instead. "All right. I'll try to do better," she whispered softly.

Amused, Aaron shared a look with Jack. This was how their sister now acted whenever she was around her fiancé. All moony and compliant. It was terribly amusing.

Jack put down the book he'd been holding. "I, for one, certainly hope that Kayla arrives here sometime soon. If we have to wait all day I'm going to be at my wits' end."

"I hate to say it, but I'm starting to find myself looking out the window as well," Daed added.

The only one to stay quiet was his mother, who looked to be contentedly knitting next to his napping baby sister.

Aaron cleared his throat. "I feel I should point out that the chances of me doing well are slim. No one should get their hopes up."

"There's nothing wrong with thinking positively, son," Mamm said at last. "If I've learned anything, it's that one never regrets looking on the bright side of things. I should've done that more often."

Aaron knew that was another veiled reference to Tim. He leaned back in his chair. That was a big step forward in their family. Though his leaving would always hurt and his absence wouldn't be forgotten, at least he was a part of their conversations now. The change was a miracle indeed.

Thinking about how far they'd come, Aaron realized his mother was right. Truly anything was possible if one had faith.

"She's here!" Tiny called out as she hurried to the door.

"Don't go out there, Tiny," Aaron said, grabbing the door handle before she could. "I'm going to talk to Kayla first."

"Really?"

"It's my test scores." And yes, he realized he was sounding more and more like a petulant teenager than a grown man.

"Fine."

Aaron was vaguely aware of Becca waking up and the rest of the family getting to their feet as he walked outside, but then he forgot all about them as he met Kayla's eyes. "Hi."

"Hiya," she murmured. "You must have seen me out the window."

"I did. Well, Tiny did. I mean, we've all been looking for you."

She smiled. "I'm glad I came over as soon as I could, then."

He couldn't take it anymore. "Kayla, did Sarah Anne call you?"

"She did. Your scores came in."

"And?"

"And . . . you passed!"

"You know, it's okay—" He stopped himself. "Wait, what did you say?"

She smiled. "You passed, Aaron. You may now consider yourself a high school graduate. Congratulations!"

He reached for her hand and linked his fingers with hers. "I can't believe it."

"You should have had a little more faith in me, Aaron Coblentz. Your future wife is a pretty good tutor, you know," she said with a laugh.

"You're better than that. You're everything. Kayla, we did it!" He picked her up and spun her in a circle.

Kayla laughed, and that laughter mixed in with his family's cheers from the open doorway. For one glorious moment the noise lit the air, bringing the sound of happiness through the whole valley.

It was a once-in-a-lifetime moment. Or, even better, a hint of their days to come.

epilogue

• RULE #36 •

Sometimes it's good to keep a list of popular series on hand.
Just in case a patron finishes a book and is anxious to find out
what happens next.

FIVE MONTHS LATER

Sarah Anne didn't think she'd ever been more excited to have an annual review. Sitting across from Ron Holiday, she could hardly keep up her professional demeanor. She really did have so much good news to share. But she hadn't reached sixty-one years of age without learning a thing or two. With effort, she folded her hands neatly over her skirt and patiently waited for Ron to look over both her report and the notes he'd taken every time he'd paid her a visit.

After a good five minutes, he put down his pen and smiled.

"It sounds like you've had quite an adventurous first year, Miss Miller."

"Indeed I have. I met many patrons, delivered books ordered by over two hundred people, and even helped one man become very proficient on the computer." She'd meant the last bit as a tiny joke. She'd helped a whole lot of men, women, and children become pros at finding information online.

"We've received a lot of praise about your demeanor." Ron flipped the paper as he adjusted his glasses. "And, a lot of very interesting comments about you as well."

That didn't sound as positive. "Oh?"

He fiddled with his glasses again. "Yes. For example, take this comment from a Mrs. Jane Shultz. She said you not only helped recommend books to help her overcome her grief, you even helped her visit a furniture store." He looked up. "That isn't part of your job description. Why did you do that?"

"Oh, well, you see, Jane has MS and needed a ride to the store. She has braces on her legs and needs an extra hand to get around. It was no trouble, and of course it was after hours, Ron."

"Hmm." He flipped another sheet of paper. "Now, here's another interesting comment. This man says you helped him find some exciting action and adventure books, and you also counseled him on ways to win back his girl. Is that true?"

She leaned over the desk and saw the note at the top of the page. "That man would be Joel Lapp, and yes, that is true."

"I don't understand why you were counseling him."

"I didn't actually *counsel*. It was more like I listened." She waved a hand. "Sometimes young men are afraid to admit when they don't have all the answers."

His eyebrows rose. "And you do?"

"Well, the books do." She smiled. "Just for your information, everything is good as gold with Joel and his girl now. Rumor has it that they've recently gotten engaged. Isn't that wonderful?"

"Ah, yes." He cleared his throat. "Moving on." He flipped through some more comments. At last, he picked up the sheet of paper and scanned it carefully before laying it flat on his desk. "Now, this one was the most concerning of all."

"Yes?"

"This letter is actually from two people. One of them says you assisted him in studying for a high school equivalency exam without his parents' knowledge?"

"That would be Aaron, and he's twenty-one years old. A bit old to have parents looking over his shoulder all the time, don't you think?"

"Miss Miller, my point is that I think that went far beyond your job description. You were interfering."

"I was not. Aaron came to me for information, and I provided it."

"You did more than that. You found him a tutor."

"Kayla is an upstanding woman and she's very smart, too. She had already taken the test. She was the perfect person to be his tutor."

"So she was English?"

"No, she is Amish. And she also loves to read romances." Sarah Anne smiled. "How sweet is that?"

"Miss Miller, what I'm trying to say is that you might have crossed the line with that couple."

"Based on what?"

He huffed. "Based on these reports, of course."

She stared at him. She thought about her options, then bent

down, opened her purse, and pulled out something she'd just received in the mail. "Perhaps this should be in the report as well, then."

He took the cream-colored envelope from her. "What is this?"

"This, Mr. Holiday, is my invitation to Kayla and Aaron's wedding."

He glanced at it. "They invited you to the ceremony?"

"Go ahead and read the note Kayla placed in it." She knew she sounded smug, but sometimes, she supposed, it couldn't be helped.

Sighing, he carefully slid the invitation out of the envelope. When a small piece of paper dropped out onto his desk, he picked it up and put on his glasses again.

Sarah Anne didn't need him to read it out loud to know what it said: *Thank you, Sarah Anne, for introducing us to each other and reminding us both about how special love is.*

She'd burst into tears when she first read the note, and she hadn't cried in a long time.

Her boss read it, then looked as if he was reading it again, more slowly. "Seems you made quite an impression on them, Sarah Anne."

"I didn't do much. I only did everything you suggested I do."

"Ah, no. I didn't ask you to play matchmaker, Miss Miller."

"That is true. But you did ask me to recommend books, talk to patrons, and help them in any way I could."

"You were supposed to help them in any *reasonable* way you could."

She grinned. "What is more reasonable than love?"

He chuckled softly. "You, Miss Miller, might be the most formidable bookmobile librarian we've ever had."

"I just might be, sir." She clenched her hands. Reviewing her list of accomplishments had made her realize just how much she loved her job, just how much she needed it. But had she gone too far?

After a long moment, Mr. Holiday closed her folder, then nudged his glasses back over his nose. "Sarah Anne Miller, I'm recommending you to continue your contract for another year."

"Thank you. I accept. I will do my best."

He looked a little worried but then cleared his throat and stood up. "Oh, I almost forgot. Here." He handed her a blue sheet of paper.

"What is this?"

"It's a new request for a bookmobile stop. Over on Gardner Way."

"Where's that?"

He walked over to the large map pinned to a bulletin board and pointed to an area on the east side of her territory. "An Amish couple." He smiled. "I actually had the chance to meet them myself over at the thrift store the other day. We got to talking, and they asked if you would be able to bring them any sort of books they asked for. I predict there's a story there."

Sarah Anne reckoned there was, too. Taking the blue form, she folded it and placed it, as well as Kayla and Aaron's wedding invitation, back in her pocketbook. "I'll get them on the schedule as soon as I can. People with a story are my favorite type of patrons." She winked as she adjusted her purse's strap on her shoulder.

She heard him chuckle as she walked out the door. Pleased that their meeting had ended on a good note, Sarah Anne looked at the rolling lush green fields just beyond the district office. Spring was in the air, and, if she wasn't mistaken, there were some lambs out.

Yes, time did move on. She'd gone from mourning her husband to waking up each day with a new sense of purpose. From worrying about numbers and ledgers to worrying about people and book bindings.

Making a sudden decision, she placed her pocketbook in her trunk, locked her car, and decided to go for a walk. She had so much to be thankful for.

So much to look forward to.

And so, with a new spring her in step, she set off. Already dreaming about what the next day would bring. After all, tomorrow, she would be on the road again.

acknowledgments

Writing the first book in a series can be a tricky undertaking. The characters are essentially strangers, the setting is new . . . and so are the themes and the conflicts. Since I'm not necessarily a very good plotter or notetaker, I'm constantly staring at a blank screen hoping that I will be able to figure things out in a reasonable amount of time.

For this book in particular, I'm very grateful to my editor, Sara Quaranta, for her guidance. She is so smart and somehow manages to both encourage and get me back on track at the same time. I'm also indebted to the whole Gallery and Pocket team, especially Sydney Morris, my publicist at Gallery. Sydney has been so instrumental in placing my books in readers' and reviewers' hands.

I owe a huge thanks to my agent, Nicole Resciniti, who is everything an agent should be. She's brilliant, hardworking, very kind, and has accomplished some amazing things for me. I love Nicole!

I'm so grateful to my Buggy Bunch readers—Team Lynne and Laurie, and my husband—who all help me so much in a hundred different ways. I also need to give a shout-out to the many librarians I reached out to with questions about their jobs and bookmobiles.

Finally, I'm so grateful to God. It's a blessing to never have to write a book alone.

reader questions

1. I've always loved going to libraries and have been fortunate enough to visit lots since I've been published. Do you frequent your local library? Why or why not?

2. Books, both fiction and nonfiction, help several of the characters in this book. Can you think of a book that has helped you in some way? If so, what book was it?

3. I enjoyed making up all of the members in the Coblentz family. Is there one character you liked the best? If so, why?

4. I really liked how Kayla kept moving forward even though she had so many things working against her. Is there someone you know who possesses the same qualities? If so, who?

5. "Perfection" and "romance" were reoccurring themes throughout the book. Both are subjective terms and can mean a lot of things to different people. What does a "perfect romance" mean to you?

6. I used the following verse from Hebrews to guide the writing of this book: "Now Faith is confidence in what we hope for and assurance about what we do not see" (Hebrews 11:1). How has faith influenced your life?

7. I thought the following Amish proverb fit the story lines well: "The trouble with reaching a crossroads in life is the lack of signposts." When have you encountered crossroads in your life?

Turn the page for a sneak peek at

An Amish Surprise

the next novel in Shelley Shepard Gray's
Berlin Bookmobile series!

one

Sarah Anne Miller often wished she had two more hands. No, that wasn't exactly the truth. She only wished that on the days when Ruth Schmidt brought her entire brood into the bookmobile.

That was when she wished she had two hands, two earplugs, and extensive experience in crowd control. And maybe in psychology, too. Honestly, anything would be more helpful than nearly twenty-eight years in accounting followed by a two-year online course in library sciences.

One needed a great many tools in order to survive the Schmidt triplets and whatever assortment of children dear Ruth happened to be fostering at the time.

But since wishes and dreams were for other people, at least in this case, Sarah Anne was on her own.

Summoning her best kindergarten-teacher voice, she clapped her hands. "Children, please. Do gather around me. And speak one at a time."

Three out of the six complied. Two boys and a sweet little red-haired girl sat down immediately in front of her, their legs crossed like pretzels and their hands in their laps. "Ah, look at you three. Would you like to hear a story?"

One of the little boys nodded before gazing warily over his shoulder, where, of course, the triplet terrors were . . . gallivanting around.

Sarah Anne didn't even attempt to hold back a sigh.

"No worries, Sarah Anne!" Ruth called out merrily. "You go right ahead. I'll tend to these wild *kinner.*"

Just then a triplet—Mary, perhaps?—held up a picture book. It had a badly ripped cover page. "Lookit!" she yelled.

"Ah. Yes. I see that." Sarah Anne smiled weakly before looking at the three sitting down, still patiently waiting for a story.

What to do? What to do? The children needed their story, but that book needed to be saved before Mary began her next round of destruction.

When the door opened again, Sarah Anne felt like screaming . . . until she noticed who it was. Calvin Gingerich, so solemn, so kind and quiet. He loved to read history and biographies. She knew he had come in to pick out a new book before returning to his farm.

But some things just couldn't be helped. He was simply going to have to step up.

"Calvin, you are an answer to my prayers! Come here," she commanded, just as one of the quiet children sighed.

After giving the seated children a wary smile, he faced her. "Ah, yes?"

Sarah Anne handed him *Mr. Brown's Barnyard Friends,* her

go-to book in times of trouble. "Calvin, do me a favor and read to these children for a few minutes, would you, please?"

He took the book—not that she'd given him much choice—with obvious reluctance. "Well, now . . . Sarah Anne, I don't have much time. Fact is—"

She interrupted. "It's a short story. It won't take you long. Please?"

Whether it was the plaintive tone in her voice, the faces of the sweet children who were still sitting and waiting, or the way Mary was grabbing at another poor, unsuspecting book, he sat down on the floor with the three little ones. "Hiya," he said. "I'm Calvin."

"I'm Miles. This here is Ethan and Minnie."

"Nice to meet ya. Are you ready to hear about some farm animals?"

When three little heads all nodded, Calvin opened the book and began to read.

And then a miracle happened.

His deep voice resonated around the room, presenting a calming influence like a big dose of lavender aromatherapy. By the time he got to page four, even the Schmidt triplets were sitting down and listening to him.

Calmed by his words, Sarah Anne quietly picked up the injured book, taped the ripped cover, and leaned it against one of the bookshelves. Ruth even stopped inspecting cookbooks and listened as well.

The peace lasted almost six more minutes. Six blessed, wonderful minutes. Until he closed the book.

Then chaos continued yet again.

When another triplet grabbed two more books off the shelf,

Sarah Anne had had enough. "Mrs. Schmidt, I'll need to be getting to my next stop soon."

"Oh! Oh, *jah*. Of course." Taking hold of one of her children's hands, she smiled at them all. "I think it's time we moved on, *kinner*. Everyone, take the book you chose to Miss Sarah Anne and then come to the door."

After glancing at Calvin and mouthing a thank-you, Sarah Anne was busy again. But not too busy to notice that one of the foster children—Miles, she believed his name was—seemed very taken with Calvin. He was gazing up at him with wide eyes.

Calvin bent down to speak with him. By the looks of things, it seemed like their admiration was mutual.

Ten minutes later, Ruth guided all six of the children out the door. "See you next week, Sarah Anne!" she called out. "Goodbye!"

"Goodbye," she replied with a halfhearted smile.

The door slammed.

And then, amid the displaced books, a wad of discarded tissue, and what looked to be the remains of two pretzels, blessed silence returned.

Calvin looked shell-shocked. "Is it like that every time?"

"Oh, yes." She smiled at the stream of children that she'd gotten to know over the last eighteen months. "Sometimes, things are even worse."

He gaped. "How can that be?"

"Some of the children she fosters are as unruly as her own."

"Wait. Those aren't all hers?"

"Oh, no. Only the triplets. Ruth and her husband have been fostering children for years." Feeling like she should stick up for the woman, she added, "It may not seem like it, but she seems to have a knack for it. She's a very caring woman . . . with a high tolerance for noise."

Calvin folded his arms over his chest. "Sarah Anne, what will happen to the foster kids? Will they get adopted?"

"If I'm not mistaken, I believe each case is different. Some will go back to their parents. Others will go to another foster home. And, God willing, some will get adopted into homes where they feel wanted and loved."

"Wanted and loved," he murmured.

"Calvin, thank you again for helping me today. If not for you . . . Well, I don't even want to think what could have happened!"

"You took me off guard, I tell you that. But I liked reading the book. I enjoy *kinner*."

Some of the shadows that were in his eyes came back. Sarah Anne wondered what made him so sad but didn't dare pry. She'd already intruded upon him enough. "Do you need any help finding books?"

"*Nee*. I came in for a couple history books I've been thinking about. I'll go see if any are available."

She pointed to the computer station. "You can always order books and I'll bring them next time. That way you won't have to read to children, and you'll be on your way."

"I know it might be quicker, but I didn't mind reading to them. It was kind of fun." Obviously still thinking about the foster children, he turned to face her again. "Sarah Anne, about how long does Ruth keep those kids?"

"How long? Oh, I don't know. Usually a couple of months. Sometimes longer. Why?"

"No reason."

He smiled in a distracted way before walking to the small nonfiction section.

She watched him, wondering what was on his mind. Anxious to not be caught staring, Sarah Anne sprayed some hand sanitizer on her hands—really, those kids were a messy lot—then busied herself by putting the picture books back to rights.

She was going to need to get on her way in thirty minutes' time.

Glancing at Calvin again, she slowed her pace. Well, she was going to leave as soon as Calvin had found what he came in for. It seemed like Calvin really *needed* this visit today. Since that was the reason she was there, Sarah Anne was happy to oblige.

to have a knack for it. She's a very caring woman . . . with a high tolerance for noise."

Calvin folded his arms over his chest. "Sarah Anne, what will happen to the foster kids? Will they get adopted?"

"If I'm not mistaken, I believe each case is different. Some will go back to their parents. Others will go to another foster home. And, God willing, some will get adopted into homes where they feel wanted and loved."

"Wanted and loved," he murmured.

"Calvin, thank you again for helping me today. If not for you . . . Well, I don't even want to think what could have happened!"

"You took me off guard, I tell you that. But I liked reading the book. I enjoy *kinner*."

Some of the shadows that were in his eyes came back. Sarah Anne wondered what made him so sad but didn't dare pry. She'd already intruded upon him enough. "Do you need any help finding books?"

"*Nee*. I came in for a couple history books I've been thinking about. I'll go see if any are available."

She pointed to the computer station. "You can always order books and I'll bring them next time. That way you won't have to read to children, and you'll be on your way."

"I know it might be quicker, but I didn't mind reading to them. It was kind of fun." Obviously still thinking about the foster children, he turned to face her again. "Sarah Anne, about how long does Ruth keep those kids?"

"How long? Oh, I don't know. Usually a couple of months. Sometimes longer. Why?"

"No reason."

He smiled in a distracted way before walking to the small nonfiction section.

She watched him, wondering what was on his mind. Anxious to not be caught staring, Sarah Anne sprayed some hand sanitizer on her hands—really, those kids were a messy lot—then busied herself by putting the picture books back to rights.

She was going to need to get on her way in thirty minutes' time.

Glancing at Calvin again, she slowed her pace. Well, she was going to leave as soon as Calvin had found what he came in for. It seemed like Calvin really *needed* this visit today. Since that was the reason she was there, Sarah Anne was happy to oblige.